THE
DELTA MISSION

A JAMES CHASE MILITARY THRILLER
BOOK ONE

Heather Kuziel,
Thank you for supporting our
military and law enforcement.
You are super sexy, so keep it up!
I wish you the best!

Tony Perez

TONY PEREZ

DRAGON
PUBLISHING

Dedicated to Tayler, Connor, Gage, Parker, Aden, and Hunter

Thank you, Karyl

CHAPTER ONE

THE GREEN ZONE, BAGHDAD

1804 HOURS – 14 NOVEMBER 2013

THE SUN WAS ALREADY SLIPPING behind the towering sand-colored buildings and tree-lined, pockmarked streets that defined the perimeter of the Green Zone, a ten-square-kilometer international fortification nestled in the heart of the Karkh district of Bagdad.

James Chase was in the dining facility (DFAC) eating what was commonly referred to as mystery meat, with a side of instant mashed potatoes and corn.

When a compact man with deep-set, faded blue eyes positioned beneath a pair of nearly invisible blond eyebrows stepped into the dining facility, a silence fell over the room. With no more fanfare than a brief clearing of his throat, Captain Edwards revealed that there would be a unit-wide briefing early the following morning, at 0030 hours.

The Delta Team remained silent, casting glances at each other, before returning to their meals.

After a cursory glance at the loosely assembled Combat Applications Group (CAG) who were just finishing up their evening meals in the base's DFAC, Edwards turned toward the young man seated closest to him. "What've you got there, Tex?"

The man glanced down at his plate, which held a half-eaten plate of mystery meat and an amorphous blob of beige mash. "They're calling it meatloaf and mashed potatoes. I'm not convinced, but every time I start to argue with it, it tries to slink off my plate. Want to grab a bite to eat with us, Cap?"

"Yeah, I'll stick around." Edwards cast a critical eye at Tex's plate and with the most minute of shrugs, turned toward the back of the room where a makeshift buffet was set out.

James considered Edwards's words. Since their assignment to this location eleven months ago, they'd already carried out several successful missions to dispatch more than a handful of High Value Targets (HVTs) on behalf of the United States Government. Such announcements weren't necessarily out of place. It was the talk that had reached their ears earlier that caused the almost reverent pause following the announcement. It had started out as mere speculation amongst the highly trained soldiers, but loose lips be damned— they weren't part of one of the best of America's servicemen for nothing. It didn't take a rocket scientist to figure out that something was looming on the horizon, so the announcement from Captain Edwards about the pending briefing came as no surprise.

James pushed away from the table and caught the eye of the Sergeant First Class sitting next to him.

The wiry black man with an easy smile of his own met his rising departure with a grin. "Gonna catch a quick nap before the briefing, Gator?"

James nodded, acknowledging both the question and the nickname. You wrestle just *one* gator in the Florida swamps and suddenly everyone thought you were America's version of Crocodile Dundee. Okay, well, maybe it was two gators. He'd lost count after the third one. "Just going to head back to my bunk for a few. Want to finish up that email to Christina before we get our next mission. She's been breathing down my neck about communication, and I don't know when I'll have another chunk of downtime to finish it."

The SFC shrugged and settled back into his seat. He tucked a sliver of dinner roll into his mouth. "Suit yourself, man. Just make sure you don't miss it, huh?"

"Speak for yourself, Hank." James clapped him on the shoulder, eliciting a throaty laugh from his friend. "If I recall correctly, you're the only member of this unit who can both sleep with your eyes open and snore with your mouth shut."

James swept his dark eyes across the dining hall one final time and, turning away from the rising murmur forming in the DFAC, exited from the same door the captain had left through a moment before.

The conflict in the Middle East was nothing new to either the United States or James Chase. While he'd missed the first Gulf War conflict by four years as he was too young to enlist in the army, the tensions had only continued to ebb and flow throughout the late 1990s. The omnipresent threat of terrorism—both foreign and domestic—continued to loom throughout the tumultuous years leading up to the attack on American soil in 2001.

James had only been seventeen when he convinced his mother to let him enlist. It wasn't some great patriotism that had compelled him to sign up for the armed forces, either. Rather, it had been the very person signing off on his enlistment papers who had partially been the driving force to get him out of the relatively sleepy city of Jacksonville, Florida. If James had been pressed to summarize his relationship with his mother in one word, he might have suggested, "Fine." Or, if he had a couple more words to play with, he may have added, "She did her best." Nevertheless, his relationship with his mother had become strained, the growing wedge between them chiefly due to the man Maria Chase had married after she separated from James's dad. Sure, Maria loved James, but as a divorced mother raising her Cuban-American son in the South, she'd struggled to find that balance between not being overbearing and letting him be himself. Frankly, James had grown tired of wondering what barrage of verbal assault and derisive insults his stepfather was going to throw at them next. He'd secretly willed his mother to grow a spine and walk out on the bastard, but she'd consistently disappointed James by refusing to stand up for herself. Witnessing her cower before his stepfather had both saddened James and tangibly disgusted him.

Maria had often been exhausted and rarely offered words of encouragement for her son, and James was damn sure not going to seek it out from his stepfather. Instead, he contented himself by staying busy with his extracurriculars. None of his exams or essays were going on the scuffed white refrigerator door anytime soon, but James hadn't minded. He'd had other things on his mind. What validation he didn't get at home, he'd gotten from his coaches at school. Some of his classmates had been on the wrestling team. Others had been varsity cross country. A few others had dabbled in soccer. James? He was part of all three. He was a formidable combination of combustive energy, quick reflexes, and indefatigable endurance. When the challenge of taking on three different sports didn't wear him out, he'd decided to start lifting weights for fun. At a slight 145 pounds soaking wet, he was still managing to bench press 325 pounds in the weight room, far exceeding even elite fitness levels in his wiry yet powerful frame.

When his Cross-Country (XC) coach pulled him aside and asked him his plans after high school, the coach hadn't had enlistment on his mind. He'd seen a scholarship to UCF or even USF on James's horizon. He'd wanted to coax James under a fifteen-minute 5K, convinced the youth could manage it. Why the hell wouldn't he? James had already been excelling at everything else he'd attempted, his studies aside. Even those could have been improved if James would have simply picked up a textbook now and again. But James had known he had to get out of Jacksonville. There was really nothing left for him there. Hell, there'd been nothing for him in Florida, period. Orlando had felt entirely too close, as had Tampa. The thought of staying cloistered within the state had made him feel uncomfortably claustrophobic and vulnerable in a way that didn't sit well with him. James had to get out of Florida and far away from his stepfather's violent outbursts.

One afternoon in the late fall of his senior year, in a lackluster strip mall that held an uninspiring assortment of fast food offerings and overpriced designer clothes, James had discovered a disinterested recruiter tucked away in an inconspicuous one-room office. Within minutes of speaking to the sergeant, he'd had an enlistment contract all tied up and neatly bundled up with a bow. James had stumbled upon his calling and knew instantly that he'd found his home with the US Army. This had all been contingent, of course, upon his mother's signature on the papers.

His mother hadn't needed much encouragement to sign the papers after James explained how much money he could bring home between his enlistment bonus and his base pay. He'd later wondered in retrospect if his mother had also done the calculations and quietly determined that the rigors of the army were still vastly superior to the hell he'd faced at home. She'd scrawled her name on the documents in her trademark script, and James had returned them to the recruiter the next day. The recruiter had given him a broad smile, extended his hand to shake, and said, "Welcome to the US Army, son."

The months between enlisting and getting shipped off to Army Basic Training seemed to fly by. He'd finished high school in the spring of 1995 and was on a plane to Fort Bliss, Texas by that following November. While other recruits groaned about how tired they were and how their drill sergeant sucked, James had marveled over how he loved absolutely everything about boot camp. If he could have complained about anything, he may have wanted a couple of minutes to actually chew his food during mealtimes, but that was a minor issue and resolved itself near the middle of boot camp.

James had finally found a cure for his chronic boredom, and he flourished under the rigidity and structure of Basic Combat Training (BCT). Where other recruits struggled to survive, James had thrived. He'd naturally excelled in everything thrown at him during the nine-week training. The marksmanship training had nothing on him. He'd marveled at the ease of hitting the targets, more often than not getting a bullseye on nearly every one of the forty targets ahead of him. Even the academic side of BCT had held his attention, his brain soaking up the lessons like an overeager, thirsty sponge.

Of course, the physical fitness side of boot camp had been a cakewalk for him too. The Army Physical Fitness Test was a joke, and he'd found himself looking around and wondering why other recruits were vomiting on their boots after an easy training run. His XC coach might have been pleased to learn that James had completed his two-mile endurance qualification run in just under eleven minutes, lapping the other recruits who had trailed after him.

James had graduated BCT in the top five percent of his class. Even his jaded drill sergeant was impressed by James's prowess, which he'd demonstrated by smoking the irrepressible young man harder than the other recruits in his unit. James had been getting bigger, stronger, and faster. He'd consistently scored greater than 350 on the extended scale on the Army Physical Fitness Test (APFT), which was no small feat when one realized that the standard APFT scale capped out at just 300. A soldier had to max out all events for a perfect score of 300 to accrue these additional points. In short, James had been born to be an American soldier, and he was finally within his element.

When asked if he was interested in trying his luck with Army Ranger training, there had been no question about whether he would qualify. He'd volunteered for the training without hesitation, and as soon as he finished BCT, he'd plowed straight through his Advanced Initial Training (AIT) in February of the following year. The first half of 1996 had been a nonstop stream of training for James, and he'd steadily progressed from AIT to Airborne School. When he finished that in three weeks, he'd transitioned to the Ranger Indoctrination Program (RIP).

It had been no surprise when James graduated RIP at the top of the class. By this point, anyone who knew him expected nothing less than the best from him. It had been a natural transition from RIP to Ranger School. Nine weeks had passed quickly for him as he mastered everything presented to him during the training. In a strenuous program that often saw a washout rate as high as 75 percent, James had seemed unfazed. He'd graduated Ranger School in June of 1996 and promptly been assigned to the 3rd Ranger Battalion, Alpha Company, in Fort Benning, Georgia.

Then 9/11 happened. James had only been twenty-two when Islamic extremists plunged American Airlines Flight 11 into the sides of the Twin Towers in New York City. The Boeing 767s colliding with these iconic buildings had transformed the country overnight. The patriotism and brotherhood that arose from the plume of dust and asbestos billowing over the rubble had been an awakening for citizens. President Bush echoed the sentiments of millions when he'd somberly intoned, "None of us will ever forget this day, yet we go forward to defend freedom and all that is good and just in our world."

A month after his twenty-third birthday, in December of 2001, James had been dispatched to Afghanistan as part of Operation Enduring Freedom. That was his first encounter with the Middle East, but he'd quickly discovered that it was certainly not going to be his last. Higher-ups again noticed his performance during that year, and when James returned to Fort Benning in January of 2002, he'd yet again been given another opportunity to demonstrate his aptitude as a soldier. A friend and advisor had suggested in passing that he should attend a recruitment briefing for Delta selection.

Why the hell not? James had already known he was a top soldier in everything else he'd tried. What did he have to lose by showing up?

He'd arrived that day with an open mind and agreed to try out for selection and assessment after the presentation. This period marked another seven months of training for him. He'd flown through the four-week assessment and after its completion, there was no doubt that he was ready for the six-month Operators Training Course (OTC). July of 2002 marked his graduation from OTC and his assignment to Alpha Squadron.

This was just the beginning of an eleven-year career and over two hundred successful missions with Delta.

James wasn't *just* an elite soldier, though. He was also a loving, albeit somewhat distant, father, a fairly decent partner to Christina, a son, and a damn good cook too. His *arroz con pollo* rivaled only his flan, but he still managed to remain remarkably humble no matter what skill he mastered next. No, James was more than that too. He was also an admittedly unflappable man who had seen a remarkable amount of shit in his thirty-six years of life.

He'd dispatched High Value Targets (HVTs) and seen innocent civilians blown into pulpy shrapnel due to a misstep on a pressure mine, yet he still managed to eat a hearty dinner every night. His sleep was often deep and dreamless and, save for the occasional fitful night of tossing and turning, he was largely unperturbed by the relentless stream of stressors he faced on a daily basis.

Work was work. Personal was personal.

James blinked at the cursor on his laptop and rubbed his eyes. The email to Christina remained unfinished, but he'd been laboring over it for an hour and it was going nowhere fast. He resigned to work on it after the mission since he had little time left that evening.

Still. Christina worried about him, and he liked to give her regular updates to put her mind at ease. She didn't like the long pauses between their correspondence, and he wondered if he was imagining that they were slowly drifting apart. With two divorces already under his belt, he really didn't want to screw up what he had with Christina. She was a reasonably patient woman, but it had been over a week since his last email to her and he could almost feel the annoyance tinged with fear from the previous message she'd sent him.

"Hey, you still alive over there, babe?" she'd written.

The humor helped both of them. Instead of tiptoeing over James's mortality, Christina liked to train her spotlight directly upon it. It was almost like a reverse-jinxing. By addressing her fears upfront, she was able to loosen their viselike grip on her imagination. She had a sharp mind and a ready wit, which is what he'd noticed second about her. Her shapely hips and full-lipped smile, of course, had been the first thing that captured his attention. And her ass. Her perky ass was definitely a plus, for sure. The problem he faced, however, was that there was very little he could say to her in these short, almost terse messages he periodically sent. He couldn't talk to her about missions. He couldn't give away their position. He couldn't say if something were a success or a failure. The US Government had his hands tied, and as much as he would like to talk to her about what he was doing over in Baghdad's Green Zone, he couldn't put his team's security at risk just to help his girlfriend sleep better at night.

What did that leave him? The day to day crap he and his unit subjected on one another would more likely than not be just a dull story that fell flat on her. She didn't care about how Hank got his call sign, though his Delta cadre had all laughed uproariously when the SFC defied expectation *and* decorum and helicoptered his family jewels at them one evening after his shower. Nah, that stuff was best kept within The Unit.

His email to her was shaping up to be a disappointment. As much as he tried to pump some warmth into it, there was truly nothing he could say to her. He loved the hell out of her, but the words weren't there. James wasn't a talking man. He wasn't into lengthy texts and gushing words of endearment. He was a doer, a man who thought quickly on his feet. Poetry wasn't his thing, and while he missed Christina, the ritual of writing emails to her almost seemed more stressful than his current mission.

He sighed and reluctantly closed his laptop with a quiet click. The briefing was going to begin at 0030 hours, and it was going on 2100 hours already. He wondered if he should try to take a nap before they convened back in the sparsely decorated conference room. He'd seen several other members of The Unit trudging back to their bunks ahead of him and they'd exchanged nods as he'd passed.

Sleep wasn't going to be a problem for him. He had a gift for grabbing snatches of shuteye no matter what kind of situation he was in. Active firefight? Heck, a quick twenty-minute doze was just the ticket to recharge him for another round of combat. Neither was feeling alert for the briefing going to be a problem. Even if he did feel groggy when he woke up, it wasn't anything that a couple of cups of strong coffee couldn't fix.

He cast another glance at his computer. Something tugged halfheartedly at him a strange but nagging urge to just hit *Send* on the email. Tell Christina that he loved her. Tell her he was doing fine, he missed her, and he'd be home soon. Tell her *anything*, really... anything that would satisfy her constant demand for updates and reassurance of his wellbeing.

James wasn't a superstitious man, nor was he a portentous one. To his knowledge, there was nothing unusual about the briefing. Last-minute notice was fairly common for them. Once the orders were passed to them from their commander-in-chief, they typically had a very narrow window before the action began. But he couldn't shake the feeling that he should just send the damn message.

Rising from the uncomfortable metal desk chair, he turned toward his bunkbed against the north wall of the ten foot by eight foot untreated plywood room. All of James's military gear, including his rifle and ammunition, lay spread over the top bunk. On the south wall sat the desk with his personal laptop. The west wall had an old wooden three-drawer dresser with a mix of personal and military clothing inside, and next to the bunkbed was a small nightstand with an old pull-string table light, some notebook papers, a small digital alarm clock, and an OTF knife. The room was small but sufficient for his needs.

Sleep it was. Even if he only got three and a half of rest, it was better than nothing. He slipped out of his boots and positioned them at the foot of his bed with their laces loosened and ready for his feet once he awoke. He stretched out on the bunk and folded one arm beneath his head. With his other arm, he reached for the cord attached to the lamp next to him and turned out the light. His eyes closed, and he felt the soothing call of slumber beckon to him. Sleep was going to come easy, as it often did. Soon his chest was rising and falling in slow, even breaths.

His sleep was dreamless and easy. His mind was calm and untroubled, and he would awake without the aid of his alarm three hours later, completely recharged, refreshed, and ready to tackle the mission ahead of him.

CHAPTER TWO

MISSION BRIEFING

0030 HOURS – 15 NOVEMBER 2013

J AMES STRODE TOWARD THE MAIN building of Delta Team's camp, seeking out a coffee station on his way to the briefing. His nap had been exactly what his body needed to prepare both mentally and physically for whatever was to come from the meeting, and now he just needed to shake off the cobwebs. A burnt mug of generic issue coffee did the trick, and he swallowed the last swig from the Styrofoam cup in his hand as he entered the conference room. He slid into the hard-backed chair in the briefing room, set the cup on the scarred, plastic-topped conference table in front of him, and rubbed the last vestiges of sleep out of his eyes. As his fellow CAGs streamed into the room behind him, he took a moment to glance around at the familiar faces surrounding him. The scraping of a battered metal chair against the tile floor drew James's attention to his right.

A man threw himself into the seat and turned to James with a wide grin. "'Sup, Gator?"

"'Sup yourself, Ginger." James offered a brief nod at the soldier, a tall and gangly man with a shock of orange hair and a nasty case of razor burn on his neck.

"You ready for the briefing?" Ginger covered his mouth, hiding a yawn behind his palm.

"Yep." James leaned back in his chair, twining his fingers over his stomach. "You?"

Someone bumped his chair as they strode past him, uttering an absent apology as they worked their way toward the back of the room. More people trickled into the room, and a quick glance at his watch confirmed that the briefing was about to begin.

"Of course. I was born ready for this." Ginger drummed his fingertips on the table, the action and the chewed flesh of his cuticles contradicting his nonchalant attitude.

Unlike Ginger, James found himself unexpectedly growing calmer before a briefing, his heart rate slowing and his respiration becoming more even. People like Ginger, though, seemed to thrive more on holding their nervous energy. As far as James was concerned, how the other members of The Unit felt during their missions was of no importance to him, and he'd quickly discovered that something as trivial as feelings had no bearing on their performance. He didn't care if they muttered a dozen Hail Marys or sacrificed a goat to Beelzebub before the mission began. What mattered was that they got the job done, they did it right, and they all came back safely.

These men were more than his brothers—they were an extension of his own body. He knew how each of them operated under pressure and had no doubt each and every one of them had his back. In turn, he watched theirs too. It was a kind of closely interwoven cooperation, and James knew he was lucky to have such a tight-knit unit in Delta to work with. Even as the briefing room filled up and the temperature in there climbed from the anxious heat radiating off the bodies of the team members, he found his own muscles relaxing in anticipation of the work ahead of him.

Ginger pointed at the foam cup sitting on the table in front of James. "Where did you find that? Any more of it left?"

James plucked it up from the table and tilted it toward the young sergeant so he could see the contents of it. The cup was empty, save for a few dregs of coffee grounds dappling the bottom of the white Styrofoam cup.

Ginger craned his chin up, scanning the room for a rogue pot of coffee.

The last thing he needed was something to fuel his tension, but it wasn't James's place to tell him what he could or could not have. If the man wanted to suck down some freeze-dried coffee crystals sweetened with creamer powder, that was his own business. James opened his mouth to reply, but his words were cut off by Captain Edwards striding briskly into the room.

Edwards flipped the light switch off, casting the room into immediate shadows. He stood in the glow of the projector, the harsh white light bathing him in a stark pallor in the darkness. He leaned forward, tapping a key on the laptop computer in front of him. A black and white satellite image manifested onto the wall behind him. Matching red banners emblazoned with the words "TOP SECRET" in blocky print lined the borders of the image on the top and bottom. There was a similar sticker on the matte black shell of Edwards's laptop. Whatever the commander was about to reveal to them—just like every other mission Delta had gone on since their arrival in the Green Zone—was classified.

The captain stepped aside from the projection and turned to face the room, his face grave and lined in the glow of the projector. A hush fell over the Delta Team, and all eyes locked on Captain Edwards.

"Good morning, gentlemen. Thank you all for making it on time. Your upcoming mission is officially known as Operation Quicksand. As you already know, this briefing is classified Top Secret and not to be shared with anyone outside of this room. As always, I expect you to please hold any questions until after the briefing." His piercing eyes lit on the room, sweeping over the faces peering back at him. "With that said, let's begin. I want to start by introducing our senior CIA analyst here in the Green Zone, Daniel Gibson. Gibson, if you will."

"Thank you, Captain Edwards." Gibson was a slim man with a slight belly and receding hairline. He addressed the men with a nod before producing a stylus from his pocket. He shook it out, extending it before him, and pointed it at the photograph on the wall behind him. "This is the site of your mission tonight. Its coordinates are thirty-three degrees north, forty-six degrees east. After several surveillance missions from the CIA drones and cross-checking with our informant, we have confirmed with at least eighty percent certainty that this is the location of our target."

With a sweeping gesture, Gibson drew small circles in the air around various features scattered across the image as he continued. "At approximately 0200 hours, you will arrive at this compound. Within this thicket of trees is the building where your target is currently located. Your mission is to capture the person of interest." He tapped this part of the picture with the stylus, glancing briefly back at it before turning back to the Delta Force unit. "Your target is one Da'wud Al Muhammad. For those of you who don't know, Da'wud is the individual responsible for the deaths of thousands of civilians in the name of his so-called 'ethnic cleansing.' He has been active in the Islamic State of Iraq and the Levant for several years and is considered a high priority target by the United States Government."

Heads around the room nodded.

They'd all heard of Da'wud before. His reputation of being a ruthless tyrant was well known, and this snippet of intel didn't come as a surprise to anyone in The Unit. James's gaze moved across the image, taking in the layout of the stronghold where Da'wud was presumed to be. It seemed nondescript, almost understated. The area around it was sparse, with low buildings situated around it and a few dirt roads leading away from the site. But that's how these terrorists liked to work, often hidden in plain sight just like Bin Laden had been. Government officials were stunned to learn that Bin Laden had been squared away in a residential neighborhood of Abbottabad, in the Persian plateaus of Khyber Pakhtunkhwa, Pakistan. Da'wud was no different. His compound was stationed in an entirely unremarkable parcel of land. Except for a perimeter wall, which wasn't entirely unheard of in this region, especially for the wealthier locals, it looked just like anyone else's home. Had it not been for their informant who had also been dabbling in swapping intel secrets with the Iranians, Da'wud may have continued to fly under their radar indefinitely.

Gibson continued. "The president has determined that this Da'wud needs to be brought to justice, and that's where you come in." His voice remained flat and even. There was no anger or bitterness. He was merely stating the facts as he knew them. "He's a firm proponent of Sharia law and takes the slaughter of those he perceives to be infidels very seriously. He will not hesitate to kill you, and if you fail tonight, he will continue to evangelize these Sharia teachings through the ruthless murder of those who oppose Sharia law. Your primary objective tonight is to capture Da'wud, but if you're unable to do so, you are to terminate him by force."

Another image flashed onto the screen—a picture of the terrain surrounding Da'wud's stronghold. Now his compound was a tiny portion of the image, contained within a white, hand-drawn rectangle on the picture. The topographic map showed relatively smooth concentric lines surrounding the compound and village. As the map moved farther away from Da'wud's residence, the lines became wavier, indicating rolling hills. A river cut through the lower south quadrant of the image, flowing from Iraq into Iran. Typed lettering labeled this river as the Nahr Mirzabad River.

Gibson's stylus pointed out features on the image as he said, "You'll see from this image that this area is flat and has minimal vegetation. You won't have any cover or concealment here, so you're going to have to focus on a swift entry into the compound once you land."

The subdued cloud had settled upon the room. James could hear Ginger's quiet breathing behind him. At least the sergeant wasn't hyperventilating anymore. He'd burned through his jitters and was now all focused on the task ahead. James returned his attention to Gibson and the next image on the projector.

A man's face appeared on the wall behind Gibson. He had thick, uneven eyebrows with rogue hairs dropping across his eyes. A tightly woven turban rested on his head, concealing the majority of his unkempt salt and pepper hair. His beard, on the other hand, was well-groomed and streaked with silver and trailed down the front of the plain white caftan he wore. The kinky growth of hair met with a trimmed mustache above an unsmiling face.

"This is your target." Gibson tapped the wall with his stylus. He glanced back to confirm the image, then returned his attention to the team of soldiers congregated before him. "Da'wud Al Muhammad. Intelligence has informed us that Da'wud is in this stronghold and has been there for the past eight months. It's believed that he is accompanied by his three wives."

Da'wud's eyes were cold and glittering beneath his bushy eyebrows. His face was bland, devoid of any emotion other than dispassionate malice. There was a calculated intelligence to this expressionless face. He hadn't climbed to power making stupid, impulsive choices, that was for damn sure. He wouldn't be an easy target, but James was confident they would be able to get him with minimal struggle. They hadn't failed at any of their other missions since arriving in the Green Zone. Da'wud would be no different.

"Here's what we know about Da'wud's stronghold." Gibson pressed a key on his computer, and the screen flashed back to the previous image. "His residence is within Mehran, Ilam. As you can see from this image, his stronghold is on the farthest edge of it, closer to the Iraqi border. In fact, Intelligence has determined that it is approximately two-point-five miles within the Iranian border, within the boundaries of the Ilam Province. You may already know that Mehran is the capital of Mehran County, but it's a sparsely inhabited region with approximately 13,000 Kurds residing there."

James knew it, and based on the nods coursing through the room, the rest of The Unit knew the region too. Even if geography wasn't their strong suit before they arrived in the Green Zone, they had quickly picked up on the local provinces and primary cities within their Area of Operation (AOP).

Gibson glanced at Edwards, then retracted his stylus with the palm of his hand. "That concludes my part of the briefing. Edwards?"

"Thank you, Gibson." Edwards cleared his throat and reached for a bottle of water sitting next to his laptop. He unscrewed the top and took a swig out of it, his face grimacing as he swallowed the tepid beverage. He tightened the lid with a quick jerk of his wrist, then returned it to the table. "Now, listen to me closely. I am going to summarize your mission one final time before drawing this briefing to a close."

Edwards's voice was crisp as he enunciated each word to the men, "You are to find Da'wud Al Muhammad. You are to capture him, but if you are unable to do so, then you are to terminate him. Any peripheral intel that you find is secondary to the mission but should be collected for exploitation. This includes any computers, thumb drives, external hard drives, paperwork, or anything else you find on site. Any non-combatant individuals found on the compound are to be captured if they do not resist. His wives, however, and any other women, are to be quickly interviewed and released on your way out of the compound. If anyone does resist or demonstrates aggressiveness toward you, they are to be terminated as well."

Edwards gazed over the room, seemingly locking eyes with every soldier one by one. "Gentlemen, this concludes my briefing. Do you have any questions before I turn it over to your team leader for your mission specific tasks?"

There was a pause. This lack of initial feedback was fairly typical for the men in The Unit. These men hadn't become part of Delta through fumbling or blind luck. They were sharp-minded, top athletes, and hand-selected because they were the very best amongst their ranks. Slow mental processing and pointless questions were not in their course of life.

"I've got a question." A voice from across the room spoke up. James threw a look over his shoulder, and his eyes lit on a man by the name of Kermit. "How fresh is the intel? Are we talking daisies here, or rotten eggs?"

Edwards glanced at Gibson.

The CIA analyst nodded.

"Very good question. Fresh. Within 72 hours," Edwards replied.

Kermit nodded, seemingly satisfied.

The age of the intel made a significant difference in the outcome of their mission. While they had operated successfully on older information, the fresher it was, the better it was for everyone involved. Except, of course, the terrorist. He was going to have a bad night once Delta found him.

Hank had a question too. "Dogs?"

Gibson shook his head. "No dogs that we know about."

"Good." Hank leaned back in his chair, his face now a serene mask. "I fuckin' hate shooting dogs."

"I hear that, man," another voice piped up. James glanced over at a stocky man with a neatly trimmed beard. It was Tex. "Sucks when we have to do that. Hey, Gibson, what about booby-traps? Electronic alarms? Anything else we need to know about the perimeter?"

Gibson's face blanched. He'd failed to give the men an essential piece of vital information. "Yes. Our informant suspects that the doors leading into the compound are booby-trapped. So, an alternate way in will probably be best, but I will leave that up to your team leader."

"Good to know." Tex's voice was wry, the drawl exaggerated and dripping with cheerful scorn. "Would hate to accidentally come down with a nasty case of, y'know, getting killed out there. Kinda hard to recover from, so I've heard."

A tinge of red crept up Gibson's collar, but he didn't reply. His lips were a thin line etched across his face as he looked straight forward, carefully ignoring the distrustful eyes boring into him. He had flubbed. Those pencil pushers didn't know what it was like to be out there in the thick of combat. Men like Gibson were more of the scholarly type, and their knowledge on these missions was frequently more technical than practical. His oversight could have cost these men their lives.

The room was quiet once more. Edwards stood patiently at the front of the room, giving them plenty of time to speak up. Gibson shifted his weight from foot to foot, his gaze lingering on an imaginary spot on the back wall. No further questions followed.

Edwards closed his computer. "Very good. I leave you to your team leader for mission specific assignments. Please convene out front for your departure to Da'wud's stronghold in thirty minutes." Without a final glance back at his men, he strode out of the room.

Tex rose from his seat and, slipping his thumb and forefinger into his mouth, let out a sharp whistle. Eyes glanced up to look at him, and he waited to ensure he had a rapt audience. His characteristic accent seemed to lend an extra note of authority to his words as he spoke. "Okay, men. I'm going to start by breaking you up into two teams. You know the drill." He pointed at each of them as he spoke, and they nodded as their names were called out. "Kermit, Rembrandt, Mooney, Bones, and Noodle. I want you working under Benjamin. You're A Team. Ginger, Hank, Gator, Dickie, and Marmaduke. You're all with me, B Team."

James stood and crossed the room to stand closer to their team leader. A glance around revealed that everyone else had a similar idea.

A loose semicircle formed as Tex continued. "As usual, you'll have a specific job once we land at Da'wud's compound. Team A is going to take and hold the bottom floor. My team is going to tackle the top floor." He raised his voice in the preternaturally quiet room, though the gesture was wholly unnecessary. "Each and every one of you has an important job to perform tonight. Kermit and Rembrandt, I want you to focus on guarding the prisoners. Keep them secured and submissive. Bones, Noodle, and Mooney, you're going to be doing site exploitation on the bottom floor. Gator, Ginger, and Hank, I want you to work on site exploitation on the top floor. Dickie, your job is to act as a perimeter lookout from the second floor. If there is any unusual activity around the compound, I want to know about it. I'll be helping you with this. Any questions for me, men?"

A somber hush held the room captive. The Delta Team stood in a thoughtful silence, ruminating over what they'd just learned from the briefing as they considered their designated assignments. This meditation was also typical for them. It always seemed to take them a good minute to assimilate the criteria of their missions before they reacted to it. While the lull was only an extremely nominal period of just a few seconds, it was sufficient. This brief passage of time was almost symbolic, as though they were giving their orders the weight of respect that they deserved.

Then Ginger said, "I think I could go for that coffee now."

"Worried about getting bored, Ginger?" The quip came from the back of the room, from a fair-skinned man with a collection of dark features on his friendly, open face. "Thinking that you're going to fall asleep on the job?"

"I'll fall asleep with your mother," Ginger shot back with no spite in his voice. His lips pulled away from his teeth in a playful grin, and he trained it on the man who had issued the witticism.

"Keep my girlfriend out of this, Ginger," another voice piped up. "She doesn't deserve your hate just because you're jealous that I got dibs on her first. You can have your turn once I'm done with her."

A crest of laughter followed. The tension in the room had broken.

The banter felt good. The camaraderie felt good. Considering the work ahead of them, James felt surprisingly good. He joined in the laughter.

Ginger flushed an impressive shade of scarlet, his face blending in with his strawberry-blond ringlets. His freckles vanished in his flush. He shook his head, chuckling along with the rest of his team, and ran his hand over his face. The laughter slowly trickled to a stop, and Ginger pointed at his own eyes with his index and middle fingers before extending a finger toward the man who had started the heckling, an SFC by the name of Rembrandt. Ginger then raised and lowered his loosely clenched fist in the air in the universal sign for jerking it.

Someone else took the opportunity to offer a suggestion as to what they would do with Rembrandt's mother, and the laughter picked up again. The smiles remained on their faces as they filed out of the room to the array of Sikorsky UH-60 Black Hawk helicopters waiting for them outside of their fortification.

James had no misgivings as they streamed out of the briefing room for just another routine mission to kill an HVT. What could possibly go wrong?

Eight helicopters were waiting when they emerged from the

building and walked onto the flight line. A glance at James's watch told him that it was closing on right about 0115 hours. Word had it that it would take a half-hour to reach Da'wud's compound from their location in the Green Zone. T-minus forty-five minutes until mission start.

James hoisted himself into the Black Hawk and fastened his seatbelt across his lap. He rested his M4 between his legs with the muzzle down, the safety securely locked in place.

Hank sat on one side of James, and Ginger settled down on his other side and leaned into James, his voice low. "I never got that cup of coffee, man."

"Sounds like a personal problem to me," James said, his voice tinged with genuine sympathy. He personally felt great. His mind was clear and lucid, his focus sharp. The cup of coffee had just been a bonus because he would have felt as good without it.

"Right?" Ginger shook his head. "You're treating me to a venti with extra whip cream when we get back. You owe me."

"I owe you?" James raised a brow at him.

"Yes, you owe me. Teasing me with that gourmet stuff in your cup. I smelled it. It was probably Kona, or some fancy Columbian brew. I know it was, and I know you're holding out on me." Ginger pulled a pack of gum from his pocket, slid one out, and unwrapped it. He folded it into his mouth, then offered the pack to James.

James shook his head no thanks.

Ginger turned to the man sitting next to him, who plucked a piece from the pack.

Outside the Black Hawk, men were piling into the other seven choppers. Eight men had fit into James's helicopter, and another eight Delta had boarded the other Black Hawk. The other three Black Hawks held twenty-four Army Rangers, each assigned to the mission to offer perimeter support. The other three helicopters were AH-64 Apache gunships, which were tagging along to provide close air support.

"I'm not buying you a coffee, man. You had your chance. It was in the canteen out front, courtesy of Green Beans. They make that fancy stuff." James shook his head. "You snooze, you lose. That's the name of the game here."

"That's bullshit." Ginger pressed the gum against the back of his rabbity front teeth, his head turning back and forth defiantly in mock protest. "I didn't know I wanted any coffee until I saw you drinking yours. You're just a coffee tease, that's what you are."

"Would you two girls just kiss and make up already?" Hank leaned forward and trained his eyes on the two men. "Gator, sorry man, but I'm going to have to side with Ginger here. You know the rules. You don't bring anything to the party unless you have enough to share with everyone else."

"Since when have there been rules?" James exchanged a glance with Ginger, then turned back to Hank. "I wasn't informed of these so-called rules. We back in kindergarten or something?"

"I just made them up right now." Hank snapped his fingers at Ginger, drawing the freckle-faced man's attention toward him. "Hey, Ginger. You got any more of that gum?"

"According to the rules, huh? That sounds suspiciously like communism, if you ask me. As a proud citizen of the United States of America, I won't put up with your red propaganda." Ginger fished his fingers into the front pocket of his Flame Resistant Army Combat Uniform (FRACU) and pulled out the pack again. He held it up for Hank to see. "You're in luck. This is my last piece."

"Red propaganda, my ass. Speak for yourself, Ginger." Hank took the gum from him and slipped it into his mouth. He chewed it thoughtfully for a moment before he spoke again. "It's a half-hour to Da'wud's stronghold."

"Yeah?" James said.

"Just thinking out loud. We finish this up and we can be back at base before dawn, I bet." Hank leaned back, his eyes focused on the matte gray wall of the Black Hawk across from him. "That is, if you don't screw it up, Gator. You think you can handle that?"

"I'm not worried. Are you worried? You sound worried, Hank." James bathed the man in a smile. There was no tension, just their usual shit talk before a mission.

Overhead, the rotors thumped to life.

James let his body sway with the rising Black Hawk as he thought of his email to Christina. Guilt nipped at the back of his mind, but he pushed the thought aside. He'd finish it when he got back. He took a breath, feeling any remaining vestiges of tension escape his body. *Focus on the task ahead right now. Worry about Christina later.*

In a half-hour, their mission would begin. Get in there, capture Da'wud, and then run a fine-tooth comb over the stronghold. Site exploitation would most likely be the most substantial part of the mission, anyway. Bureaucracy and intel always took up a good chunk of time after a mission had finished. Capturing Da'wud was going to be the easy part. He'd be getting a hot shower and thinking about bed in less than three hours.

As the helicopter closed the distance between the Green Zone and Da'wud's stronghold, James let himself relax.

CHAPTER THREE

THE GROUND RUSHED UP TO meet the team as the Black Hawk began its descent into Mehran, and in an almost Pavlovian response to this change in tempo, James felt the muscles in his back tighten. On the ride over, he'd been loose and comfortable. His breath had come out in a measured meter, neither languid nor frantic. However, with the imminence of the task ahead of them, his body stiffened in expectation of the aching fatigue he knew he was going to experience once the mission was over.

Then there was a jolt and the Black Hawk was still. James rose to his feet. Around him, his team also stood. Their faces were undoubtedly a mirror of his own. The tension of their pending mission had temporarily aged everyone. James saw lines in their faces that hadn't been there an hour before. By the time they were back in the Green Zone, they would all look their respective ages again, save for a few extra gray hairs as a reward for their hard work.

"Don't fuck this up, Gator," Hank said, slapping him amiably on the back. "We're all counting on you."

"Speak for yourself, man." James nodded at him, his smile breaking through his silver-streaked beard.

Hank returned it without hesitation.

This would be the last of the shit talk for a while. He may as well soak it all up now. Once they stepped out of the helicopter, they'd be too focused on their mission for heckling one another.

Tex silenced them with a glare. "Let's stop the chitchatting. C'mon, move out, B Team." The easy smile was gone from his face. He was all work now, the down-to-earth, good ole boy persona a distant memory. Once they were done with their mission and back at their base in the Green Zone, he'd be the Tex they knew and loved once again. But for the time being, he was all grim concentration and determination.

Tex led the way to the sliding doors of the Black Hawk and, with a grunt, hoisted the handle and slid the door open. One by one, the men filed out and paused to consider the terrain ahead of them.

Da'wud's compound loomed some five hundred yards before them, a stout black building squatting against the dark horizon on the west side of Mehran. A few other buildings, spartan rectangles set against the skyline, remained unlit. Everyone was asleep, or at least, bore the semblance of slumber in the subdued stillness. The only activity seemed to come from a sewage treatment plant in the distance, but even that was minimal. No glow emanated from it, but James recognized it from the map that Gibson had shown them during the briefing. Its presence also explained the repetitive rushing sound ebbing in the quietness of the hour.

The night was clear and starless, an inky expanse spread out like a velvet blanket overhead. Not even a sliver of moonlight illuminated the compound or the area around it. Off in the distance, James could see a faint hint of ambient light from the closest building, but it was dim and had no bearing on their visibility this far out in the rural region. The night was extraordinarily dark and strangely peaceful and, save for the men pouring out of the Black Hawk helicopters, it was wholly untainted by light pollution and human noises. Only a few minutes before, the low but resonant burr from a swarm of desert locusts and the mechanical churning of the sewage plant had been the only sounds interrupting the otherwise perfectly tranquil setting. Now the raucous cacophony of the elite team's arrival disrupted this formerly idyllic scene. That serenity would be broken in less than five minutes. James and the rest of Delta would undoubtedly see to that. It was the stereotypical calm before the storm, and they would be unleashing one hell of a tempest upon Da'wud in just a few minutes.

No words were necessary between these highly trained, elite men. They knew what they needed to do.

James slipped his night vision goggles (NVGs) down over his eyes and, with a flip of a switch near the front of his modulator integrated combat helmet (MICH), turned the device on. The world was suddenly bathed in a green glow, sharp and crisp in the unnatural lime hue. Sickly green or not, he could see again. He tested the gear by turning his head first to the left, then to the right. Hank materialized in front of him, and James could see a hint of a grin, which could have just as easily been a darkly cheerful sneer, beneath the man's own ballistic helmet. Even with the promise of a potential firefight ahead of them, Hank always somehow managed to remain levelheaded. The man was the embodiment of good humor, even when others were feeling tense or uneasy.

James could understand Hank's strained grin, though. While he personally tended to be more reserved, he knew the almost jocular energy the man felt. He was sure his own face was taut with anticipation of the mission ahead. He returned the expression with a nod of his own.

Satisfied, Hank turned away from him, his body blurring slightly in the lens of his NVGs.

Tex's voice was in his ear, a distant hiss muted by the static of his radio. "C'mon, let's go, men."

James could see his team leader's broad-shouldered form ahead, his arm bent at a 45-degree angle next to his head, his palm flat and facing forward. He fell into a trot behind Tex. The rest of B Team assembled behind him, and they trekked steadily across the sandy landscape toward Da'wud's compound. Their footfalls were muffled on the soft turf, and were it not for the whumping sound of the rotors of the Black Hawk helicopters, they may have flown in completely undetected. James strongly doubted they would have such good fortune to go entirely unnoticed. He hoped, though, that they would be able to maintain the upper hand in the upcoming mission. They didn't necessarily need to sneak in. It wasn't as though stealth was on their side. But he didn't want to draw any needless attention to himself or any of his men. Why give away their position unless absolutely required?

The sounds of the helicopters faded away as the men closed the distance between themselves and Da'wud's compound on foot. Despite the weight of his equipment, James's legs and lungs felt strong and steady as he jogged across the sand. The world around him bounced dizzyingly through the spectral glow of his NVGs, but James barely noticed the jolting jerkiness as he narrowed the gap between himself and the compound.

The members of The Unit stopped in front of a looming, eight-foot wall. Someone coughed, and another man cleared his throat as they stood alongside the perimeter barrier. Even though the short jaunt was nothing compared to the thirty-something miles they each ran every week, the dry air was still an irritant to their sinuses. Twenty paces to their left was the main entrance to the compound, but both logic and intel provided by their informant dictated that they needed to find an alternative way in. The risk of encountering an improvised explosive device (IED) was too high. The door to the compound was almost surely boobytrapped. The Delta Team needed to forcibly enter Da'wud's stronghold.

The wall was comprised of pale, sand-colored bricks and topped with a dully gleaming coil of razor wire. Da'wud evidently wasn't taking any visitors tonight. Well, hell, they'd gone all this way to come see him. Not having a friendly welcome mat set out in anticipation of their arrival wasn't going to deter them, though.

From James's peripheral vision, he saw Ginger pull something out of the front pocket of his Kevlar vest. As their resident tactical demolition expert, it fell upon him to help them infiltrate Da'wud's makeshift fortress. He operated quickly, affixing a linear shaped charge against the towering obstacle.

James stepped back, giving the explosive and its handler the respect they were due. Everyone else in their party moved back, giving Ginger sufficient space to move freely as he worked. James aimed his M4 at an undefined point in the distance, and even though no verbal command was issued, all of the other members of The Unit followed suit. They knew their responsibilities to their fellow team members and didn't need constant reminders to look out for one another. Because Ginger was exposing himself to the danger of enemy fire by setting up the explosives, he was entirely dependent upon his men to keep him protected while he operated. Their vigilance was both an automatic and ingrained behavior.

Ginger's face was a resolute mask of concentration beneath his NVGs. He carefully yet rapidly attached the firing system—a cylindrical tube connected to a fuse ignitor. Then, with a low grunt of satisfaction that was barely picked up by his radio, he pulled the key on the M60 ignitor and announced, "Firing!" He took several lunging steps toward the Delta Team, turning his back toward his explosive device.

A moment later, a loud pop resounded, breaking the silence of the witching hour.

James drew back from the sound, an involuntary reflex rather than a flinch. A smoking hole stood where the wall once was, a pile of rubble collected at the base of it. They now had their access to the compound.

"Ladies first," a voice chirped in James's ear.

He suspected that it was Rembrandt from the New Jersey accent, but he held back from stepping through the opening. He sure as hell wasn't going to indulge the young SFC's folly and be the recipient of pithy remarks when they got back to the Green Zone. He raised his M4 carbine in the air before him, his eyes abruptly alert and scanning the terrain ahead. The air was thick and choked with floating dust particles that danced and drifted in the faint glow of his NVGs. Then he was through the plume of debris, and the courtyard of Da'wud's compound sprawled out before him. He swept his gaze in a wide arc, his attention on high alert for any sign of movement.

There was none. Except for the twelve men who had just penetrated the compound, they were alone.

James moved briskly, his weapon steady in front of him. His finger was on the trigger guard, ready to fire. So far, there was no sign that the compound was inhabited. He could see the motion of his men advancing steadily upon the fortification. Nobody spoke. The only sounds in his ear were the low and rhythmic echoes of his own breathing.

At the back entrance of Da'wud's residence, James turned toward Ginger. The man was already moving toward the door. He produced another shape charge from his kit and quickly assembled it against the metal door. The men drew away from the explosive as Ginger's voice cried out, "Firing!"

A booming explosion jostled the steel door free from its hinges, and it swung forward before falling to the ground with a crashing thud.

James glanced around, seeking out Tex in the haze. He could see a hint of the man's shape and his raised palm, then Tex stepped through the door and the rest of the men slipped through the opening one by one. James cast a final glance back over his shoulder, confirming they were still alone in the courtyard, and stepped through the shattered doorframe. He peered over the shoulder of the man standing in front of him. The room was empty. He swept his firearm to the left, taking another cautious step into the room. From his peripheral vision, he could see another teammate moving past them, but his initial assessment had been correct. There was nobody in the entryway, though it would take a methodical room-by-room sweep from the A Team to verify with any degree of certainty that the first floor was empty.

A less trained individual might have thought someone had tipped Da'wud off and held the mistaken suspicion that their target had fled in advance of the team's arrival. Or they may have believed their informant had double-crossed them, feeding them false intel for their enemy's gain. Hell, one couldn't even be sure the CIA's intel was fresh enough to be relevant. But James knew better. They weren't alone. Yes, the house was enshrouded in an oppressive hush, but they would find Da'wud shortly. He was confident their target was still hiding in this house somewhere. And, with twelve elite soldiers on his trail, they would find him rather soon.

James's training kicked in. He crossed the room briskly, falling into place behind a pair of wide shoulders a couple steps ahead of him. Alpha Team split apart from the group, and James watched as they moved into position, led by Benjamin and tailed by Kermit, to go room by room to clear the first level of the house. Kermit slipped from view, and James turned away, his focus returning to the task ahead.

In a moment, James would be alongside B Team upstairs, performing a similar ritual on the second level.

The process of clearing a building was a fairly simple yet methodical one. James and the rest of Delta Team had been trained extensively on procedures that combined older and newer methods for both a swift and effective clearance of the quarters. The concept was deceptively basic, belying the amount of trial and error that had gone into its development. Working together, the stack would need to not only anticipate their enemy's moves, but also the movements of their own team. By combining strategic movement with quick thinking and banishing the methods that were only upheld merely because it was repetition at that point, the casualty rate of this task soon dropped for Special Forces soldiers.

In the past, the US Army had relied upon older training techniques to clear a room. These methods, while successful when facing a hostage or a rescue situation, had quickly proven to be largely ineffectual when translated to close-quarters battle (CQB). They weren't there to rescue hostages. They were there to kill the enemy. Nobody would disagree with that, yet they still found themselves caught in the groove of doing things in a conventional and unproductive manner. In a conventional hostage rescue (HR) situation, the objective was to distract the enemy from their primary target, their hostages. By flooding the room with soldiers (or, in these cases, members of a SWAT team or other rescue operation), they would be able to complete their objective with minimal casualties. Up until the war in the Middle East, this had proven to be a seemingly foolproof method. After all, it had worked time and again in these hostage situations and had even been integrated into the Battle Drill 6A. Why change what worked?

Because it wasn't working, and men were dying due to these flawed and antiquated techniques. Even a split-second delay in the second group of soldiers was enough to give their enemy an advantage. Furthermore, in a hostage situation, they were operating under more offense than defense. In CQB, the stack needed to be more defensive. Not only did their enemies know they were present, but they were also heavily armed and had a mutual goal of killing their opponents. Merely bursting into a room repeatedly was no longer doing the job. What was there to diffuse if there were no hostages to rescue?

It was also worth considering that during other military conflicts, soldiers had faced a more diverse terrain for combat. The jungles of Vietnam were vastly different from the flat desert of the Middle East. And while the training techniques from SWAT teams and hostage negotiators were adequate in predictable, domestic situations, the Middle East was a whole other ball game. Enemy soldiers were no longer ducking behind trees or making tiger pits to suppress their enemies. The insurgents were instead using whatever cover was readily available. In the smooth surface of the Baghdadi or Iranian wastelands, that translated to urban combat. Any building could provide shelter for enemy combatants, and because of this shifting tide of combat, new training protocols were deemed necessary.

Humans also had another disadvantage: they couldn't outrun bullets. No matter how quickly they burst into a room, a round from an enemy firearm was much faster. Perhaps they still maintained some semblance of surprise in the first couple of rooms, but as they advanced upon their enemy, their location was no longer a mystery.

And since there were no friendlies to rescue, there was no need to prevent lethal crossfire from harming an innocent non-combatant.

By changing the way they approached urban combat, shifting their training from an HR situation to a CQB one, Special Forces soon started to see a decline in combat mortality. They no longer needed to storm a room, clear it, then make way for their team members behind them. They could instead let their bullets do the heavy legwork for them.

Tex led B Team up the stairs, his boot-clad feet landing on each step quietly yet swiftly, remaining on each one only long enough to push him to the next riser. Despite himself, James felt his pulse quicken slightly. Of all the places in the house, the stairs were arguably the most dangerous position. Anyone could throw a grenade down the stairs or release a barrage of bullets upon them, and there wasn't anything they could do about it. Acutely aware of their vulnerability, James didn't like it one bit. His shoulders were square and tense as he climbed the stairs behind his team.

Of course, Da'wud had to have a multilevel compound. It wasn't enough to have a palatial garrison to hide away in. He had to loom over the rest of the city in his two-story house. *A smug little prick, that's what he is,* James thought sourly.

He cast the thought off. There was no point dwelling on it, much less wasting emotion by attributing anything more than professionalism to the job ahead. He needed to remember that his conflict with Da'wud was not his own. He was acting as an extension of the United States Government, there to do a job, not to seek out petty revenge on behalf of everyone killed by the terrorist.

The heightened risk of danger in the narrow stairwell wasn't exclusively due to their trapped position there either. It was also the fact that there were so many angles where their enemy could hide. This particular stairwell had an L-bend in the middle of it, leading to a brief landing before they resumed their journey to the second level of the house. Anyone who had any intention of putting a swift and judicial end to B Team would have no problem completing this task while the men ascended the narrow stairs.

While clearing a room may take slow and deliberate movements, clearing a stairway was different. Speed was of the essence. Yes, they still needed to be methodical and not careless. Still, there was no time to carefully tiptoe up them and hope they were going largely undetected. They'd already announced their presence. Their enemy, were they hidden away upstairs as James suspected, knew someone was coming for them. They weren't up there enjoying a light snooze but rather were acutely aware of the intruders.

They crossed the landing, rounding an open corner, then the final dozen steps loomed before James. He monitored the void ahead of Tex as the man crested the last series of stairs, his weapon aimed and ready in case he needed to use it. While he couldn't see anything except the ceiling from his position on the landing, he monitored their flank. As Tex approached the top, Hank flattened himself against the wall opposite him and waited for Tex to lift his hand in signal that the hallway was free from imminent danger, giving them the go-ahead to join him in his current position.

Despite no evidence to suggest that they were anything but alone in Da'wud's compound so far, James acknowledged the nagging voice of suspicion in the back of his head with little more than dutiful recognition as he waited for the go-ahead to crest the final series of stairs. His eyes bore holes into the back of the soldier standing directly in front of him. Ginger's tall and wiry frame was practically thrumming with tension as he waited for the signal from Tex that they were safe to proceed.

A resonant boom from downstairs met James's ears as he loitered impatiently on the landing. A stunned stupor fell over him, giving him a moment to puzzle over the source of the sound as his legs buckled beneath him.

What the he—

Then he fell to the ground, his body collapsing to the cold tile floor with a weighty thud. All sound was sucked out of his ears, replaced by a high-pitched, keening note.

But James didn't have to guess what had just transpired. Based on the plume of dust and sand enveloping the men on the second floor and inside the stairwell, the reverberating whine in his ears, and the shouts coming from downstairs, he knew what had happened. Someone downstairs had managed to trigger some sort of explosive device. He felt a knot of dread in his stomach because whoever had done it was surely dead now. He knew this with unwavering certainty. Such an explosion was not survivable. He also knew from experience that the magnitude of the explosion probably meant collateral damage as well. Someone else may have been mortally wounded in the explosion too. A parade of faces marched past James's open eyes, each one taunting him as it drifted past. In a rapid stream, he vividly saw every one of the men downstairs.

Rembrandt. Kermit. Mooney. Bones. Noodle. Benjamin. Who was the unlucky man? Who unwittingly triggered the explosive?

James rose unsteadily to his feet, needing to get downstairs and tend to his fallen brother. Or possibly even brothers. He had no idea how many had been taken out or wounded by the explosion but felt a pressing urgency to get there and help triage them. Yet, even as he found his footing beneath him, he heard ululating shouts of the enemy arise suddenly from down the hall and several weapons being fired all at once.

It was an ambush.

Whoever was lurking upstairs had been waiting patiently until the right moment. Like a snake that watched its prey without moving, stalking it until the ideal time to pounce, Da'wud and his company of insurgents had finally found their ideal opportunity to begin their strike against Bravo Team. In the midst of the chaos arising from downstairs and the opaque fog of dust and sand creeping up the stairs, James and the rest of B Team were actively under attack.

CHAPTER FOUR

INSIDE DA'WUD'S COMPOUND

0225 HOURS – 15 NOVEMBER 2013

A T APPROXIMATELY 0224 LOCAL TIME, Kermit stepped on the pressure plate. It wasn't that he had been careless or not paying attention, and it would be appallingly unfair to blame the sequence of actions on his lack of training or recklessness. He hadn't been distracted at all. If anything, because he was the tail of the formation, he had possibly been on higher alert than any of the other men in the room. Benjamin had just cleared the first level kitchen and beckoned the A Team to follow with his open palm, and Kermit had followed his footsteps religiously. After all, if it had been a safe enough route for Benjamin, why wouldn't Kermit place his boots exactly where his team leader had stepped? It made perfect sense. Except Kermit had failed to remember that Benjamin was taller, with longer legs and a wider stride. Kermit had boasted no more than five and a half feet of height to his name on a good day. With his boots on, it gave him another inch or so of lift. Benjamin towered over him at well over six feet, and while Kermit wasn't necessarily petite per se, he was the shortest man in The Unit by at least two inches. So, where everyone else had easily stepped over the pressure plate, concealed by a creaky floorboard in the unlit room, Kermit had the poor luck of resting his full bodyweight directly upon it.

The result? A cataclysmic explosion that changed the course of their mission entirely. The moment his foot landed on the pressure plate, the percussive force of the explosion immediately blasted his legs off and sent pulpy shrapnel of the young man in all directions. The explosion also immediately claimed the lives of Mooney and Noodle, who had been following Kermit closely. While Kermit had become a fleshy projectile, Mooney and Noodle suffered a slightly different fate. A wicked shard of shrapnel had damn near separated Mooney's head from his shoulders, and he'd collapsed to the ground without hesitation. A rain of barbed edges had pierced Noodle throughout his torso and neck and one particularly nasty piece had gouged through his left eyeball.

None of these men would serve on another mission for the United States Government. Thanks to Kermit's untimely and ultimately tragic misstep, they immediately retired from their service with Delta Force and became another unfortunate casualty in the war on terrorism. They would be posthumously awarded several medals for their heroic actions on behalf of the United States. Within forty-eight hours, their widows would get a call, sympathetic condolences, and a gentle yet heartfelt reminder that their husbands had saved several other men's lives through their heroic actions during the mission.

A white fog of dust radiated from the blast, bathing the entire first floor in a haze of thick sand and debris. With nowhere else to go, the particulates whooshed upstairs from the convective force of the explosion.

A handful of seconds passed after that initial explosion. There was something curiously muffled about its aftermath, lending an eerie pseudo-calm that descended upon the men inside Da'wud's stronghold. Then, after only the briefest of delays to recognize and assimilate what had just transpired, Alpha Team reacted to the tragedy.

A natural leader, Benjamin had been chosen to be Alpha Team leader because of his unflinching leadership instinct when under extreme duress, and his characteristic mindset swiftly took over. Grasping an exposed beam jutting from the wall, he hoisted himself to his feet. His face was a white mask of shocked dismay, and twin trails of blood trickled down the sides of his face where the concussion of the explosion had ruptured his eardrums. He turned, fumbling in the whiteout, and extended his dusty hand to the man to his direct right.

Bones clasped it, and Benjamin stumbled back, using the wall as leverage so he could help the staggering man to his feet. From the smoke, another ghostly form materialized, and Rembrandt drifted into view. His eyes were wide, dark pinpoints punctuating his face, and his mouth was locked in a dumbfounded *O* of disbelief. He bore his own matching trails of blood on his cheeks from ruptured eardrums.

Benjamin's training took over, and upon recognizing that these two men didn't need any immediate or lifesaving assistance, he ignored the muffled whine reverberating from within his destroyed ears and spun in the direction of the explosion. There was no need to issue verbal commands. Nobody would be able to hear them anyway. He arrived at the heap of bodies first.

There wasn't enough left of Kermit to immediately identify, and it took several moments of visual scanning for Benjamin to locate enough evidence to determine that the quiet Frenchman was no longer alive. The largest piece of him was his arm, which still held the battered leather watch he'd always insisted on wearing, claiming the timepiece was lucky. His superstition had finally failed him.

Mooney and Noodle were easier to identify, and while Benjamin's combat medic training gave him the skills to staunch blood flow or treat a severe bodily wound, he knew right away that there was nothing he could do for the two men. They were beyond salvation. He produced a bandana from the front pocket of his vest and, making eye contact with Bones through his NVGs, nodded. With an understanding nod of his own, Bones withdrew one from his own pocket and, with a shake of his wrist, unfurled it. Taking measures to avoid the pit in the floor and possibly avoid triggering another explosion, the men knelt and gently draped the cloths over each corpse's face. It wasn't much, and it was a damn poor eulogy, but resting the square of cotton over Noodle's unseeing eyes offered a degree of closure to the sergeant major. Bones let his own scrap of fabric settle onto Mooney's face, which listed at an unnatural angle by a thin thread of exposed tendon on the man's neck. Rembrandt pulled his own cloth from his pocket, but after a fruitless glance around the room, returned it to its original position in his vest. There wasn't enough Kermit for him to cover. The corners of his mouth dragged down, instantly aging him several years.

The unforeseen action on Kermit's behalf had been enough to give Da'wud and his fellow insurgents the opportunity to strike. Above Alpha Team's heads, the rattling sound of a firefight and a litany of shouts interrupted their somber reverie.

Bravo Team was under attack.

James was trapped in a surreal nightmare. Just like a dreamlike state was often accompanied by a sense of detachment and numbness, he felt oddly distanced from the events unfolding before him. It wasn't that he didn't fully grasp what was occurring. It was just the analgesic balm of his training taking over, pushing him through his natural fight or flight drive. His training allowed him to view the world through a lens of acute clarity, to set aside any hesitation or excessive deliberation for long enough to take care of the urgent matter developing around him. He could feel the rush of bullets cutting through the air, pummeling the wall behind him. He could hear both the high-pitched whine as they zipped past and the explosive report as they peppered the stairwell where he stood. But his visibility was next to zero due to the milky haze of smoke rising from the lower level, and each mote of dust and sand glowed in a brilliant, emerald tint. Between the chaos of the explosion downstairs and the unexpected assault directly in front of him, James staggered in a momentary blackout of disorientation.

His training, however, didn't require his conscious wits. Even before he'd fully assimilated what was going on around him, he was already lifting his M4 and storming up the stairs to join his team. The entire span of time from the explosion downstairs to him cresting the top of the stairs was a delay of less than five seconds. It took less than a half dozen heartbeats for James to assimilate the situation and react. His shoulder clocked off Hank's as he mounted the stairs and aimed his firearm down the hallway, and he uttered a perfunctory and automatic apology, but the man didn't seem to recognize that James had stopped next to him. The good cheer was gone from his face, a contortion of savage fury now in its place.

"Hank and James, aim left!" Tex's voice cut through their radio. "Ginger and Marmaduke, I want you to hold the center. Dickie, I want you to aim right, with me."

Hank's entire body suddenly jerked violently as his MICH helmet flew off his head, and James had a moment to realize that where once Hank's easy smile resided, a gaping void now existed. From James's vantage, he could see that the lower part of Hank's jaw was a shattered and gory mess, revealing the white bones of his jaw and teeth. Then he was tumbling down the stairs, and James understood immediately and acutely that his friend was dead. The calculated numbness of his training offered a momentary shield from emotion, but it wouldn't protect him from receiving his own tattoo of bullet holes if he lingered on those thoughts. He had no time to grieve or mourn, nor could he justify it in that moment. He had to focus on the assault directly in front of him.

James barely had a moment to register Hank's death when another body collapsed to the ground. A glance down revealed that the obliterated face peering up at him had once belonged to Marmaduke. The towering man had been both soft-spoken and unexpectedly gentle despite his role as a formidable fighter in Delta. It had been a running joke amongst The Unit that Marmaduke didn't seem to know his own size nor strength, and the man had been the epitome of the gentle giant in their team. Now, though, he was yet another casualty of war.

Those sons of bitches!

It hadn't been personal to James before that moment. Work was work. He knew that. He'd always known that and always taken great pains to separate his job from his emotions. What good would it be for him to get angry at his enemy? Anger was a distraction and compromised his skill, resulting in impulsive actions. But it didn't change the bubbling wrath that churned the acid in his stomach. Sure, it was just a job before, but now? James was about to unleash holy hell on those motherfuckers for Hank and for Marmaduke and for whoever had been killed or maimed downstairs.

It was virtually impossible to make out the shapes of their enemy through the swirling debris, much less discern the precise location of the assault. Even the amplified luminosity from his NVGs did little to improve the clarity of the setting. But while he couldn't make out any tangible human forms, the muzzle flash of the enemy's AK-47 gave him a fairly good idea where the attack was coming from. James pressed his shoulder against the left side of the wall. To his right, Ginger already had his own carbine raised and was firing, his weapon aimed straight down the center of the obscured hallway. Tex and Dickey aimed at the right side of the hall and even through the darkness and particles of dust in the air, James could just make out their shoulders jostling from the recoil of their weapons.

James pressed his M4 against his pectoral muscles, positioning it near the groove of his armpit, and gripped the stock with his left hand as his right hand closed around the grip and trigger. The butt of his rifle skimmed his bearded lower jaw, and he peered through the scope as he aimed the weapon down the hallway. He widened his stance, leaning forward slightly as he aimed. He knew he wasn't going to be able to see his enemy clearly, but that didn't worry him. The insurgents were directly ahead of him, and the ammunition firing from his carbine would help level out the playing field. As long as he fired in the correct general direction, fussing over the nuance of precise aiming wasn't a huge problem. What he lacked in precision he would make up for in volume. He let out his breath, then depressed the trigger on his M4, releasing the first of a steady onslaught of bullets in the general direction of the insurgents. The semi-automatic rifle fired smoothly in his hands until it clicked hollowly, and James reached deftly into his utility vest pocket and produced another magazine. Without missing a beat, he dropped the empty mag out of his M4 and replaced it with a fresh one, slapping the side of the firearm to slide the bolt forward.

A large chunk of plaster bounced off the wall less than an inch away from his face, but he barely noticed the sharp material lacerate his cheek as it bounced off and tumbled to the floor at his feet. His focus was too honed, too intent on killing his enemy to let frivolous things like a small scratch on his face distract him. Who cared about a nick on his skin when he could be facing a brand-new hole in his body?

"Cease fire!" Tex cried out suddenly.

James immediately removed his finger from the trigger and, keeping his weapon aimed down the hallway, turned to face his team leader. Standing directly to his right, Ginger also removed his index finger from the trigger and propped it against the guard, then he spun toward Tex, his carbine still trained on the darkened hallway before him. Dickie was the last to respond, his body reluctantly turning to face Tex as he kept both his weapon and one eye trained in the direction of the enemy.

Silence finally reigned over the upper level of the residence. Sometime in the past thirty seconds, the insurgents had stopped firing upon them. Either they'd retreated or they'd been killed.

James strongly hoped it was the second option.

"Dickie and Ginger, I want you to come with me. James, check on Hank and Marmaduke." Tex's voice was flat on that last sentence as it filtered through the radio, and James suspected the man knew exactly what he'd seen with his own eyes.

James cast a glance down the hall. Through the glow of his NVGs, he could see the shapeless forms of the terrorists in a hunched posture at the end of the hallway. Around them, the walls were peppered with holes. In some places, entire chunks of the architecture had been completely demolished. Gaping holes formed a rough, patchwork pattern on the far walls and doors, and James suspected his team would find corpses when they made their way down there. He exchanged a brief nod with his team leader and the other two men before turning to face the slumped bodies of his fallen comrades on the stairwell behind him.

James wasn't a squeamish man, but he didn't want to see the faces of Hank and Marmaduke. He already knew what he was going to find. He'd already seen the immediate aftermath of their faces versus an AK-47. But an order was an order, and protocol required that he confirm they were dead. He took a step down the stairs and knelt, pressing his fingers against Hank's neck as his brother stared up at him with unseeing eyes. No pulse. James shook his head and slipped his hand down his friend's face, closing the man's eyes for the last time.

An examination of Marmaduke's prone body revealed matching results. The large man had no face left to speak of, and James didn't bother feeling for a pulse, as his head had almost been completely detached from his body. He rose to his feet, his knees cracking as he stood. The men were dead. There was nothing James could do for them. He made a mental note to grieve for them later. He would empty a bottle of his finest whiskey onto the desert sand in their honor when he got back to their base inside the Green Zone. It would be a piss-poor tribute, but the private ceremony would give him a modicum of peace.

He was turning to ascend the stairs and help the rest of B Team clear the upstairs level when the sound of a weapon being discharged rang out from down the hall. Multiple shots followed in rapid succession, followed by a bellowing scream. James didn't hesitate. Raising his M4, he gripped the stairway railing for momentum and launched himself down the hall. He sprinted, pausing before the slightly ajar door only long enough to kick it open with his boot. He wasn't sure what he was going to find when the door swung the rest of the way open but was ready to take action and defend his team. He aimed his weapon, his eyes scanning the small room as he tried to locate the source of the commotion.

To his surprise, his eyes lit upon Da'wud Al Muhammad staring back at him. He was sitting on the wooden floor with his upper body propped against the twin bed and an AK47 still in his hands but lying in his lap.

CHAPTER FIVE

END OF MISSION

0237 HOURS – 15 NOVEMBER 2013

J AMES AIMED HIS M4, HIS finger tightening automatically around the trigger. Then, after a brief pause as he considered the terrorist looming before him, he lowered the weapon and afforded the bearded man a more thorough inspection. His dark eyes lingered on his enemy's ashy countenance. Da'wud's own eyes were blank and unseeing, and James realized that a blossom of blood was spreading across the enemy's cream-colored robe.

Ginger spun to face James, his pale features blanched in the aftermath of his encounter with Da'wud. The lower portion of his face, which was barely visible beneath his MICH helmet, had taken on an especially sickly pallor through the green glow of James's NVGs. The slim man shook his head, his Adam's apple bobbing in his throat as his voice filtered into James's ear through his headpiece. "We had to shoot him, Gator. He was going to shoot us first."

Tex's voice was calmer. "He had an AK-47 and was drawing upon us when we entered the room. Unfortunately for him, we shot first."

James nodded. Their instructions were to capture Da'wud Al Muhammad, but if they were unable to do so, they were to execute him. His men had done nothing wrong. A thorough briefing once they returned to the Green Zone would verify that they'd acted in an appropriate manner in killing the terrorist. There would be several interviews with James and his men, and all of the reconnaissance data gathered from their mission tonight would be noted, documented, and then hidden away in a classified folder that would probably never see the light of day while James was still alive.

The mission had come to a successful end, depending on how one defined success. Had they killed their target? Sure. But what had been the cost of their success?

The mission wasn't entirely done just yet, though. They still needed to perform their site exploitation and finish clearing the house. There could be valuable intel hidden away within Da'wud's compound. James felt a sudden wave of fatigue, but he pushed it away. There was so much more that needed to be done before he could go back to the base and get his shower. Despite the horrors he had seen tonight, he would still try to get some sleep. Would he be successful? Perhaps. He'd lost men before, but none as close to him as Hank had been. Even Marmaduke had been a damn fine soldier and a good buddy.

"What did you find?" James asked Tex.

"Five insurgents," Tex said. He glanced toward the open door where the pile of insurgents lay in a huddled heap, then back at James. "Plus Da'wud. It appears Da'wud had retreated when we started returning fire. We checked the bodies and confirmed the kills, then started the process of clearing the rooms."

James nodded. It made sense. He couldn't argue with Tex's logic or his report of the actions of himself and his team. He would have done the same thing had he been in their shoes. Second-guessing oneself or hesitation could lead to men getting killed, and they'd suffered enough losses already that night. It was a shame that Da'wud was killed, as a leisurely interrogation of him could have divulged some highly valuable intel to The Unit. For instance, Da'wud might have known where other HVTs were hiding out. Maybe he wouldn't have given this information up willingly, but there were ways of making people talk.

Oh well. Killing him is just as good after what just happened.

"Well," Tex said after a moment, "there's been a slight change of plans. Gator, I'm going to have you do site exploitation with me. Dickie and Ginger, I want you to perform site exploitation on the south side of the residence. If you see anything unusual, I want to hear about it right away. We're going to have to double down our efforts tonight since we're down two men. I know you're not going to loiter over garbage, so I'm mostly just stating the obvious here. But as you already know, we have to be especially efficient now if we want to get out of here on time."

James nodded again. He understood what Tex was telling him. It wasn't a request, and getting out of there on schedule also wasn't optional. They had to lift off from Da'wud's compound well before dawn. Sticking around after the sun rose was a death sentence, and nobody wanted to be seen there after morning broke. James fell into step behind his team leader.

Tex cast a final glance over his shoulder, but Dickie and Ginger were already headed toward the south-facing side of Da'wud's house. They didn't need to be told twice what to do.

The importance of a comprehensive site exploitation could not be stressed strongly enough. As one of the more essential means of gathering crucial intel, it was an invaluable part of any Special Forces task. Yes, capturing or killing their HVT was almost certainly the most important consideration of their mission. However, detaining their enemy was only one facet of their job. In fact, it could be argued that it was almost secondary to site exploitation when it came to advancing and supplementing government intelligence.

The concept of site exploitation relied upon five core concepts. These activities helped ensure the data soldiers gathered was not only reliable and important, but that it would be accurately categorized and put to good use later on. By adhering to these five principles, it became much easier to quantify their efforts and recognize the quality of their intel.

James knew these concepts by heart: detect, collect, process, analyze, and disseminate. When Tex had reminded him to not linger over garbage, he'd been talking about detection. Knowing what was important and what was trash was a highly important distinction. James knew better than to spend too much time sifting through a stack of paperwork to find a specific sheet of data. It was better to set it all aside and let someone else go through it. The same could be said for any computers or USB drives found on site. That moved into the next steps, all the way down to the very last stage, dissemination. At that point, it would be out of James's hands.

Frankly, the finer details of site exploitation were of little relevance to James. The key focus for him, at least in that moment, was gathering the intel for later dissemination. He kept this in the back of his mind as he swept through the second floor of the compound. He carefully yet swiftly sifted through everything he encountered to determine if it was trash or relevant. By the time he'd finished clearing the two rooms assigned to him, he had a nice pile of material to bring back to the Green Zone. Tex had also added to his pile, and they stacked everything on a scarred and battered wooden table. There wasn't much, but James suspected there was sure to be something good in the meager stack of data. Among the collected material, James counted several computer devices, scores of thumb drives, multiple hard drives, and even the shattered cell phones from the pockets of the insurgents.

Tex jerked his head at James, and James followed him down the hall to where Da'wud's corpse was cooling off in the room where he'd been left. Tex stood over Da'wud's body and, raising his face toward James to ensure he had the younger chief warrant officer's attention, withdrew his Yarborough from a sheath attached at his hip. James understood immediately and stepped across the room, gripping the collar of the terrorist's tunic. Without preamble, Tex slid his knife smoothly across Da'wud's beard, removing a lock of the coarse facial hair. James fished a zip-top bag from his pocket and shook it open in the otherwise quiet room, then Tex slipped the hair into the bag. The DNA would serve as an identifier later, in case anyone doubted they'd actually eliminated their target during their mission. Tex ran his fingers along the seal, closing the bag, then returned his blade to its sheath. He held the baggie in his closed fist, and his face turned down toward the body of the terrorist one final time. Even through his NVGs, James could sense the look of contempt on his team leader's face.

James held Da'wud's head aloft by his coarse hair as Tex captured a series of photographs of the terrorist with a small, handheld camera. He closed his eyes against the bright flash as Tex took the pictures. He felt a mounting need to get downstairs and see what had happened to Alpha Team, but he pushed the feelings of impatience aside. Per their training, Alpha Team had stayed downstairs and Bravo Team remained upstairs while they worked. The two teams would not meet again until they'd finished their assigned responsibilities. But as they wrapped up their work upstairs, James couldn't help but wonder who had stepped on the plate and who was still alive down there. Other than the initial blast of the explosion, he hadn't heard any commotion or sounds rising up the stairs.

When his headset picked up ambient sounds of radio chatter, the voices seemed calm enough and James let out a breath he didn't know he'd been holding. He trained half an ear on the chatter as he searched the south quadrant of the room, which contained a table with one chair and two boxes. One box contained female clothing with a mix of children's clothing, and the other box contained what appeared to be pirated movie DVDs, two hard drives, and one thumb drive. James took possession of the hard drives and the thumb drive and placed them in an antistatic bag. Yes, some of his men had been killed tonight, but based on the overlapping voices playing in his ear, several had also survived. He recognized some of the chatter as discourse from the Ranger element that had joined them to provide perimeter support. They'd secured the outside of the compound, and a discussion was unfolding as to how they were going to carry the deceased Delta members out of the compound. From the sounds of it, there had been three casualties in the explosion. He could hear Benjamin's voice distantly in his headset. According to the report coming from Alpha Team leader, Kermit had been the unfortunate man who stepped on the pressure plate. Mooney and Noodle had been additional losses. In their case, it was a matter of being in the wrong place at the wrong time. Then there were low grunts as the men hoisted the fallen soldiers and started the process of carrying them outside to be returned to base. In a few minutes, they would start working their way upstairs to see if Bravo Team needed their assistance too.

"Let's move out," Tex said finally. "I already cleared the body, so there's nothing left in here for us to deal with. His personal effects are on the table with the other material we retrieved. We'll do one final sweep with our camera before we head out, but I think we're just about done here."

"Sounds good to me," James said. He led the way out of the small room and, speaking into his headset for Ginger and Dickie, repeated to the men what the plan was.

A moment later, both men strode into view.

James arrived at the stairs first and carefully avoided looking down at the bodies of Hank and Marmaduke, which were still lying in unnatural angles at the lip of the hallway. It wasn't that the bodies were repulsive. James had an exceedingly strong iron stomach, and his unflappable expression in the face of the macabre often stunned those who witnessed it firsthand. But if he dwelled on the fact that his friends were now dead, he'd let the worm of sorrow wriggle its way into his brain and distract him.

Grieving can come later, he reminded himself firmly. *Focus on the task at hand. You can pay your respects to them once you're out of here.*

The mantra worked. He'd taught himself to compartmentalize his feelings early on. His inherent aptitude for being a soldier wasn't just in his physical prowess. He had a higher than usual mental fortitude, and things that would break another individual rolled off his back more often than not. Resilience was a cornerstone of his identity, whether he liked it or not. Sometimes he almost wished he could experience that candid anguish like other people, but he knew this weakness was also his strength.

What happened next would haunt James. Perhaps it was because he'd been distracted by his fallen friends despite his best efforts to remain focused. Or maybe anyone would have failed to notice that the structural integrity of the stairs had been compromised in the blast from downstairs. He would ruminate and question his memory of the event, wondering how he'd failed to notice he was stepping on a trap not unlike the one Kermit had discharged over an hour before.

———※——※——※——※——※———

Tex froze at the top of the stairwell. A moment ago, Gator had been standing directly in front of him. Then, without warning, Gator was suddenly gone from his sight. He marveled silently to himself at how he hadn't even heard Gator utter a single word as he slipped through the staircase. Just one second he was there, and the next, gone. The only noise that signaled something had even happened to his fellow team member was the loud crack of the wood splintering and the resonant boom of Gator's body thudding against the ground below.

"Gator?" Tex's voice filtered through the radio, but no reply met his ears. He raised his voice, speaking clearly into his radio. "Gator, can you hear me? Do you copy?"

"What the hell just happened?" Ginger crossed the hallway to the landing, but Tex thrust his arm out, holding the tall redhead back. Ginger shot a glance at his team leader, then leaned forward, peering down into the gaping hole sprawled open in front of him. "Holy shit. Gator?"

"Back," Tex said sharply. "I don't want you falling through too."

Ginger took a step back, then gripped the railing and peered down into the blackness yawning before him. Gator's body lay sprawled out some thirty feet below him. "What happened, Tex?"

"He fell," Tex answered. He spoke into the radio again, pausing between each sentence to give his friend an opportunity to respond. It proved to be a futile consideration. "Gator, man? I repeat, Gator, can you hear me? Gator, this is Tex, do you read me? Do you copy?"

But Gator didn't read him, nor did he copy. He lay motionless on the subterranean floor below them, his body contorted at a crooked angle.

Tex trained his NVGs on the seemingly lifeless body of his

friend, but from this distance, he couldn't get a clear view. Gator wasn't moving, and the silence coming from the motionless body didn't give him much optimism either. He shook his head and took another step back from the edge of the precipice.

"You think he's dead?" Ginger asked, a note of anxiety finding its way into his voice.

"Do I look like a fucking psychic to you?" Tex pushed away from the stairway, spinning on his heel to face Ginger. Tension had worked its way into his voice too. "We need to find another way down. I guess the explosion weakened the stairs. Shit!"

Dickie stood silently in their peripheral vision, and at the last string of words out of Tex's mouth, he turned toward them. "I think I saw some scrap boards in the back when I was guarding the back window. If they're sturdy enough, I bet we can throw together a makeshift bridge here so we can step over this hole. Shouldn't take more than a few minutes. There were some cinderblocks back there too, so they won't budge. I'd trust them more than these boards, at least."

Tex considered this option and was about to say something, but before he could, a booming explosion rang out far off in the distance, beyond the perimeter of Da'wud's compound. He muttered an expletive under his breath, the profanity barely audible in the radio feed.

Ginger jerked his face toward the sound. "What the hell was that?"

Before anyone could answer him, another familiar noise rose up in the darkness.

Tex listened to it for a second, then shook his head. It was the sound of several weapons being discharged, and from the sound of it, they were coming from multiple people. Were the Rangers under attack now? With an exasperated growl, he took off in the direction from where Dickie had shown up. They needed to get off this second level right now, and there were no guarantees that Dickie's suggestion of fabricating a makeshift bridge would even work. And they still needed to retrieve Gator's body too. He hadn't been able to see for himself, but it wasn't outside the scope of reality that Hank and Marmaduke's corpses had fallen through the hole in the floor also. As much as he wanted to feel sadness over their losses, he set that urge aside. He would do his own private grieving later. But he also found himself fighting off a flash of irritation. He wanted the hell off of this compound, but it didn't look like he would be getting that wish anytime soon.

As he strode toward the far back of the residence, his footfalls blending in time with the steady sound of the firefight outside, he thought crossly, *Can this night get any worse?*

CHAPTER SIX

THE FIREFIGHT

0322 HOURS – 15 NOVEMBER 2013

T EX SURVEYED THE PILE OF boards and blocks with a critical eye. Yes, they certainly did look stronger than the planks that currently comprised the remainder of the stairwell. With a shrug, he said into the radio, "C'mon. Hurry up. I want off this damned level. It sounds like they need our help downstairs."

Moving swiftly, the surviving members of B Team shuttled the boards from the back room to the stairwell, piling them up as they accumulated a decent sized pile.

After two trips to the back, Tex nodded in satisfaction and pointed to the longest board of the group. "Dickie, help me grab that board. Ginger, we're going to place it across the gap. As soon as we do, I want you to stabilize it with the cinderblock."

"Understood," Ginger said. He knelt, hoisting the brick up with surprising ease. He may have been lean and rangy, but he wasn't weak. He held it patiently as Tex stepped over the plank and gripped it with his fingertips.

"Lift," Tex said.

Dickie hooked the board in his hands, shuffling his legs until the board spanned the breadth of the gap. The board wasn't heavy, but its size made it unwieldy.

Tex eyeballed the opposite side of the hole in the ground, the board hovering over the opening. When he was satisfied with its position and that it wasn't settled on a weak part of the flooring, he said, "And lower." He lowered himself to his knees, setting the board on the floor.

Dickie released the board on his side, and it dropped the remaining inch to the floor with a loud clatter.

Ginger sprang into action, the tendons in his neck straining as he placed the cinderblock onto the board.

"Again," Tex said into the radio, pointing to another lengthy board.

Dickie moved into position, grabbing it, and they repeated the actions two more times, until they had a sturdy-looking albeit questionable bridge spanning the hole.

Tex held up a closed fist, and Dickie and Ginger fell back, waiting patiently as he tapped the board with his foot. It wobbled slightly but didn't seem to bow excessively beneath his weight. With a shrug, he placed his full weight onto it. The gap couldn't have been more than four feet across at its widest point, but the fact that they were trying to maneuver downstairs made the trip especially challenging. One wrong move and he could wind up in the hole with the other downed men.

He held his arms out on both sides of his body, using them as a counterweight to steady himself as he crossed the opening. The board creaked and jostled beneath his weight, but it held steady. He didn't glance back, nor did he glance down. He was sharply aware that the lifeless body of at least one of his men was sprawled beneath him as he spanned the hole in the floor.

Then he was across and turned back toward the other two men. On this side of the hole, he could see the crumpled bodies of Marmaduke and Hank hidden behind the bend in the stairs. They must've tumbled down the stairs when James fell, ricocheted down the stairs by the recoil of the boards breaking. He assessed their remains calmly, then signaled to Dickie. His face didn't reveal his discovery to his subordinate.

Dickie nodded at the command, his face moving up and down

in the darkness. Then he was stepping on the board, his feet moving carefully as he navigated the gap. He kept his gaze trained on Tex as he walked, and in a few seconds, he was leaping nimbly off the corner of the plank. If he noticed Hank and Marmaduke, he didn't indicate it.

It was now Ginger's turn to cross. He eased his weight onto the board, extending his arms on both sides of his body for balance. He glanced down into the hole and shook his head slightly. In his earpiece, he muttered, "I fuckin' hate heights."

Ginger started across the board, his breathing slightly ragged in the microphone. If he were nervous, he didn't reveal it to the other men. He inched across it, his boots finding purchase on the downward slope. He was over halfway across the plank when the board creaked unexpectedly. He spat out an invective as a loud crack followed. His arms pinwheeled in the air as the board dipped and then he was leaping the final foot of the bridge toward the stairs. Tex was waiting for him, his arms open and ready to catch him. Ginger harmlessly bounced off his chest, then skipped a couple of steps farther before crashing against the wall with a loud thud.

The board bounced and jiggled from Ginger's weight but held steady. Had he remained on it a moment longer, however, it might have been a different story.

Dickie turned toward the taller man, clapping him on the back even as he spun back to face the two remaining men in Bravo. Genuine concern showed on his face, albeit partially hidden by the NVGs. "You okay, man?"

"Yeah, I'm fine." Ginger's voice was breathless and strained, but he was telling the truth. It had been a close call, but he'd made it across unscathed. That was more than he could say for the other three men in B Team. If he saw the other two bodies around the corner, he kept his comments to himself.

"Let's go." Tex jerked his head, and the two men fell into place behind him.

He led them down the stairs, moving as quickly as he could justify. He knew he'd lost James because the floorboards that made up the stairs had been weakened by the explosion. While he wanted to get downstairs as quickly as possible, he had to be mindful of the risk of another one of them falling through another surprise weakness in the floor.

The sounds of the firefight seemed louder the closer they got to the first level, and Tex glanced in the direction of the sound as he descended the final riser of steps.

Benjamin's strained face greeted him at the foot of the stairs. "What happened up there?"

"I could say the same for you," Tex countered. His eyes swept over the Alpha Team leader. "We need to provide combat support to the Rangers. It sounds like hell out there."

"Yeah, I know. We were just waiting on you. Wasn't sure you were alive up there, then I heard that loud crash. I decided to wait. Sounds like I made the right call." Benjamin shook his head. "We lost Mooney, Noodle, and Kermit."

Tex allowed this new information to sink in. If it affected him, he didn't allow his expression to change. Their loss didn't change their upcoming work outside. Well, that wasn't entirely true. It did change it in the sense that they were down by six men, but they would have to adapt to the new body count. Tex turned his head and noticed Ginger lower his head in a moment of respectful reflection for their loss. Tex said, "We lost Marmaduke, Hank, and Gator."

"Shit," Benjamin said.

"Yeah." Tex cleared his throat. This wasn't the time to dwell on it. For all he knew, they were losing more men by the second outside. "Let's move out."

Just like that, Benjamin was relegated from being the Alpha Team leader to falling into rank behind Tex. He gave up his authority willingly. While he was a natural leader, deferring to someone else took the onus of responsibility off him. More importantly, he trusted Tex and his guidance without hesitation. He nodded and jerked his head at Rembrandt and Bones, and the two men fell in behind Tex. The brawny man led the way, hurrying out of the house and into the firefight outside.

Tex paused by the perimeter wall, his left hand held up in a fist. The surviving members of The Unit stopped, their weapons high and ready to use at his signal. He scanned the distance for any sign of the enemy, his ears on high alert for any indication that they were nearby. He didn't need to tap into any special senses, though, to locate them. He could see the muzzle flashes from the enemy as they assaulted the Rangers a couple hundred yards away.

Tex could see the 12-man Ranger element on the east side returning fire on the enemy force. He knew the other 12-man Ranger element was still holding on the west side, and it sounded like they were busy as well. Then he noticed the support helicopters fly overhead, firing at the enemy toward the east.

The assault was seemingly coming from all directions, but the majority of the Iranian Islamic Revolutionary Guard Corps (IRGC) appeared to be largely situated to the east of the compound. While he couldn't immediately see them, he could clearly hear the steady report of the enemies' AK-47s as well as the follow-up sound of the M4 carbines the Rangers bore. It made for a steady rattle in the chaotic night, a repetitive tattoo in the inky blackness.

He held his left hand high for his men to see and, folding his ring finger and pinkie in, pointed to the right with his index finger. The enemy was to the right of them, clustered together on the east side of the compound wall. Then Tex flattened his hand, his palm facing forward, and jerked it down slightly, and the men fell into a trot behind him.

Moving at a steady pace, Tex jogged across the sandy expanse toward the sound of the fighting. Then, as the wall turned at a sharp angle, he paused. He had to strike a fine balance between not leading his men into a slaughter while simultaneously providing necessary support to the Ranger team. If they didn't intervene soon, there was a high likelihood that it would be a complete massacre and the Rangers could all but be wiped out before they even sprang into action.

A bullet zipped past Tex's head, and he jerked away from the high-pitched whine of the round passing so close to his helmet.

Instead of tracking its trajectory, though, he turned his head in the direction from where it came. That's when he saw it: the enemy they were up against.

Through the vibrant green haze of his NVGs, Tex could see the sheer numbers of the IRGC compared to the 12-man Ranger element lending defensive support to the Delta Team. The survivors of the original twenty-four men were vastly outnumbered and surrounded. The enemy stood in a wide semi-circle in the distance and were steadily closing the distance between themselves and the Rangers. A cold sweat broke out on Tex's forehead as he sized up the forces they were up against. With dawning clarity, he realized there was a very strong likelihood that he and all of his men were going to die that night.

Well, they weren't going to die without taking down a few of those Islamic Revolutionary Guards in the process. Fair was fair. It was an eye for an eye on this chilly night, and Tex and the rest of the men in The Unit were going to blind the fucking hell out of their enemy.

In his mouthpiece, Tex said matter-of-factly, "Ten o'clock, fifteen Tangos. Twelve o'clock, ten Tangos. Two o'clock, ten Tangos."

"Thirty-five of those bastards?" Ginger said incredulously in his ear.

"Did I stutter?" Tex returned flatly. "Eyes sharp. Move out, men."

Tex raised his weapon and, keeping his body hunched, launched himself into the fray. Immediately he felt bullets zipping past him. Something stung his arm, and he resisted the urge to probe the wound. He would worry about injuries later. For now, they needed to do some culling of the enemy. The Rangers were almost backed against the wall and, being this far out in the rural region of Mehran, had no viable cover they could use. They were completely exposed, sitting ducks for the IRGC to pick off one by one.

How the hell did this happen? Where did they all come from?

It didn't make any sense. There was no way they should have gotten surrounded like this, unless it was an ambush or somehow arranged in advance. But that still didn't answer the question as to *how* the enemy had managed to get into position so quickly and catch the Rangers off guard. These men were just as skilled and proficient as the men in The Unit. They hadn't been asleep on the job. With growing dismay, Tex suspected for the first time that they'd walked into a trap.

He fell into position behind a cluster of Rangers. He couldn't make out the identity of the nearest soldier in the darkness, but he could see from the tension in the man's body that he was already exhausted from the ongoing firefight. Two of his men lay within ten feet of him, their bodies crumpled and lifeless. Many more lay scattered about them on the desert sand. Tex didn't bother counting how many were downed. He could tell by the ones still standing that their forces had already been dramatically diminished.

The enemy was a hundred yards ahead and rapidly closing in on them. Tex hoisted his M4 up to his chest, wedging its butt into the groove of his armpit. With a calculated glance across the clearing ahead, he aimed his firearm and took in a slow breath. Then, releasing it slowly, he depressed the trigger on his weapon, sending a spray of bullets in the direction of the IRGC soldiers. His body vibrated with the recoil as he released a steady barrage of ammunition at their opponents, sweeping his firearm back and forth while trying to find a balance between careful aiming and callous indifference as to whom he eliminated. As long as he didn't inadvertently hit one of his men, he was perfectly content to be indiscriminate in his targets.

A body in the distance spasmed, and with grim satisfaction, Tex watched as one of the enemy soldiers dropped his weapon and fell forward, his body landing silently on the sand.

One down, thirty-fucking-four more to go.

The Ranger he was covering jerked and collapsed, and Tex took an involuntary step back as the body pinwheeled back into him. He glanced down at the ruined face. It was one of the men he'd known in passing in the hallways but never really gotten to know. He would never have the opportunity to befriend him now.

"We're outnumbered!" Ginger bellowed into his earpiece.

"Hold your position," Tex replied crisply.

Until he got the surviving Rangers out of this mess, they weren't backing down. If they retreated now, they would be leaving these men helpless and at the mercy of the IRGC. Even if he ordered a tactical retreat, they would still be pursued. While dying was certainly not something he was looking forward to with any degree of pleasure, he was less enthusiastic about any of them getting captured. It would be an absolute fiasco if any of them wound up in enemy hands.

A glance around the clearing showed that they were still vastly outnumbered, and their own men were dropping steadily. Everything was going to hell. The enemies, though? They were holding on strong. Tex could see the familiar forms of Rangers in various positions across the terrain. Less than half of them remained standing. The lack of cover combined with being pinned against the perimeter wall of Da'wud's compound had put them at a marked disadvantage.

He heard a scream in his earpiece and his stomach sank as Rembrandt cried out, "Shit mother*fuc*—!"

When the Jersey accent was cut off abruptly, Tex knew Rembrandt was gone too.

He surveyed their position again. As their team leader, it was on him to make the best tactical decision for the remaining men. If they held their position any longer, there was a good chance none of them would survive. But if they retreated now, it didn't automatically ensure their survival. A strategic retreat didn't mean they wouldn't be pursued. Their enemy could continue to chase them down and pick them off one by one until they were all killed. They wouldn't stop just because Tex called his men off.

He had to make a choice, and he had to make it soon.

Directly to his right, he saw another body jerk. He couldn't afford to cast a glance at the fallen soldier, though. He had to maintain his focus on the threat immediately ahead of him. But he didn't need to look to know who it was. He heard a forlorn groan in his earpiece as Ginger gave him a complete play-by-play of who was getting killed around them. "Aw, shit. That was Benjamin."

Tex tightened his lips into a firm line. His weapon spasmed harmlessly in his grip, and he pulled out the clip, reloading it with a slap from the flat of his palm. For some reason, he'd always seen Benjamin as immortal. Yes, they all would die eventually. But death was something reserved for the enemy and the lower ranks of men. It was a cruel way of looking at it, but there was a certain halo of imperviousness to certain men in The Unit. Losing any of them was like losing a limb. It would hurt, and he would miss them every day for the rest of his life. He could live without an arm and, as much as he hated to admit it, his life would go on without Hank or Rembrandt or Kermit. But men like Benjamin seemed somehow different. Untouchable. Like they would live forever, even long after Tex himself was lowered into the ground. Benjamin had been a stoic and unflappable force, much like himself, and he had Tex's complete respect both in and out of combat. He'd been selected to be Alpha Team leader for his own undeniable prowess in combat and it had seemed as though those steely gray eyes of his never missed anything. Well, evidently the enemy's bullet hadn't missed Benjamin tonight.

Around him, the bodies piled up. And yet, even as he saw his own men falling, the swarming hoard of enemy soldiers seemed immutable. As much as the soldiers tried, they could not successfully reduce the enemy's numbers. They were losing this battle. Tex hated to admit it, but he was leading his men into a death trap. He couldn't in clear conscience allow them to remain in the enemy's crosshairs any longer.

"Fall back, men." Tex's voice was resigned as he spoke into his mouthpiece. "I repeat, fall back."

But his command was in vain. There was nobody left to fall back. It had been his duty to protect his men, but somehow the enemy had managed to overpower them. It wasn't his fault, and he hadn't made any errors in judgement. It was simply the fact that they'd been outnumbered by the IRGC soldiers. Despite doing everything they could to pick them off and pull the Rangers out of the firefight, he'd only succeeded in getting the majority of his men killed. This failure would live with him for the rest of his life.

Tex lowered his head and turned away the enemy. His booted legs carried him across the clearing, the soft earth sending up plumes of sand with each footfall as he retreated. He kept his M4 aimed in a defensive position as he sprinted across the terrain, squeezing off a round as an IRGC got close enough to justify the bullet.

Then his back was pressed against the wall. The sound of AK-47s continued reverberating in his headset, a steady clatter over the sound of his heart pounding in his chest. He flattened himself against the wall, sucking in deep breaths of air. He'd made it out of the firefight alive. It was a pyrrhic victory. What was the cost of his engagement with the enemy?

The Blackhawk helicopters lay five hundred yards ahead of him, and he was sure he had enough energy left to make it to their escape. But first, he needed to make sure the rest of his men got out of the fight alive.

Tex kept his weapon raised as he ventured a glance around him. Any minute now the rest of his men would tear around the corner and they would all retreat together toward the choppers. He cast a glance around the lip of the wall, ready to provide defensive fire for the remaining men. If he needed to, he would readily go back in to make sure they all got out. But the only body careening toward him was the familiar gangly shape of Ginger. Even without being able to see his face, Tex could make out the distinct form of their demolition expert flying across the sand, his legs pumping beneath him as he tried to escape the attack. Then Ginger was throwing himself against the wall. A litany of profanity mingled with prayer graced Tex's earpiece as the man drew in heaving breaths while he slumped against the wall next to Tex.

A heavy lull descended upon them, tense and uneasy. Tex pushed himself off the wall and turned toward Ginger. "Once the rest of the men round that corner, we're making a break for the choppers. Be ready to provide defensive fire if they need it."

"The rest of our men?" Ginger trained Tex in the scope of his NVGs and shook his head. "Tex, there aren't any of our men left. It's just us."

"The hell it is." But even as he said it, he knew Ginger was telling the truth.

Nobody else was going to be joining them on this side of the wall that night. Despite his training and best intentions, Tex had led his men to their demise with his orders. Nobody else had made it out of the firefight alive. Tex regarded Ginger coldly. A part of him wanted to hate the man for his remarks, but he knew Ginger was merely the messenger. It was himself that he was silently hating in that moment. With a resigned sigh, he quietly accepted that the other man was right. There was nobody left to wait for.

Together, the two men headed toward the Black Hawk helicopters as the sound of the firefight faded into a dull roar in the distance. As the only survivors of the failed mission to capture Da'wud, they had an obligation to make it back to the Green Zone. If they didn't, then nobody would ever know what had happened that fateful night.

The weight of their burden rested heavily on their shoulders as they let the compound fall away in the distance behind them. Their responsibility, though, loomed ahead of them. Neither man looked forward to it, but both of them were ready to do whatever it took to make it back to the Green Zone alive and give their report of what had transpired.

CHAPTER SEVEN

DA'WUD'S BASEMENT

0755 HOURS – 15 NOVEMBER 2013

I

N THE QUIETUDE OF THE compound's basement, James Chase groaned. A flare of pain shot down his spine, burrowing deep within his lumbar vertebrae and jolting him from his restive state of foggy unconsciousness. Both silence and darkness enveloped him, cloaking him in a stifling grip of disquiet. He shook it off, and the shroud of oblivion loosened its hold on him as awareness slowly infiltrated his senses. With another grunt of pain, the man opened one eye, then the other, and peered blearily into the gloom around him.

While his sense of pain was heightened, it also seemed to be working a double shift to compensate for his lack of vision. Oppressive blackness enshrouded him, and James blinked several times, trying to cast off the shadowy caul of blindness. But his eyes still refused to work. He closed them again, squeezing so tightly that a bright sparkle flashed behind his eyelids. Satisfied that he had nothing lingering in them to obscure his vision, he opened them back up again.

The room remained pitch black.

I'm blind, he thought with mounting alarm.

The impact and concussion had somehow managed to take his vision, putting him at a great disadvantage and rendering him vulnerable in a way he acutely disliked. He turned his head slightly, his unseeing eyes scanning his environment for any clue that he had any remaining sight. A dazzling ribbon of light flared before his open eyes from the exquisite pain that arose from the movement, but as it slowly faded away, he realized he was in fact unable to see.

He turned his head again, blocking out the flare of light and pain that followed. Now his head was facing upright, and he realized for the first time that his head was bare and resting against a hard, solid surface. Somehow, he'd lost his helmet. Should a rogue round or shrapnel decide it had his number, he wouldn't have any protection. This knowledge filled him with unease, and he took a deep breath, steadying himself.

What the hell happened? Where am I, and where is my helmet?

Nothing made a bit of sense, and James's stomach twisted with growing fear. He wasn't the type of person to give in to fear, and now was no different. Yes, he was concerned. And yes, he was also confused. He didn't like his situation at all and certainly was no fan of the fact that he had no idea where he was or what had happened to him. Regardless of the ambiguity of his situation, however, there had to be a plausible explanation. Panicking would do him no good and could actually increase his risk of inadvertently endangering himself.

James released the air from his lungs, then took in another gulp to replace it. The repetitive motion of breathing calmed him, and after a moment, he found his wits returning to him.

Something had knocked him unconscious but not senseless. The blow to the back of his head had made him dizzy and disoriented, but he was neither an impulsive nor a flighty man. Despite the throbbing pain emanating from his skull and body, he was still James Chase, a highly elite, trained member of a Delta Force team. This turn of events didn't change that, nor did it undo his years of advanced military training. If anything, it served as a stark reminder of what separated men like James from the rest of the population. While others may have succumbed to the tension and uncertainty of such a dire situation, he had the mental fortitude to remain focused and on task. Now that he'd shaken off the rest of the state of oblivion, he needed to verify if he was still in one piece.

I need to make sure nothing's broken. The pain radiating from his neck and spine concerned him, and he realized that he may have fractured a bone or two. *What happened to me? Was I bludgeoned and kidnapped? Did someone shoot me?* For all he knew, he was permanently disabled and helpless, but until he confirmed it, he wouldn't know for sure. The next step was to determine if he was injured and, if so, what was the extent of those wounds.

He already knew his neck turned, but for good measure, James moved it ever-so-slightly again to face the right and then to the left. The bloom of light was smaller this time, and the pain more subtle. Yes, he could move his neck. At least it wasn't broken. He opened and closed his mouth, testing his jaw. A smaller jolt of pain followed this movement, but it hinged with ease. That, too, still seemed to be intact. He ran his tongue over his teeth, performing a perfunctory catalog of them. All present and accounted for. His mouth, while dry and powdery, was not blemished by the taste of his own blood. He wriggled his fingers, starting with his right hand. They moved without issue. Then he checked his left hand. The results were the same. He raised his shoulders off the ground before easing them back to the floor. Each shoulder rotated in its socket without pain, and bending his arms at the elbows revealed he was still functional at least from his arms up.

Now entering the trickier zones of his body, he approached them with a modicum of trepidation. While he could probably inch himself out of his unknown prison on his elbows, it would definitely be considerably easier if he had use of his lower body. His booted feet moved on a pivot, one at a time. He clenched his toes, balling them up and releasing them. Then he raised each leg, feeling the strong, ropy muscles beneath his FRACUs flexing. His legs felt great. No pain followed this motion. There was one final test to perform: could he sit up or was there undetected damage in his spine somewhere? The pulsating ache in his lower back seemed to indicate that the region wasn't permanently damaged, but there could be hidden nerve injury he didn't yet realize.

Hell, there's only one way to find out.

Using his palms, James pressed his hands flat down on the surprisingly cool, dry ground. With a low grunt, he pushed himself upright into a sitting position. Brilliant spots of light danced before his eyes, and he reeled from them, shaking his head at the barrage of flickering that spread out before his field of view. A magnificent bolt of pain shot down his back, but then he was sitting upright, his tailbone seated against the sandy floor. Yes, he hurt like a son of a bitch at that moment, but the pain was almost a welcome relief. It meant nothing was severed or broken. He was more than a little bit battered and bruised from his trip down into this recess, but at least he was fully intact.

He swept his hands over his body, carefully patting his FRACUs as he searched for any sign of injury or blood on his person. His legs were dry, and the fabric was intact, as were his arms. Then James's throat tightened as he discovered an alarmingly vast quantity of liquid at the base of his back. He probed his fingers over the damp surface, then rubbed them together briskly, testing the texture of the fluid. Relief washed over him as he realized the liquid wasn't viscous enough to be blood. Further inspection revealed the frayed material of his water pack. Evidently, landing on his back had been too much for it to bear and the pack had ruptured upon impact.

His thoughts were becoming clear and lucid once more. Memories of the instant before the fall flooded back to him as he considered his position in the room. He vaguely recalled standing at the head of the stairs, ready to move down to the first level of Da'wud's compound. They'd just finished their site exploitation and collected a DNA sample from the HVT. Then Tex had ordered him to move out, and they'd rallied the rest of the remaining members of B Team together to regroup back downstairs. James had led the group. He remembered taking measures to avoid looking at his fallen men, possibly distracting him. He searched his memory, then reluctantly acknowledged he was not to blame for falling through the floor.

Something else had come into play, leading to him plunging into the dark void. He wouldn't have let his private grief divert his attention or make him careless. It simply wasn't in his character to not be vigilant at all times. No, something else had caused him to fall. As he reflected upon it, he realized that it was more likely than not that the floor had been weakened when Kermit triggered the pressure explosion.

In the blurry haze of his memory, James remembered that he'd barely placed his weight on the upper stair when the floor dropped out from below him with a loud, splintering crack. Everything else was a gaping vacancy in his recollection. He couldn't recall the journey down, nor the landing. That, at least, was still a mystery to him. But that trivia no longer mattered. It wouldn't do him any good to dwell on the event, regardless.

James's next order of business needed to be confirming whether or not he had vision loss or was just in total darkness, then locating an exit from his current position. He could worry about finding his team later. Residual blindness after the impact wasn't outside the scope of possibility. He'd seen other men go temporarily blind on other missions, whether from an impact or some other trauma. While they'd eventually regained their sight, James wasn't especially thrilled about sustaining even a temporary loss of vision.

A thought occurred to him, and he raised a hand cautiously to the back of his head, feeling for the telltale sign of a goose egg there. Did he have a concussion? It would explain the momentary confusion he was experiencing. But there was no lump on the back of his head. He prodded through his thick, black curls, but no scale of blood or open laceration seemed to blemish his skin.

It was another small victory. James was evidently racking them up left and right. His luck, albeit poor already, was sure to run out soon. He pulled his hand away from his head, then patted the front pocket of his Kevlar vest. His fingers closed over the familiar shape of his SureFire flashlight and he pulled it from the pocket. His thumb slipped over the push button, followed by a bright wash of light flooding out the business end of the light, both simultaneously bathing the room in a stark, bright light and confirming with an indisputable degree of confidence that James had not lost his vision after all.

He sucked in a breath of air in unexpected relief. At least he had that going for him. His body wasn't broken in a half dozen places, and his eyes could see just fine. Check and check. Things were starting to look up for James. He tallied up these two victories and set them aside on a mental shelf with his other dubious luck so far. As it were, he didn't seem to have much else going for him at that moment. Several of his closest friends were dead, he was in a mystery room somewhere on Da'wud's compound, and he wasn't sure what the hell was going on with his current situation. But sure, he could both recognize and acknowledge the small moments of better-than-mediocre luck when they occurred.

James swept the light in a slow arc across the room, taking in his surroundings. Yes, it looked as though he'd fallen through the stairs into a hidden room in Da'wud's compound. None of their intel had revealed to either the CIA or his team that this room existed, and he suspected Da'wud had wanted it to be that way. The room was bare and unfurnished, almost cave-like in its presentation. The walls were made of a coarse, stone-like material resembling the rough, porous texture of limestone. The floors were hewn of the same material, smooth except for a fine dusting of sand. There was no evidence that this room had been used at all in recent months.

The spartan furnishings of the space meant only one thing: this was a completely hidden compartment in Da'wud's compound that served one singular purpose. Da'wud must have created it as a quick escape route in the event that he ever got surrounded by enemy forces. James enjoyed a small glimmer of satisfaction in knowing that he and his men had taken out Da'wud before the terrorist had an opportunity to flee.

James trained the flashlight over his head, probing the beam at the ceiling from where he'd fallen. His eyes traced over the pattern the light was carving out in the darkness, taking it in. He swept his gaze from the ceiling back down to the floor. A rough estimate of the distance informed him that he'd fallen at least thirty feet. It was no small miracle that he hadn't broken anything on the way down. He owed a debt of thanks to his helmet and durable, bullet-resistant vest. They were strong enough to withstand both bullets and a stone floor rushing up to greet you from thirty feet below.

Somebody, he thought, *needs to trademark that slogan.* He made a mental note to file that thought away for later. He, or someone else in The Unit, might appreciate his dark sense of humor. Tex might even get a chuckle out of it. Right now, though, James needed to find a way out of this room.

Overhead, someone had haphazardly shut the opening from where he'd fallen. His flashlight played over the hole, and he considered it with a trace of confusion. How had it been covered so quickly? The seal seemed hasty, as though someone had thrown an assortment of random materials over it and hoped nobody would notice. How long had he been down here in this cavernous pit exactly? James frowned as he considered it. The crisscrossing bars of cracked wood that covered the hole matched the planks of the stairs, and a moment of investigation from his flashlight's beam confirmed that the jutting chunks of cement probably also came from the destroyed stairway.

He was quite literally buried alive.

James transferred his flashlight to his left hand and, using the gloved knuckles of his right hand, pushed off the ground. His legs were a little bit shaky, but no worse for the wear. They bore the entirety of his weight after only the slightest complaint. His vision swam in front of him as he rose to his feet, and he felt a momentary rush of lightheadedness as sparks danced in the corners of both eyes. Then the dizziness passed, and he was able to see again. He switched his light back to his right hand and glanced around the room once more. It was so damned dark down here.

Again, he wondered how much time had passed since he fell. It didn't seem that long, but time had a curious tendency to be somewhat unpredictable during their missions. And the closed-off hole aroused his suspicion, as did the curious quietude of the room.

If his men were still there, wouldn't he be able to hear them moving around above him?

He raised his left arm up to eye level, training the beam from his flashlight on it. A brow raised as the number registered in his vision. His watch certainly was broken, because there was absolutely no way in hell that it was 0758 hours. He tucked his flashlight into his mouth, steadying the beam onto its reflective surface, and pressed the largest button on its upper right side. The screen blinked and the readout changed, revealing the current date. The GPS seemed to be working too. So did the temperature setting. James puzzled over the screen for a moment longer, then switched it back to the time setting. No, the watch wasn't broken. That was confirmed. Yet it was still stubbornly reading 0758 hours back at him.

James's thoughts swirled around in his head as he calculated the current time. It was nearly 0800 hours. They'd arrived at Da'wud's compound at approximately 0155 hours. They needed to be off the compound before dawn, yet his watch was showing him that it was now 0800 hours in the morning. Outside, the sun would be fully up, blazing its scorching heat down on the steadily warming desert sand. While the fact that he was still on the compound defied all forms of sensible logic, James couldn't dispute the facts. He wasn't back at the Green Zone where he belonged, but instead, hidden away in some strange cavernous basement level of Da'wud's stronghold during the daytime.

And if he was still there, then that meant something must have gone horribly, terribly wrong.

CHAPTER EIGHT

CONFUSION

0812 HOURS – 15 NOVEMBER 2013

A SOUND COMING FROM DIRECTLY OVERHEAD jarred James from his reverie. He glanced up, startled at the unexpected noise. Instinctively, he covered the lens of the flashlight with his hands, smothering the beam as his thumb pushed down the power button to turn it off. With the suppression of his only source of light, he was plunged into total darkness again. He turned his face toward the sound, his ears attuned to any audible clues to its source.

It was coming from the hole that he'd fallen through some four hours or so before. He tilted his head, a frown crossing his face as he listened. It sounded as though someone was frantically digging into the pile of rubble, and he could hear repetitive scraping sounds as someone fumbled with the pile of boards and concrete overhead.

Could it be the surviving members of The Unit coming to rescue me? A surge of hope soared in his chest. A Delta Team member would never abandon a fellow team member. It wasn't that preposterous of an idea.

A small beam of light filtered through the wreckage of the stairwell, and James took a step back as a stream of dust and sand drifted down to the floor where he stood. Then, with a shake of his head, he turned away from it. There was no way it was his men. It wasn't possible. As much as he would like to believe they were coming for him, it was merely a dangerous fantasy and nothing more. Just as he knew the dangers of being in Iranian territory after the sun came up, so did the rest of The Unit. While they were all devoutly loyal to one another, it was an extremely calculated and even potentially irresponsible risk for them to take just to rescue him.

Still.

James glanced up once more, then pushed the flashlight's power button back on. As much as he wanted to believe it his team coming back for him, without proof, he wasn't going to stick around to find out. At least, not without confirming first. He trained his beam on the floor, sweeping it around. If he could find his radio, he could try to contact his men. If they answered his call and verified it was indeed them working overhead, then he could sit and wait until they lowered down a rope. If not… Well, James didn't want to think about that. It was much easier to believe it was his men working steadfastly overhead to pull him out of his cellar prison. If it weren't the remaining members of his Unit, then James would have a whole other set of problems on his hands.

James searched the cool, dry basement. He recalled that his radio had still been on his vest back while he and the rest of the team were sweeping Da'wud's compound. When he patted down his body to check for injuries, he'd realized that it had somehow gotten dislodged from his person. So, where was it? He swept the light beam methodically back and forth over the floor, his dark eyes scanning for any sign of the misplaced piece of equipment.

Ah, there it was. The radio was several feet away, half hidden under some wooden planks, and the helmet and NVGs were close by and still connected with each other. James walked over and leaned forward, ignoring the sharp jab of pain that seared across his back, and grabbed for the radio. His fingers closed over his helmet and his NVGs in the same motion, and he straightened his back, his equipment dangling from his fingers.

Do they still work, though?

James hefted the sturdy weight of his radio and NVGs up to eye level and shined his light on them. The equipment issued to him and his fellow team members was of the highest quality the government could justify. For missions like this, the defense spending was higher than usual. Even if the military cut corners in other places, such as serving questionable chow in the DFAC, they didn't typically stoop low enough to issue junk to their Special Operations soldiers. James clipped his radio to his vest, then drew the cord from the mic and the earpiece toward it, connecting the two components.

A quiet beep sounded in his ears, letting him know the radio was on and operating. He was slowly getting back into business. If he could get his NVGs to work, then he would be in a much better place than where he was just a minute before. He slipped his flashlight back into his mouth, holding the beam on the exterior of the ballistic helmet. Spinning it in his hands, he examined its surface. Except for a little bit of a scuff, it still seemed intact. With a shrug, James placed the helmet on his head. He withdrew his flashlight from his mouth, flipping the power off, then raised his hand to the power button on his NVGs and, with a silent prayer, switched it on.

The cave was instantly painted in a vibrant shade of green. Despite himself, James felt his face spread in a grin. Now he could focus again. If he actually got through to his team and confirmed they were the party working directly above him, he would finally be able to relax. He cast another glance up at the opening. Through the bilious hue of the NVGs, he could see that they were making good progress in clearing the debris. A few more specks of light streamed down, and he could see the dust particles floating in the air through his lenses.

Clearing his throat, he spoke directly into his mouthpiece. "Gator to Green Team?"

He waited.

Whoever was listening in on the other end would immediately recognize his call sign. While using their nicknames was a strange and almost awkward bonding mechanism amongst the men in The Unit, their call signs also served another purpose. Sure, it was a great way to give one another a hard time, but each and every call sign had to be earned. They couldn't just choose one for themselves at random. Hank and his flailing genitals. Ginger and his rubicund hair and freckles. Benjamin and his penchant of throwing twenties at the young women in the clubs when they returned stateside. Even Gator's name was rightfully acquired. He would never admit that he'd never held anything larger than a juvenile gator in his arms, and even that was over at one of the myriads of theme parks back in Florida. But the moment they'd told the men he was from Florida, they'd drawn their own conclusions him. If they thought he liked to wrestle alligators in his spare time, then he wasn't going to be the one to dissuade them from that belief. But no, the call signs were more than just a clever inside joke. They were also a way of protecting their identities when they did need to communicate with one another on the radio. Yes, his own men could be listening on their comms, but who else also had an ear on their chatter?

No answer.

James ran his tongue over his dry lips and tried again. "Gator to Green Team?"

The only response was the incessant hiss of the static in his ear. Either they couldn't hear him through the rubble or they'd already moved out.

James stole another glance up. More light was breaking through the hole in the ceiling. Whoever was trying to dig down to him, they were making better progress. And he had a mounting suspicion that they were decidedly not friendlies. His stomach sank. As nice as it was to think someone was coming to rescue him, more realistically, it was the enemy working relentlessly above his head.

James ran the calculations in his head again. It was now past 0800 hours and fully daylight. Maybe his team would have come to get him within the first hour or two after he'd fallen, but a whole six hours later? It wasn't likely at all, and the more he thought about it, the more he realized there was absolutely zero chance that the people moving around above him were from his team. As much as he wanted to hope it was them, his men weren't idiots.

There was no reason for any Delta Team members, or even an auxiliary support team, to be out in Iranian territory during daylight. To do so would be the equivalent of a death sentence. A swift execution at the hands of their enemy would be a highly grim best-case scenario if one of them got captured. More than likely, capture by the Iranian Islamic Revolutionary Guard Corps (IRGC) would put the United States in an extremely bad political position. It would give the Iranians an advantage James was certain the US did not want to relinquish to a hostile country. Trying to negotiate the release of civilian hostages was already a tricky enough situation to maneuver, so if someone as high-profile as a Delta member were taken?

James shook his head. No, the US wouldn't risk it. Those weren't his men above his head. Period.

He cast another glance up. His pursuers were unrelenting, and he could tell from the amount of noise they were generating above and the amount of light filtering through the hole that they were getting closer to breaking through the rubble. James knew that, at that rate, it was a matter of minutes before they would be directly on top of him. He needed to get the hell out of that cave, and fast.

James turned away from the opening and trained his focus on the other side of the cave. If Da'wud Al Muhammad had used this space as a hideout, then surely he would have fabricated an exit from which he could escape. This wouldn't be information the high-profile terrorist would want to be made public, either. It would be an exit that perhaps only Da'wud and a handful of his closest lieutenants would know about, at the very most. If there were an escape, and James was certain that there was one, then it would be hidden away somewhere discreet.

He took a step forward, his eyes focused on the craggy walls of the cave as he searched for telltale evidence that Da'wud had built in an escape route for himself. He furrowed his brow as he traced along the walls of the cave for any indication that there was an exit built into it. His gaze landed on a narrow opening concealed behind a lip of the stone wall, and then he nodded triumphantly. There it was: his way out.

James dropped to one knee. Before he left, he needed to perform an equipment check. He didn't want to leave anything behind for the enemy to find. Not only that, though, he wanted to make sure he wasn't entering enemy territory in broad daylight without a full arsenal of necessary equipment to survive. To an outsider, it may have appeared as though the Delta member had overpacked for his brief stay in enemy territory. But to James, it was a matter of ensuring he had every possible tool he may need for every potential situation he may encounter.

He knelt down on one knee on the sandy floor and, touching his equipment with his fingertips, mentally categorized his arsenal. As his fingers brushed over each item, he whispered the name of each piece of equipment aloud to himself. Saying it aloud, and hearing it in his ear, helped him confirm every item's presence. His M4A1 rifle with its attached grenade launcher. The multitasking carbine was one of the more essential tools he had, and he nodded as he tapped its stock with his hand. Check. At his hip, he found his Colt M1911 .45 pistol with its suppressor. This weapon was better in close-combat situations where he needed to dispatch an adversary without drawing unwanted attention to himself. Check. His Yarborough blade. Check. The only casualty of his tumble into the cave appeared to be his water pack.

Ammunition? James inventoried that as well, and his ammo check revealed that he had six M4 magazines, each with thirty rounds in them. That afforded him 180 rounds for that weapon. He also counted a total of twelve grenades for the grenade launcher too. Check and check. His 1911 pistol also needed ammunition, and he probed along his belt to confirm that he had six magazines for it, each clip providing him with seven rounds each. That was an additional forty-two rounds, not including the one already in the pistol. He was looking good on ammunition, at least. Finally, he tallied up four M67 hand grenades. James was, in that moment, ready for a fight.

"Equipment check is done," James announced to the empty room, his voice echoing hollowly in the basement cavern. "Now it's time to get the hell out of here!"

The digging above his head had taken on a frantic note, the individuals above his head now tearing through the pile of rubble much more quickly as they found themselves making progress in accessing their target. In a moment, they would break through completely and successfully infiltrate the basement.

James didn't want to still be in there when they did finally break through. Using his hand for leverage and minding the steadily diminishing ache in his back, he pushed himself back up to a standing position.

The exit was directly east, and he took a wary step toward it. The floor seemed to be smooth and free from any visible tripwires, but he proceeded with caution. He couldn't afford to be reckless so close to the exit. His gaze scanned the floor and walls and ceiling, bouncing between them as he strode carefully across the room. He strained to see if he could pick up any indication of the faintly gleaming filaments of a rogue tripwire. Boobytraps weren't outside the scope of possibility. Just as Da'wud had likely used this basement cave as a hideout, it was also highly probable that he wouldn't want anyone else to use it without his knowledge or consent. And, if some unauthorized party did happen to stumble upon it, it would have been in Da'wud's best interest to stop them. Who knew what they would report if they managed to escape from it? Because of this risk, it was fairly common for these hideouts to be fully rigged with a wide cache of boobytraps. James had seen for himself the results of someone who accidentally tripped on one of them. Hell, poor Kermit himself knew firsthand what would happen when one of them was activated. One wrong move, and a tripwire attached to an explosive could put an expedited end to an operator.

With this knowledge secured away in the back of his mind, James steadily narrowed the distance between himself and the opening in the far end of the basement cave. Despite covering a dozen yards at a methodical pace and steadily increasing the gap between himself and the Revolutionary Guardsmen, the sound of digging hadn't grown fainter. If anything, it was progressively becoming louder. He didn't risk a glance back over his shoulder to verify that his enemies were still in active pursuit. He didn't need to visually confirm that they were still advancing when he could hear them just fine.

James's boot stopped before a large stone, and he paused, considering it thoughtfully. He knelt, picking up the hunk of limestone with his left hand, and hefted its weight in his grip. As he clutched it in his hand, he reckoned it to be easily eight or nine pounds. Such a sturdy hunk of limestone could come in handy later. James curled his left arm up, drawing the rock closer to his body.

He continued toward the exit. That he hadn't encountered any tripwires so far didn't mean there weren't any lurking outside his field of view, though. It merely meant there were none he could visually confirm so far. He stopped at the mouth of the exit. It was a crude and rough-hewn tunnel, probably dug out by a handful of Da'wud's men over a relatively brief period of time. From where he stood, there was a sharp grade or slope at the beginning of the tunnel, though it appeared to level out after a dozen feet or so. After a moment of consideration, James pulled his flashlight out of his vest, pushing his thumb over the power button. He was rewarded instantly with a circle of brilliant light illuminating his path, its intensity amplified significantly by his NVGs.

James cast a critical eye over the tunnel, measuring it out. From his estimations, it was approximately three feet across at its widest point, though it tapered to almost-claustrophobic proportions in some segments. It couldn't have been more than five feet high, and he suspected that he would have to hunch over and almost creep by in some parts to successfully get through. While it wasn't the most elegant exit, it would have to do. Beggars couldn't be choosers, especially with an unknown number of men tailing him.

A triumphant cry broke through the hole, and James glanced back at the sudden noise. A bright shaft of light poured down through the opening, and he could now see the shifting shadows of people crowded around it. While the voices had been muffled just a moment before, they were almost crystal-clear in his ear now. Even through the low hiss of his earpiece, he could make out snatches of his pursuers' words. It was unmistakably Farsi. The low murmur of their voices made James think he hadn't yet been discovered. While they undoubtedly suspected he was in the cave, they still didn't know his precise location. It was a small advantage, but one that would vanish if they spotted him.

The presence of the enemy directly over his head combined with the fact that he was still in Iran well after sunrise served as a somber reminder of his position. He wasn't amongst friends. He wasn't back in the Green Zone with his fellow Delta Team members. He wasn't even within radio signal of help. He was utterly and completely alone, a one-man solo mission to escape. Not only did his life depend upon it, but the integrity of his role as a member of The Unit did also. Were he captured and not afforded an opportunity to end his own life, James knew he could wind up serving as a reluctant bargaining chip for his enemy. While he also knew he would never divulge any secrets willingly, he didn't want to put the United States in such a compromising position.

James had no misgivings about the implications of his current situation. If the men above discovered him standing near the opening of the tunnel, they too would be privy to this tactical information. While they may not have known who specifically they were going after, they probably had a pretty good idea that the man in the subterranean cave had played a role in killing someone in IRGC leadership and would stop at nothing to either capture or kill him.

CHAPTER NINE

ESCAPE

0834 HOURS – 15 NOVEMBER 2013

J AMES FINALLY CAST A GLANCE over his shoulder, venturing the nominal delay to determine if he could see the individuals who were trying to find him. He turned and craned his neck so he could see the opening, his gaze landing on a bearded face perfectly illuminated in the circle of a flashlight beam. Then the beam was trained on his own face, and James muttered an, "Oh shit," under his breath.

In the glow of James's NVGs, the Revolutionary Guard's eyes seemed to shine from within. It almost looked like the eyes of some apex predator out in the wild, feral and caged. James regarded the face with a combination of contempt and a type of detached indifference that surprised him. His eyes lingered on the man's own for several beats, and the two men seemed to consider one another in the silent cave.

These bastards are the reason my men are dead. James's lips narrowed at the thought, and he turned away from the man, returning his attention to the tunnel.

It would have been a grave disservice to the order and organization of the Iranian Islamic Revolutionary Guard to dismiss them as nothing more than primitive barbarians. Founded in 1979 as a means to help maintain the integrity of Islamic control in Iran, the IRGC recruited youths and shaped them into killing machines in order to help the agency assert their authority. By targeting their trainees at a young age, they were able to generate an unwavering loyalty from these men. What respect they couldn't earn through totalitarian authority, though, they made up for in throwing copious amounts of money at their recruits. Either way, it worked handsomely.

Because of their fervent and dogmatic view of anyone who didn't agree with them, the IRGC readily employed ruthless, secret-police type penalties on disobedient Iranian citizens and unflinchingly utilized cruel and inhumane tactics against those they perceived as dissidents. Resorting to acts of terrorism wasn't out of the question for them. In fact, it was just another day on the job for most members of this government agency. While they could be quite narrow-minded and vicious in their methodology, they still underwent rigorous training to bring them to the level of skill many of them possessed. A lack of formal education didn't automatically equate to an inferior enemy.

While their training methods varied greatly from American or even other western military regiments, they still had their own semblance of hierarchy and protocol. Even if their worldview was largely corrupt and inherently paranoid, founded on the basis that they were acting as emissaries of Allah, it didn't mean they didn't cling to their ideologies wholeheartedly or wouldn't quite readily die to defend them. Their training included both armed and unarmed combat techniques along with an applied reading of the Quran. What good was a trained body if they didn't have an equally manipulated mind?

Each and every one of the IRGCs steadily digging through the pile of rubble firmly and earnestly believed in their mission that day. They had a good idea of what type of person they were going after as they set aside handfuls of splintered lumber and hunks of craggy concrete. While they weren't completely sure what they would find when they cleared the debris from the hole, they had their suspicions.

To them, they'd categorized their potential quarry into two different classifications: either it was a local who had wandered astray and needed a little bit of strong-arming to correct, or it was an infidel.

If it were someone in the first column, they had ways to handle him. If it were the second category, though? There was an electric thrum of anticipation as they dug. To lay their sights upon an American would be the ultimate prize, and as they shouted orders to one another, they couldn't contain their mounting excitement. What if they did have an American cornered? While none of them spoke the thought aloud to one another, they were all thinking it. There would be a handsome reward in store for them if they brought him back alive. Of course, if they failed to capture their target? That was also something they were not discussing. One side of the coin was positive recognition. The other side was a public reprimand and brutal beating.

Regardless, they worked tirelessly in removing the debris from the opening of the hole. A jagged circle finally appeared in the middle of the mess, and a lower subordinate trained his flashlight beam into the hole. At first, he saw nothing. As he fumbled with his light, momentarily blinding himself as he accidentally aimed it on his own face, he spotted what they sought. The gear the man was equipped with was unmistakably American. Sure, his skin was darker than expected and the facial hair was not unlike their own. But it was undeniably an American. His attire and bearing gave him away, even if his outward appearance didn't. How fortunate for them!

They suppressed their excitement as they got back to work clearing the debris from the opening. In a moment, they would be able to lower down a rope ladder to help them gain access to the cave and then they would have their prize.

The IRGC who had spotted the infidel brought his lips away from his teeth. While the expression could be mistaken for a savage snarl, the owner of the expression knew what he wore on his face. It was a smile. He was darkly happy, a sensation that was few and far between for his ilk. The black joviality never left his face as he cleared the opening. An equally large mountain of debris was forming behind him as he threw the clutter over his shoulder, now haphazardly as he sensed himself closing in on the enemy. Then, with a shout of triumph, the soldier stopped digging. The hole was now big enough for him to enter. He took a step back, making way for a more senior soldier to take over.

In a couple of minutes, they would have their American. The IRGC soldier would be highly praised for his efforts, but that wouldn't come until later. For now, he was still single-mindedly focused on the task ahead. He still needed to capture his enemy. The smile never left his face as the rope ladder was unfurled into the hole.

James wasn't about to wait around to see if the guard would zero in on him. Based on the muffled thuds coming from behind him, they were rigging up some sort of ladder or rope to help them wriggle down into the cave. He wasn't especially concerned about the technicalities of how they would get down. All that mattered was that he wasn't there when they did manage to set foot in the cave. He'd lingered long enough in the entrance to the tunnel.

He swept his flashlight's beam over the tunnel, watching for any glint of metal or sign that it had been boobytrapped, but there was nothing. He extended his arm, feeding the light into the tunnel. It appeared to be vacant. He squeezed his thumb over the power button, and the glow of the flashlight blinked out. He tucked it into the front pocket of his vest and unholstered his 1911 pistol. Now entirely reliant upon his NVGs to proceed, he took a careful step forward in the darkness of the tunnel.

The opening itself was smaller than the general breadth of the cave, and James found himself drawing his limbs close to his body as he advanced. Between his own stocky frame and the bulk of his equipment, it was proving to be a tight squeeze. Despite the urgency to find out where this tunnel ended, he realized he wasn't going to be making very expedited progress. The risk of accidentally triggering a tripwire, especially with the weight of his equipment on his body, was significantly hindering his progress. But dumping his equipment wasn't an option, and so James continued on doggedly. He held his pistol in his right hand, the stone still firmly held in his left. He continued to sweep the surfaces of the tunnel for any IEDs or tripwires blocking his way. Behind him, the IRGCs had found the opening to the tunnel, and he heard a surprisingly shrill voice yelling out orders in Farsi. The guard's voice echoed off the stone walls of the tunnel, seeming to surround him from all sides. He didn't know exactly what they were saying, but he wouldn't have been surprised to learn that it was some variation of, "Get the American infidel!"

James ducked his head, stooping to avoid a particularly jagged edge of rock jutting out from the ceiling. Checking carefully, he found nothing hiding behind it. He tightened his abdomen, then squeezed through another tight gap in the wall. His shoulders brushed against the wall, and he paused, monitoring the craggy surface before he proceeded. These were all ideal locations to hide a tripwire, and he was highly aware of his vulnerability as he navigated through the tunnel.

Ahead of him, a stone outcropping concealed a tight passageway, and James dropped to one knee. A quick visual inspection confirmed there were no tripwires. He considered it thoughtfully. Even a slimmer man would have to turn his body at a 45-degree angle to creep past this constricted channel, which made it the ideal spot for James to drop an IED.

From his position on the floor, he worked quickly yet methodically. He eased the rock onto the tunnel floor, then reached into his vest and withdrew an M67 fragmentation grenade. The baseball-shaped orb weighed less than a pound in his hand, clocking in at just fourteen ounces of gross weight. The body managed to pack six and a half ounces of combustible TNT and RDX explosives encased in a robe of steel, but it had an impressive 50-yard radius when activated. In this tight passage, it would be more than enough to serve the purpose James was rigging it up for.

With steady hands, James carefully pulled the safety pin on the grenade. He glanced around the tunnel, then with a shrug, slipped the pin into his pocket. There was no point in tipping the Revolutionary Guards off early by leaving evidence of his handiwork out for them to find. While the soldiers came from a more primitive culture than his own and hadn't received the same level of training he had, James wasn't foolish enough to think they were ignorant. Yes, they were brainwashed, religious zealots, but it would be dangerous to mistakenly believe they were outright stupid.

He placed the fragmentation grenade on the floor of the tunnel, taking measures to avoid jostling it as he operated. With his free hand, he carefully positioned the rock on top of it, depressing the lever onto the side of the grenade. The stone had a smooth surface, and when James released the stone, it settled onto the grenade. As it was in the moment, tucked beneath the weight of the rock, the explosive was inert and harmless. If one of the IRGCs stumbled upon it, they would jostle the rock, activating the grenade.

James nodded to himself in quiet satisfaction. His handiwork was only as good as the hapless man who would trip over it, but in this darkened juncture, they were all but guaranteed to encounter it. With both hands, he scooped up handfuls of sand, piling the material onto the impromptu trap. Then he stood up and admired his handiwork. The combination of stealthy placement and the darkness of the tunnel made it a fairly high likelihood that someone would unknowingly set a foot down upon it, slowing them down and even hopefully eliminating one or two of them. He stepped carefully over it, giving his IED a wide berth.

He resumed his laborious trek through the tunnel. A juncture guided him to the left, and he turned, following it attentively. If anything, the lack of measures made him more suspicious. If they weren't rigging up IEDs here, where *would* he find them?

But James's concerns were soon laid to rest. His flashlight beam danced over a thin filament, and he froze. Above him, running along the ceiling of the tunnel, a hint of metal caught his attention. He swooped to the left, ducking beneath it as his gaze lingered on the almost-imperceptible string glinting in the darkness. The rogue wire curved into the wall, and James gave it a sidelong glance as he slipped past. Had he become complacent and not been paying attention, he could have easily bumped into it, putting a sudden end to his mission and himself.

He continued along the cold walls, dodging suspicious rocks. Here, Da'wud or some other insurgent had exerted more effort to make the passage difficult. It was as though they'd hoped that anyone steering through it would grow lazy once they realized no other traps had been placed. And because the walls were close together, it was getting very difficult to both simultaneously squeeze through them and avoid tripwires. He contorted his body in creative positions to avoid the obstacles. In some places, the passage was so tight he had to draw in his breath and hold it to squeeze through.

James counted his paces away from his boobytrap as he shuffled through the tunnel. Ten yards separated him from his creative IED, then twenty. He turned and found himself steering right, and another thirty yards served as a buffer between him and the trap. He navigated the tunnel slowly, pausing frequently to verify the route he was taking wasn't going to put his life in imminent danger. Then, as he zeroed in on a hundred yards past his IED, he spotted his exit. A ladder, clearly handmade and comprised of crudely assembled steps, rested against the stone wall.

James slowed his pace, then eased to a stop. The ladder seemed rickety and weak, but there didn't appear to be any boobytraps hidden on or around it. He sheathed his pistol, switching to his flashlight, and leaned forward, fixing the beam of light on the backside of the ladder and then drawing it across the wooden surface. It also appeared to be completely clear of any signs of hidden traps. He stepped up to it, then paused at the bottom rung, craning his neck up. The ladder was approximately twelve feet in height, and although it was difficult to tell with any degree of certainty, it did seem to be the way out of the tunnel. He trained the flashlight onto the ceiling. Even with his NVGs on and the aid of his flashlight, he struggled to get a good view of the exit, but the ladder appeared to lead to an equally decrepit wooden door. Both the ladder and the door seemed to be crafted out of the same material, a raw, unfinished type of pale wood. A round object was stuck to the door, and James turned his head in the darkness, trying to identify the mysterious shape. After a moment's contemplation, he realized he was peering up at a combination lock.

There was only one way left for him to go, so he returned his flashlight to his vest pocket, gripped the closest handrail, and stepped up onto the bottom rung. He waited for the familiar crack of the wood splintering, but the rung held. Despite its flimsy appearance, it seemed as though it would support him without issue. He'd made it up three of the rungs when a booming explosion sounded behind him from the direction where he'd just come.

A grin spread across his face. With a glance back toward the source of the noise, James whispered, "Sounds like they found my present."

With the immediate threat of his pursuers now resolved, he climbed up the ladder more rapidly. He didn't want to be in this tunnel much longer. Not only was it getting harder to see in there from the dirt and debris dislodged from the explosion, but he also knew the noise was going to draw more attention to him. James wasn't worried about any threats approaching him from behind. Nobody was going to be able to get past the rubble his explosive had generated. Still. He had no idea what, or who, was on the other side of the door or how much they'd heard from his side of it.

James reached the top of the ladder and paused to consider his next move. The air in the tunnel was thick with dust particles, and he coughed into his sleeve as he rested on the top rung. The temperature in the tunnel was climbing, and he found his brow breaking out in beads of sweat that carved out a path on his grime-streaked face. If the combination lock proved to be a bitch to pick and he didn't get through quickly, he might need to come up with a makeshift air filter with his handkerchief. First, though, he was more interested in determining if he could get past the lock.

The bulk of the NVGs was proving to be more of a hindrance than a help, and James briefly debated the merits of removing them. He would be emerging from the tunnel in a moment, which meant he probably wouldn't need them in just a few minutes anyway. And while the NVGs were great for allowing him to make out the broader details of objects in darkness, for this type of detailed work, he needed to see the lock with his own two eyes. He flipped the NVGs up and out of the way, then reached into his vest for his flashlight once more.

With the tunnel plunged into complete blackness, James marveled at the intensity of the absence of light as his thumb slid over the power button of his flashlight. He trained the white beam on the circular lock. Upon scrutinizing it, he saw it was a standard combination lock with Arabic numerals demarking the various codes one could use to try to crack it. James frowned as he studied it. It looked like a fairly new addition recently attached to the lever door. Someone had been feeling especially cautious when they'd added this lock.

James tilted his head, turning his ear toward the door. Silence greeted him, but he stood patiently on the ladder, waiting. If the sound of the explosion had drawn anyone's unwanted attention, he would know shortly. He wasn't about to pop his head out only to get it lobbed off by some twenty or thirty IRGCs. He listened for the sound of booted feet falling heavily onto the door or even shouts in Farsi, strong enough indications that there was company waiting for him on the other side. He counted silently as he waited, recording the seconds in his mind.

Ten seconds passed, then twenty. No noise, shouts, or footsteps suggesting he wasn't alone.

Satisfied there was nobody guarding the exit and feeling growing pressure to get out of the damned tunnel, James extended his hand toward the combination lock. The dial spun easily enough beneath his fingertips, and he rotated it back and forth as he peered at it. While it was a newer lock, it didn't appear to be impregnatable. He pressed his fingers against the lock's hasp, feeling where it met with the wooden slab. It wiggled beneath his touch, hinting at weakness. With a determined nod, James transferred his flashlight to his mouth, turning his head to steer the circle of light. He pulled his

Yarborough out of its sheath and, bracing his wrist on the highest rung of the ladder, probed at the hasp with the blade's tip.

The distance between the hasp and the wood widened as James worked, and he noted with satisfaction that the metal component was steadily prying apart from the latch despite his slower progress. Then, with a quiet creak, a screw fell from the hinge and landed on the sandy floor below. He watched it fall, then returned his attention to the hasp. The second screw tumbled to the floor and then the hasp fell away from the wooden door.

James slipped his Yarborough back into his sheath. A low ache throbbed in his *shoulder*, but he ignored it. The combination of working on the hasp with an already bruised arm had upset the recent injury, but the pain was more of an annoyance than a genuine problem. He opened and closed his hand, flexing his fingers. After a moment, the pain subsided. He thumbed off the light on his SureFire and returned it to his front vest pocket. With his right hand, he reached for his holster, withdrawing his pistol.

In the catacomb-like silence of the tunnel, James waited. He breathed through his mouth as he listened for any signs of company overhead. Except for a monotonous whine in his ear, a residual artifact from years of exposure to loud explosions, there was no sound to be heard. As far as he could tell, he was wholly and completely alone.

CHAPTER TEN

OUT OF THE TUNNEL

0840 HOURS – 15 NOVEMBER 2013

J AMES POCKETED HIS FLASHLIGHT ONCE more and flipped the NVGs back over his eyes. A flip of the switch on his NVGs caused the ladder to spring back into his field of vision, a wan green in the darkness. Yes, it was cumbersome, but that was a minor annoyance he was more than used to contending with.

If someone had been in the room above the tunnel, they may already be aware of his presence, and he kept that knowledge in the back of his mind. While he'd been as quiet as possible when he worked on the hinge, it didn't mean the enemy wasn't lurking above his head with equal stealth. He gripped his pistol in his right hand, holding it close to his body while aiming it toward the exit.

"Let's do it," he muttered as he reached his left hand cautiously above his head, his fingers fumbling for purchase in the darkness.

With a deep breath, James pushed on the wooden door. To his surprise, it was heavier than expected, and he strained to get the cumbersome wooden slab to rise high enough that he could peek out it. The door rose laboriously underneath his palm, and when an inch-wide gap formed, he justified a peek through the small opening.

The darkness that greeted his eyes surprised him. He had his NVGs on, so why couldn't he see into the room?

James raised himself another rung on the ladder and, using his injured shoulder as a brace, pressed his arm against the door again. His fingers probed the narrow gab, and realization dawned on him as they met against fabric. It was a rug. The door was pinned down beneath a rug. He shook his head at the absurdity of it. He'd come all this way, only to be smothered beneath a musty old rug. He wasn't going to let the scrap of cloth hold him back, though.

He shifted his weight again, throwing his strength into his back and shoulder and using them for leverage against the burden over his head. A flare of pain shot down his spine, and he winced away from the sudden, sharp discomfort. He gritted his teeth and pushed again. A twinge in his shoulder wasn't going to prevent him from escaping the tunnel.

I'm this far. Might as well go all the way.

The door rose to a 90-degree angle, high enough that he could slip the barrel of his pistol through the slight opening. Gripping the door with his left hand, he wedged the business end of his pistol through and nudged the rug, then prodded at it, jostling it with his firearm. The rug rose and fell, flopping around as he poked at it. Then the edge of the rug flipped over, and the door was no longer weighed down by the rectangle of Afghan wool. It swung wide, thudding quietly as it landed on the floor of the room.

James didn't hesitate. He gripped his pistol in both hands, sweeping the firearm back and forth. His body pivoted on an axis on the ladder as he scanned the room, his fingers gripping the trigger of his pistol as he sized up the space for any threat. But there was nobody to greet him. His original assessment had been correct. He was still alone. At least, for now.

He switched his pistol to his right hand and pressed his left arm against the lip of the exit. Swinging his leg up, he climbed out of the tunnel, his knees dragging on the sandy floor. He pushed himself to a standing position and, using the toe of his boot, hooked it beneath the wooden door. It rose easily enough, and he hoisted it with his foot until it was parallel with the wall. He grasped it with his left hand and eased it to the floor, lowering it quietly back to its original position.

The rug lay bunched in a pile next to the door, and James kicked at it, unfurling it with his boot. It flopped open, sending up a plume of dust and sand into the air. He smoothed it out with the flat of his foot, stepping on it to work the creases out of it. The rug shifted and slid on the floor as James scooted it around until it was more or less back in the same spot he assumed it had been when he arrived. As far as he could tell, the room looked exactly the same as it had before. If anyone happened to find this room after he left, it was unlikely they would have any inkling that someone else had ever been in here.

James glanced around the room through his NVGs, seeing that he was in some sort of basement dwelling. Directly ahead of him, a frayed cord caught his eye. It appeared to lead to a bare bulb suspended from the low ceiling of the room, and James nodded to himself. He flipped off the power on his NVGs, then reached for the cord.

An instant later, wan yellow light flooded the room, casting it in a weak glow from the low-wattage bulb. The light did little to chase away the shadows in the room as he spun in a slow circle, taking it in. It was a surprisingly spacious rectangular room, spanning some hundred feet across and another sixty feet wide. Its unadorned walls were the same color as the desert sand, pale beige in the warm light cast by the lightbulb. Even though it was well after dawn and the room should have been filled with the bright and dazzling sunlight that was endemic to this region, the lack of light was easily explained by the lack of windows.

The room was remarkably unbalanced, with the majority of its adornment shoved somewhat haphazardly to one side. James's gaze flickered across the room as he took it in. Whoever owned this house was clearly using this room for storage. On one side of the room, a dozen or so boxes were shoved into the corner, stacked on top of one another. No handwritten script indicated their contents, but if he had to venture a guess, he imagined they held an assortment of junk and other surplus supplies that locals had a tendency to stockpile. In addition to these boxes, the room also housed a remarkable number of bicycles in various states of disrepair. He counted no less than four bikes in various states of repair propped against the wall, and several open boxes revealed even more bike parts. Chains, gears, and even a few bent wheels peeked out of the top of the battered and scuffed cardboard containers. The nearest wall wasn't entirely sparse, but instead of boxes, it held a variety of storage containers. A bulky metal safe took up a large portion of the wall, but a cabinet and dresser also occupied some of the real estate there. This wall also held its own share of boxes, and judging from the heaps of fabric piled high above them, they were filled to the brim with old clothes. The final wall had no personal effects and featured a rickety-looking staircase that led up to a single door.

James's eyes went back to the pile of boxes nearest to him. There was a fairly decent chance that something in those boxes might actually fit his muscular frame, and if he wanted to survive in Mehran, a wardrobe change was in order. He needed to stay one step ahead of the locals and blend in while staying on the move, because looking like an American soldier was the easiest way to get him singled out with a glaring target on his back. He glanced down at his black FRACUs and utility belt. While they were efficient for completing a mission, they would make him stick out like a sore thumb here.

Curiosity tugged at him, and James took a step toward the safe. Kneeling before it, he reached out and yanked on the handle. It was locked. He shook his head in slight disappointment, then turned his attention to the piles of boxes to his immediate right. He wasn't feeling picky about his fashion choices today. All he needed was something that fit his frame and wasn't designed for the female persuasion. He plunged his hands into the box, pulling out a pile of the musty, stale-smelling garments. The clothes fell to the floor in a heap, sending up a small cloud of dust. He wrinkled his nose but sifted through them resolutely. It didn't matter if they were soiled and filthy with dirt and sweat. It was better to stink of the locals now than be painted in his own blood later. He held up a few pieces, sizing them up with his dark eyes. Many of them were too small or too ornate, hinting by their cut and style that they were for women.

A handful of them, though, seemed viable and would allow him to blend in seamlessly with the current Iranian dress code, and he set them aside as he dug through the box.

Soon he had a complete ensemble in a lump next to him, and he stood up, brushing off his knees as he rose. Keeping an eye on the door, James started undressing. He unbuckled his MICH helmet, then dropped it. The rest of his equipment soon followed, and he lay his utility belt and weapons in a pile next to him. He pulled his shirt over his head, ignoring the pain in his shoulder, and let it drop to the floor. After a moment, he was standing in the warm room in his underwear and simple black undershirt.

The set of clothes he'd found were definitely menswear and wouldn't lead to him being on the receiving end of questioning looks by the natives, but they were cut for the physique of an overweight male and held the lingering stench of body odor. The excessive fabric of these clothes was actually a non-issue and worked in his favor. The larger garments would make it easier for him to conceal his equipment, facilitating his ability to arm himself as he maneuvered through town. James shrugged and went about putting the items on. He pulled a pair of surprisingly clean socks on over his bare feet, then slipped into a pair of basic pants. The shirt would follow later, after he accessorized himself with his equipment. A woven wool hat, a popular style for the men in Iran, completed the outfit.

He considered his equipment. His own belt would serve to hold up the too-large pants while also giving him a place to store his weapons. He held up the length of leather and wove his holster and magazine pouches onto it, then wrapped the belt around his waist, tightening it around his midsection. His bullet resistant vest was also a vital part of his equipment, but James frowned as he considered it. While its thick padding would help shield his body from piercing bullets, it was also extremely easy to detect beneath his clothes due to its unwieldy bulk. He couldn't justify the added heft from it, especially since there were many other pieces of equipment he still needed to take with him.

Using his fingers, James pried open the Velcro fasteners that held the heavy-duty ceramic plates inside his bullet resistant vest. The material came apart with a low ripping sound, revealing the durable material underneath it. He slipped his hand into the pocket and pulled the ceramic plates out, throwing them onto the mound of clothes one by one. The ceramic landed with a soft thud onto the pile, clattering against one another as James stacked them haphazardly. He pulled the vest over his head, tugging it down to his waistband. Then, reaching behind him, he drew the Velcro straps around his body to tighten the vinyl garment. There. With the excess material removed, the vest was much less obvious.

James slipped a long-sleeved shirt on over his arms, then ran his palms down the front of the garment. Now he looked merely husky instead of suspiciously bulky. If he had a mirror, he would see a man in his mid-thirties with intense brown eyes set beneath a pair of bushy eyebrows and a thick, gray-streaked beard. His apparel would make him look heavyset, a jarring contrast against his lean face, but his facial hair helped conceal the sharp angle of his jaw. He glanced down at his body. Without a reflection, he could only make broad assumptions about his appearance. But with his dusky complexion and dark hair, he was confident that he would fit in relatively well with the locals.

As James was reaching for his pistol, the door by the stairwell creaked open on its hinges. His head jerked up in the direction of the sound, then he wrapped his fingers around his pistol and his blade and, ducking his head, padded across the grainy floor toward the nook beneath the stairs. He lowered his body into a crouch, obscured by the long shadows in this corner of the room. His blade was held in front of him, ready to use if needed, and his finger rested loosely on the trigger guard of his pistol.

A series of thumps sounded overhead, and James drew in his breath, holding it. Whoever it was, they were coming down the stairs. James slowly let the air out of his lungs, his body turned at an angle toward the stairwell, his eyes fixed on the newcomer. From his vantage point, he couldn't determine with any degree of confidence if the individual was male or female. The person seemed frozen in place, their head tilted at an angle as they stared at a distant point in the room. With dawning realization, James recognized that they were peering at the light, perhaps wondering who had left it on.

Shit. James shook his head ruefully. *Too late to turn it off now.*

He traced the trajectory of their gaze. In a moment, the stranger would probably figure out that someone had been sorting through the boxes. All of James's equipment, as well as his American-style black military-issue clothes, were also sitting out in the open for the person to stumble upon. If they spotted it, there would be no doubt as to who had been loitering in the room before they arrived. James's only advantage at this point was that he was still undiscovered. If the person decided to peer over the railing of the stairs, even that slight advantage over them would instantly be lost.

James scooted closer to the space beneath the stairs, moving as quietly as feasible. His body was all but concealed in the crevice now, and he tensed as the person descended the rest of the stairs and stopped again. He kept his body taut, his weapon brandished in front of him, ready to strike if the person had the poor enough luck to glance in his direction. But they were more fixated on the mess in the middle of the room as they scratched the back of their head and took a tentative step toward it.

James saw the hint of a beard casting a shadow on their face. His gender was no longer a mystery. It was a man of medium height and stature. He had close-cropped black hair and a slim build, his dark green pants perhaps a little bit too short on him, belying his poverty. His feet were bare, and his faded blue T-shirt was baggy, stained, and frayed on the hem. The young man couldn't have been much older than twenty, and James regarded him with a detached type of sympathy. If he hadn't been confident the person would kill him on sight, he might have been able to muster up enough pity to spare his life. Out here, though, in Iran? It was kill or be killed. There was no middle ground.

The young man stopped in front of the pile of boxes, and James could almost hear the gears in his head as he contemplated the equipment. He could see as the man's head turned slightly to the left, where James had abandoned his personal clothes. Then the man's face swept to the right, where the rest of the equipment lay. The man paused for a moment, then knelt, picking up the M4 rifle. He turned it over, the matte black paint reflecting dully beneath the glow of the single lightbulb.

James knew his opportunity was a slim one. As the young man inspected his M4 carbine, James pushed off the wall, his feet moving soundlessly on the sandy floor. His knees popped as he eased out from beneath the nook, and he froze, his breath catching in his lungs. The sound seemed immense in James's ears, and he was certain he would be discovered. But the man didn't move from his position, his attention riveted to the weapon in his hands as he manipulated it, turning it over and over in his palms. Raising his feet off the ground with each step to avoid causing any sound as he moved, James advanced steadily upon the boy. He breathed through his mouth, his eyes pinned to the scrawny back beneath the blue shirt. The young man glanced up suddenly, and James froze, his pistol drawn before him. But the boy was looking in the opposite direction, at James's MICH helmet. The NVGs and ballistic helmet held less sway over him than the weapon, though, and he returned his attention back to it.

As James drew closer, he realized that the single bulb was casting erratic shadows in the room. His own shadow flowered out around him, causing a ghost of a shadow to appear. If the kid happened to look down, he would notice James was directly upon him. James shook his head, glancing up at the light before returning his gaze to the young man. He was close enough now to smell the heady stench of sweat on the youth. He raised his pistol, aiming it at the kid.

Instead of tightening his finger around the trigger, however, James brought the weapon around, his hand gripping the barrel of it. Calculated mercy for this unknown young man prevailed. He raised his arm over his head, then brought it back down sharply. The butt of the pistol collided with the boy's head with a thud, and the young Iranian crumpled to the ground without uttering a single sound.

Even as the boy collapsed, so did the weapon. James watched

as the M4 slipped from the youth's fingers and clattered to the ground. The sound was sharp, sudden, and terrifyingly loud. James recoiled from the noise, his face drawing back in a wince. His eyes instinctively went to the door. If someone had heard the weapon slamming against the hard floor, he would know shortly.

The boy lay on the floor in a heap, a small pool of blood forming behind his head where his face lay against the floor. His eyes were open and unseeing, and his mouth lay open in a stunned gape.

James returned his pistol to the holster and sheathed his knife, then dropped to his knees in front of the young man. Even though the boy had a lifeless expression on his face, James could see his chest rising and falling slowly each time he took in a breath. While he was possibly seriously injured and concussed from the injury, he was still alive.

James reached out, gripping the collar of the shirt, and dragged the boy across the room. He needed to get the body out of sight and check to make sure nobody was descending upon him from upstairs. He hauled the body to the space beneath the stairs, then dusted his hands off. He needed to move quickly. James drew his pistol and rounded the corner, throwing himself up the stairs. He mounted them rapidly, two at a time, and paused before the door. It remained ajar, as the boy had evidently forgotten to shut it behind himself when he stepped into the basement.

After a beat, James slipped his sock-clad foot into the small opening and kicked the door open. It swung wide, bounced off the far wall, and started to swing shut again. He lunged into the opening, his weapon high and aimed into the dark void ahead. But there was nobody standing there to greet him. The door lead to a hallway, narrow and short, which opened up to what appeared to be a kitchen.

James gripped his pistol as he stepped into the hallway. From his angle, he couldn't see any movement ahead, but that didn't mean he was alone in the house. Someone could just as easily be hiding around the corner. He moved rapidly, then paused as he reached the end of the hallway. He threw his body against the opposite wall, aiming his weapon directly in front of him. The room remained still and quiet. The only person standing in it was James.

The house was small, and it didn't take James long to clear it. He moved from the kitchen to a cramped living room, to a sparsely furnished bedroom, to a bathroom with a single hole carved into the floor. Each room he cleared confirmed that the only individual in this house other than himself was the young man downstairs. The entire process took no more than a couple of minutes, and James cast his eyes over the house a final time before turning back toward the hallway leading to the basement.

How much time had passed since he initially woke up and worked his way through the tunnel? James held his watch up to check. In the stream of light coming from the windows, the face was easy for him to view. He regarded the time with a momentary flash of surprise. It was only 0840 hours. A mere forty-five minutes had passed since he'd first roused from his unconsciousness. It felt curiously longer.

The passage of time triggered the first twinge of anxiety in him. He was spending far too much time in this house. He had a very limited amount of time before he was discovered. He'd been fortunate so far. The only person who had encountered him was unconscious and bleeding beneath the stairs. That didn't mean he was home free, though. Every second that ticked by was another moment bringing him closer to a face-to-face encounter with his enemy. While he wasn't entirely sure why the IRGC hadn't found him yet, he suspected their ignorance about his location probably had to do with the tunnel and the fact that they were unaware of the house it connected to.

But time was steadily running out, and James was sharply aware of this as he hurried back down the stairs. He kept his pistol aimed as he descended, but a glance over the railing revealed that the boy was still unconscious. James approached him, nudging him with his foot. The youth didn't respond. No, he wasn't faking it. James had clocked him good when he brought his pistol down onto his head. It would be quite a while before he roused again.

James turned toward the boxes on the far wall. While he

suspected that they contained an assortment of random supplies and bicycle parts, they also probably stored some cords or other sort of rope inside them. He hastened across the room, his stockinged feet moving soundlessly on the floor. The first box held nothing more than old electronics and bicycle equipment, but the second box held plastic-coated power cords. A cursory glance inside the box didn't reveal anything else that could help restrain the boy, so the electrical cords would have to suffice.

He jogged back across the room to where the unconscious young man waited. He knelt, and after a moment's consideration, pressed his index and middle finger against the boy's beard-stubbled throat. There was a pulse, albeit weak. The boy was still alive. James regarded him with muted sympathy. He didn't want to kill him, but he wasn't especially enthused about the prospect of getting captured and killed. He turned the youth onto his stomach, then gripped the boy's arms, drawing them behind him. A couple of twists with the makeshift ligature seemed to do the trick, and James double knotted the wires to ensure the young man wouldn't be going anywhere anytime soon.

With the issue of the unconscious youth out of his way, James was now free to focus on getting out of the house. He jogged toward his belongings and assessed them with a glance. There was no way all of his possessions would be able to fit on his person. He would have to be choosy about what he decided to equip himself with. After a moment's consideration, he bent over, picking up his equipment one by one. The pistol and the suppressor, along with the six fully loaded magazines, were a no-brainer. They absolutely had to come with him. The Yarbrough combat knife was also a vital piece of equipment, so he kept it sheathed in front of his vest. Finally, he scooped up his three remaining M67 fragment grenades. Those just might come in handy later. The rest of his equipment would have to be left behind. James pursed his lips as he assessed the items, but trying to take them along would prove to be an exercise in futility. He had his most essential items, and trying to smuggle it all along with him would merely lead to him becoming discovered as a soldier. If he wasn't going to be able to take them, though, he didn't want to leave them out and exposed for anyone else to grab. Not only did leaving them out act as a beacon to anyone who stumbled upon them that an American soldier had been in the room, James also didn't care for the idea of someone turning one of his own weapons against him.

He trained his gaze upon his rifle with its grenade launcher. The weapon had served him well, but it was now relegated to a non-essential item. Moving with rapid expertise, he disassembled the weapon, removing the firing pin. He shoved it artlessly behind the cabinet, then took a step back, casting a critical eye over it. The shadows behind it would be adequate to conceal it from the casual looker.

His clothes would be easy enough to hide beneath the piles of clothes in the boxes. James overturned one, dumping its contents onto the ground. He crammed his bullet resistant plates into the bottom of the box, pressing them into the box with the flat of his hands. His helmet with the NVGs followed, and he dropped his combat pack onto it. The material sagged over the MICH helmet, and he gave the shape an approving nod. The remaining twelve grenades for the launcher went on top of his pack, and a few of them tumbled beneath the folds of thick canvas fabric. Finally, his black FRACUs settled on the very top of the pile. The box was almost full now, but James was sure he could cram as much of the old clothes back into it as possible. He scooped them up, dumping them on top of his belongings. There. Nobody could tell at a glance that anyone had even been in this room. Of course, the unconscious young man would certainly report his presence to anyone with ears once he awakened, but that was something James would have to worry about later.

A black shirt hung over the lip of the box, and James reached out, plucking it out from beneath a rust-colored tunic. He shook it out, and a small rain of sand flew out. The fucking sand was everywhere in Iran, and he was frankly quite tired of it. When he made it back to the United States, he would bypass the inviting turquoise beaches of South Florida and make a beeline for the mountains for some much-needed relaxation. For now, though, he had to focus his efforts on actually getting the hell out of this godforsaken country.

James draped the shirt over his shoulder, then pushed himself to a standing position. He nudged the box back into its original position with his socked foot. The only thing he needed to do was put on his boots and get out of this basement. He laced them up quickly, then turned to the spot of blood on the floor. It was a small smudge, and head wounds were notorious for seemingly excessive blood loss due to the sheer number of capillaries near the surface of the scalp. The boy would be fine, and the stain wasn't his problem anymore.

James turned toward the exit and reached over his head, grabbing the yellowed chain link cord that operated the light. The basement was plunged into darkness once more. Using the mental image of the layout of the room as a map, he tracked his way toward the stairwell. Then, without a final glance back at the dark and still basement, he slipped through the door and into the main part of the house. If his memory served, there had been a house phone in the living room, and he had an urgent call to make.

CHAPTER ELEVEN

CONTACT

0847 HOURS – 15 NOVEMBER 2013

J AMES HAD TWO PRIMARY GOALS as he moved through the small house. One, he needed to find a set of keys. Keys indicated the presence of a functional vehicle, and a set of wheels was critical for his escape. Secondly, he needed a phone. He was certain that he'd been left for dead, and it was imperative that he notify the Tactical Operations Center (TOC) that he was, in fact, still alive and in vital need of a rescue from his current position.

He hadn't seen any keys during his initial sweep of the house, but that didn't mean there weren't any. Most people in Iran had some sort of motor vehicle, though the poorer families had to make do with automobiles that were barely held together by duct tape and a prayer. A glance around the living room didn't reveal any keys, nor did the kitchen counter hold them. However, the kitchen counter did hold an old rotary phone, and James's eyes lit on it with renewed optimism. He had the TOC's phone number memorized, and once he found the keys, he would make a brief outbound call to them.

The keys weren't hanging on a nail by the front door. James was starting to get discouraged, and a part of him worried that someone had walked out of the house earlier with the keys still in their pocket. But his search ended in the kitchen. He'd been so fixated on the phone, his eyes had completely swept over them during his initial glance through the room. The keys were hiding underneath a soiled and damp dish rag, and he plucked them up with a quiet cry of triumph. The ring held four keys, and one of them looked decidedly like a car key. His search had not been in vain.

James slipped the keys into his pants pocket, and they jingled slightly as they slipped down into the folds of the fabric. With that order of business out of the way, he was now able to focus on contacting the TOC. He scooted the phone across the kitchen counter, drawing it toward himself. Holding the receiver up to his ear, he heard the familiar sound of the dial tone. It was almost a sweet melody from one of the most beautiful hymns to his ears. This normally grating sound was his connection to a way out of Iran.

James slid a pinkie into the opening of the rotary phone, dialing the number to the TOC from memory. He muttered the numbers aloud as he dialed, his voice a quiet whisper in the silence of the kitchen. "Zero, seven, six, zero. Zero, three, zero. Three, six, four, six."

He held his breath as the phone rang, the sound muffled and distorted by the distance and the poor connection. A gnawing anxiety in his stomach wondered if they would pick up, or if his call would even get through. Who knew what the quality of the phone service was way out here in the rural parts of Iran?

To his surprise, a familiar voice answered, albeit choked by the steady drone of static hissing relentlessly in the background: "Task Force Green, Specialist Osborne. How can I...you?"

In a voice that was perhaps too frantic, James cried out, "This is Gator from Operation Quicksand. I'm still on site. I need to speak with the commander!"

The voice that replied was both stunned and barely concealed delight. "Holy shit! You're still alive! ...thought you had...!"

James pulled the phone away from his ear, giving it a sour frown. The static was making it almost impossible to make out what Specialist Osborne was saying. He returned it to his ear, enunciating each word as he spoke. "What? Say again?"

A burst of static followed James's response, then he heard Specialist Osborne's voice saying, "I'll…the commander."

The monotonous hiss of static ensued. James impatiently tapped his foot as he waited for the line to connect again. It sounded as though it was getting worse, and the connection hadn't been especially good in the beginning.

"Shit!" James slammed the handset down onto the phone, a spray of spittle flying from his mouth from his exasperated cry. He absently wiped at his mouth with the back of his hand as he reached for the phone again.

The phone was dead. There wasn't even the distant buzz of a dial tone now.

He raised the hook switch and released it again.

The silence persisted.

James dropped the handset onto the phone base, then snatched it up an instant later. He wasn't going to give up on trying to reach the commander—or hell, any listening party—at the TOC without first putting forth a solid effort. But only a steady drone of hissing static greeted his ears.

"Shit," James said again, dismayed and resigned.

He wouldn't be getting through to the commander after all. He considered making one more attempt when distant weapon fire drew his attention. James spun to face the sound, his feet carrying him across the tile floor. He paused at the front door, then nudged it open with his left hand as he trained his pistol before him with this right. He peered through the front door as it swung open. The door led to a cramped courtyard sheltered by an eight-foot-tall stone wall. A heavy-looking green metal gate that served as the only entrance and exit to the courtyard occupied a car-wide space on the far side of the wall. And the courtyard was completely barren of any people.

James took note of the few artifacts that lay scattered around the yard. A small, white car in a state of severe decay lay hunkered nose-first on the opposite end of the courtyard. The windshield had a meandering crack spiderwebbing its surface and rust gnawed at the tire wells. An uncertain smile crept across his face. That was probably his way out of there, if the thing was even capable of starting.

Further examination of the courtyard also revealed some clues as to the owner of the house. There was a decrepit fountain standing in the middle, its brick edifice bleached by the sun. It probably hadn't seen water in many years. There were a few odds and ends scattered throughout the yard, including a smattering of toys. More bicycle parts lay rusting in the brilliant morning sunlight, and a sun-faded soccer ball lay in the shadow of the fountain. Propped up on a corroded kickstand was a small motorbike, with its own scars and share of rust, as well.

James scanned the horizon once more, his ears straining for any additional gunshots in the distance. There were none, and after a moment, he swung the door open the rest of the way and stepped out into the blinding sunshine. He fleetingly wished he had a pair of sunglasses with him to help protect his eyes from the bright light, but nobody could have predicted his presence in Mehran after dawn. He blinked, shielding his eyes from the light with his cupped palm, and turned toward the rust-eaten car once more.

A name was inscribed on the front of the vehicle, and he peered at it, sounding it out to himself as he circled the automobile. *Paykan.* Those cars hadn't been made in almost a decade, and from the looks of this one, it was one of the older models. He shrugged as he rounded the car, not caring in the least about the cosmetic blemishes on it. If he could get it running, the unwritten law of possession decreed it would become his. He gently rapped on the hood with his knuckles, the sound resonating hollowly in the tranquil courtyard. The vehicle was solid-steel construction, a relic from the slowly dying Iranian automotive industry. In the past, the purchase of a car built in Iran had been a subject of pride for the locals, but in recent years, the industry had been falling apart and so had their cars. But James didn't care about the reputation of the local car manufacturers or if the corroded Paykan sedan was a death trap or not. All he was concerned about was if it actually ran and would successfully get him out of this town. Everything else was secondary to that objective. No working air conditioner? No worries, the windows could be rolled down. Only got ten miles to the gallon? Who cared? Just as long as it ran and had a little bit of gas in the tank, James would be perfectly content with it.

He tried the handle. The ancient bar was stiff but responded reluctantly to his touch. It was unlocked, but corrosion and age had formed a solid seal. James's heart sank. This was already a bad sign as to the state of the vehicle. He yanked on the door, and it swung open with a low creak of protest. He glanced over his shoulder, his gaze darting across the yard and flickering to the gate. The courtyard was still empty. He returned his attention to the car and took a slow breath before steadily releasing it. In a moment, he would find out if this old beater had any life left in it.

He lowered his body into the driver's seat, and a plume of dust and sand rose up around him. A faint hint of mildew greeted his nose, and he made a downward grimace of distaste at the subtle stench. The keys dug into his thigh, and James fished them out of his pocket, turning them until the largest one was pinned between his thumb and forefinger. He slipped it into the ignition and turned the key.

Silence. Not even the low chugging of the engine trying to turn over greeted him.

He turned it again.

Again, silence prevailed.

James frowned, considering this new turn of events. While he hadn't pinned too much hope on this car after his initial assessment, this was much worse than he'd originally anticipated. If there were a battery beneath the hood, it was probably flatter than a pancake and coated in a thick cake of acid and corrosion.

"Well," he said to nobody in particular. "That's not good."

He balled his hand into a fist, then lowered it again. While punching the steering wheel might have helped relieve some of his stress, it could also put him in a much worse position. If the horn inside the sedan were one of those old-fashioned horns that wasn't dependent upon the battery to operate, it still might sound in the quiet courtyard. He didn't need to risk drawing unnecessary attention to himself when he was so damn close to escape. A frustrated outburst could come later. For now, he needed to keep his cool and see if the issue with the car was something that he could fix.

James sighed, then opened the car door again, swinging his legs out. As almost an afterthought, he pulled the keys back from the ignition, returning them to his pocket before rising to his feet. He closed the door behind him, and it bounced off the latch before lying still. He moved to the front of the vehicle, stopping at the nose of the car, then ran his fingers along the bumper and fumbled beneath the strip of chrome for the hood release. A moment later he came in contact with it and depressed his index finger, triggering a low thump as the latch sprung. He raised the sun-warmed metal of the hood to reveal the inner guts of the vehicle.

A dour expression settled on his face as he inspected the engine block. *Well, shit.* He wasn't going anywhere in this car anytime soon.

It wasn't so much that the battery's connectors were coated in a thick, yellow film of sulfuric acid or that the belt had completely fallen off the water pump, but the engine itself was missing several critical components. Its metal intake pipe had completely snapped off, and the rubber vacuum hose was brittle and had visible holes from age. This car had clearly not run in many years.

"Damn." James took a step back, lowering the hood down with a quiet thud.

His dark eyes surveyed the courtyard once more. He wasn't especially looking forward to walking the two and a half miles out of Iran in the dry, cool November day, but it was shaping up to be his only option. It wasn't just the fear of being discovered that made him hesitate, though. He hadn't had a drink of water or anything to eat since before they left for Da'wud's compound, and the risk of him sustaining serious injury from dehydration was a considerable one. And any chance of getting rescued was largely contingent on him getting out of Iran and back into Iraq.

James again swept his gaze over the courtyard. There were many partially assembled bicycles in this house, but he wasn't sure he would have enough time to repair one. By the time he cobbled something together from the various odds and ends, the IRGC could very well be on his ass. Then his gaze landed on the motorbike. In his fixation on the rusty white car, he'd completely overlooked it. It didn't look much better than the car, but it was better than nothing. He frowned as he considered it. Actually, it didn't look that bad at all, at least from this distance.

With a cautious glance around the courtyard, he took off in the direction of the motorbike. A small crest of hope rose in his chest, and he suppressed it with barely contained optimism. It was too soon to tell if it was functional. Hell, he'd thought the car was an option, and what good had that done?

James jogged briskly across the courtyard. The motorbike was propped against the wall, but first he had to slip past the gate to get to it. He paused, then steered toward the courtyard wall, drawing his body alongside it as he covered the distance. He approached the gate, and a quick peek around the corner verified that there were no enemies hiding immediately on the other side of the wall. He moved quickly past the ten-foot span, then he was closing in on the motorbike and found his pulse quickening in bridled excitement. It looked good. It looked surprisingly good, in fact. Yes, there was a layer of rust on the body and the vinyl seat was ripped and faded, but the tires were still inflated and a cursory glance over the engine didn't reveal any critical issues. The optimism surfaced again, and James suppressed it once more. He could peer at the bike all he wanted, but until he threw his leg over and actually tried to start it, he wouldn't be going anywhere.

In the distance, closer now, another report from a firearm sounded.

James's head jerked in the direction of the sound. Judging from the familiar tone of the report, it was undoubtedly from an AK-47. He had a mounting suspicion that the IRGC would be rounding the corner any moment now. He had no time left to waste in this courtyard.

He fumbled in his pocket, hooking the keyring with his index finger, and pulled the set of keys out. He flipped them over in his palm one by one, quickly sizing them up. A shorter key, bronze in appearance, seemed to be the most likely option out of the remaining four keys. He pinched it in his fingers, then straddled the bike and slid the key into the ignition as he held his breath.

James sent a silent prayer heavenward as he pulled the lever on the choke. While the bike may have run without this action, he wasn't about to gamble with that risk on this brisk morning. By pulling on the choke, he was letting just enough air into the engine to ensure it would actually start. His wrist moved forward, and he turned the key. A dial readout confirmed that the gear was in neutral, and he squeezed the clutch. His silent prayer continued as his thumb found the start button, and he pressed it firmly.

A low sputtering sound reached his ears, and a cloud of smoke billowed out from behind the matte black motorbike. It was tarry and had a heady stench of burnt oil, but the bike was actually running.

A jubilant grin spread across James's bearded face. *Alright. Back in business. I might actually get out of this godforsaken place on a pair of functional wheels after all.*

He glanced up at the cloudless sky and clasped his hands together, locked his fingers over one another, and brought them to his chest. He hadn't stepped foot in a church in years, but the habit from his early years in Sunday School was still ingrained in him. Regardless, this small victory arguably justified the subtle gesture. Had any of the IRGC seen this motion, he may have been shot on the spot. But in that moment, James didn't care. In a voice that was for his and the Big Guy's ears only, he breathed, "Thank you, God."

The smile remained on his face as he hopped off the motorbike and strode over to the gate. For the moment, things were finally starting to look up. At the very least, he knew he would be getting out of this courtyard. Even better, he wouldn't need to do it on foot. Would he actually make it to Iraq alive and in one piece?

That remained to be seen, but James was ready to take that chance.

CHAPTER TWELVE

GETTING OUT

0856 HOURS — 15 NOVEMBER 2013

USING ONE LEG FOR SUPPORT, James maneuvered the sputtering motorbike toward the green gate. It moved forward with surprising ease. Despite how old and careworn it appeared, someone had taken pretty good care of this bike. He paused by the gate, then swung his leg over the saddle and stood beside it. Instinct told him to keep the engine running. He'd gotten lucky once, and there was no guarantee the motorbike would start again if he shut it off. James hooked the kickstand with his right foot and locked it into place, then quickly walked over to the gate.

How much time had passed since he climbed out of that basement, searched the kitchen, tried calling his commander, and actually found a functional vehicle? James held up his wrist, pushing up the billowing sleeve of his tunic shirt, and turned the watch face toward him as he stood by the gate. The sun bounced and reflected off the glassy surface as James peered at the numbers. It was 0856 hours. From his initial recovery in Da'wud's compound to now, almost an hour had passed. That was too long. He'd already spent far too long in that house, and every passing minute was an opportunity for the enemy to gain ground on him.

James wasn't entirely sure what he would find on the other side of the gate. He'd barely afforded himself much more than the briefest of glances through it, merely to verify there were no imminent threats to his person standing on the opposite side, as he'd hurried past it during his approach to the motorbike. He had no idea what he was about to walk into when he opened the heavy wrought-iron gate. Now he was seeing the town of Mehran for the first time in broad daylight, and the vista was both nondescript and, to his jaded eye, predictable.

James opened the gate about two feet and peered out. To the west of the residence, a two-way street meandered off into the horizon. Even out in the more rural parts of Mehran, someone had taken initiative to pave this road. A thin layer of desert sand coated the street in a taupe powder. If someone had bothered to come out with a broom to sweep it up every morning, it would simply pile back up again by that evening. Trying to remove it would be a Sisyphean act, entirely redundant and fruitless. The winds coursing through the flat desert terrain made for vast, sweeping dunes and a fine layer of the coarse dust on every visible surface.

At this time of day, the town was already bustling with activity. A couple strolled side by side on the sidewalk that ran alongside the road, the taller, heavyset man leading the pair. The smaller form, no doubt his female companion, trailed behind him by several paces. It was hard to determine any of her features through her colorfully patterned linen hajib, but she moved with the lumbering pace of a person who was exhausted from the rigors of day to day life in the Iranian desert. The man didn't bother to glance back at her, nor did he acknowledge her existence. He knew she was behind him, and she wouldn't dare disrespect him by either trying to catch up with him or falling too far back.

An armored personnel carrier (APC) was parked at the nearest intersection, effectively blocking traffic in both directions. James swept his gaze over the olive-green vehicle, taking in the black and gold emblem of the IRGC on its side. His lips flattened into a frown. This might prove to be a problem. Nobody was crossing the intersection without first going through the two guards stationed on either side of the vehicle. Each guard bore an AK-47 and a determined expression. One faced in the direction of the eastbound traffic, and the other monitored the westbound flow of pedestrians and cars.

James's vantage point behind the gate gave him a surprisingly strategic position. He watched as a door opened in a squat, single-story house across the sand-swept road and six soldiers filed out. They paused in a loose cluster in front of the door, their hands moving as they animatedly discussed something amongst one another. Then the one in the front nodded, and they took off in unison toward the next house on the street. The leader of the group strode toward the door, his hand reached out in front of him as he approached it, and then he was walking through the door and into the house with four of the men behind him. A lone guard stood outside, his eyes fixed at a distant point in front of him. James realized they were performing a meticulous sweep of the house, and the man loitering outside the door was serving as a lookout to ensure nobody entered or exited during their search. It was clear they were looking for something—or someone—specific.

He needed to see more of what was happening, so after a cautious glance around to make sure nobody was going to spontaneously blow it off, he poked his head out of the gate. While the APC was stationed on the west side of the block, the east side of the street seemed to still be clear of any military activity. James knew instinctively that he was the subject of both the barricade and the search, and the longer he lingered in the courtyard, the greater the risk was of him being discovered. Across the street, the six men were done searching the house and now advancing onto a house just two down from where he stood. At their rate of speed and level of efficiency, they would be closing in on him very shortly.

James considered them quietly. It was as though they knew he would be making a beeline out of the Iranian boundaries via this specific route, and the most practical way out of Mehran was now closed off by the guards and the APC. They were blocking his exit completely. He would need to find another way out.

He glanced east. It was still clear, at least for now. In a moment or two though, he would be trapped. He needed to leave right now if he planned on getting out of there alive.

With steady hands, James reached out and pushed on the metal gate. It swung open with a low creak, abrupt and grating in his ear. He cast a wary glance to the west, but nobody was paying attention to him yet. The guards were still working their way through the residence two houses over, and the walking couple were trying to discreetly monitor the activity without calling unnecessary attention to themselves. The guards on the APC were more focused on the traffic meandering down the street than the dark-skinned man slipping through the gate. James let out a slow breath, then turned back toward the motorbike.

It was still sputtering quietly where he'd left it. James gripped its handlebars and wheeled it toward the gate, then nosed it through. He led it beyond the open gate, then released it to stand idling on its kickstand, and turned back toward the gate. His heart thudded loudly in his chest, but his exterior demeanor was calm and tranquil. As long as he acted as though his actions were completely normal and not out of place in this desert borough, nobody would pay him any mind. As far as they could tell, he was just another local carrying out his routine daily ritual of going to the market or visiting with family.

The soldiers searching the houses were now close enough that James could hear the crescendo of their voices as they spoke amongst one another. They were now searching the house directly across from him, and based on the contorted expressions on their faces, unhappy that they weren't finding what they were looking for. He could sense palpable frustration emanating from them. They'd been told they would find their quarry on this block, but they'd searched almost the entire street and still come up empty handed. Either they were about to zero in on their target or they'd been fed inaccurate intel. They were equally excited and irate, and James could sense the determination coming off them in fetid waves.

The gate squealed in protest as James swung it shut. He kept his jaw set as the noise sounded loudly, betraying his current position. With how close the soldiers were, he didn't need the damned gate announcing his location to everyone within earshot. He stole another glance to the west, and his heart sank as he made eye contact with one of the soldiers.

The man watched him with a sort of detached curiosity, no doubt realizing he didn't recognize the face of this newcomer. Then the soldier's face twisted in a frown of contemplation.

James made a careful point to ignore him as he moved deliberately and smoothly, his hands steady as he latched the gate. Then he turned back toward the bike and swung his right leg over it. He'd settled into the saddle when the first shout rang out behind him. He ignored the Farsi cry, his eyes trained ahead of him. If he didn't acknowledge the soldier, the man might think he hadn't heard him. The bluff would work for a moment or two, and the soldier would call out to him one more time before he raised the alarm to the other guardsmen.

James squeezed the throttle, jerking it toward him, and the engine revved in response to his touch. Its roar drowned out the second shout, and he smiled ever so slightly. He nudged the kickstand up and let the motorbike surge forward.

Another voice joined the original one to deliver sharp cries of outrage in Farsi.

James maneuvered the motorbike down the eastbound road, his back drawn and tense as he picked up speed. The soldiers were armed, and a new hole puncturing his back was not outside the realm of reality as he sped off.

The road split off to the right some fifty yards ahead, merging onto a cross street. James kept his eyes trained on the juncture in the sandy road ahead. The polished texture of the sand would act as a liquid beneath the wheels, and he knew if he turned too sharply at the intersection he would hydroplane. He didn't need to lose control of the bike with escape so close and tangible. He could wipe out as soon as he crossed into the border of Iran. That would be just fine. But for now, he needed the wheels to stay steady beneath him and the sky to remain directly overhead.

James rounded the corner, and as the bike hugged the curb,

he ventured a glance back. The soldiers behind him had given up their pursuit. His escape was almost too easy, and his brow knit in suspicion as he headed southbound on the motorbike. They hadn't given up on him that easily. No, that wouldn't make sense. They'd spent a larger part of the morning searching for someone who probably matched his description, then a man on a motorbike had taken off while also disregarding their direct commands. They were perhaps just regrouping, and James was confident that he would encounter another obstacle on the road shortly.

Approaching another intersection, James slowed down. This intersection was bustling with activity too. He turned his head first to the right and then to the left, verifying with a perfunctory glance that the street was clear and safe for him to cross. As he looked west, his eyes lit upon a large truck not unlike the one he'd left behind a few hundred yards back. He narrowed his eyes at it. A cluster of soldiers moved along the street like the ones behind him had, and James realized the entire town of Mehran was being canvassed by the IRGC. They were not going to give him any opportunity to escape if they could avoid it.

Directly ahead, a soldier had a two-way radio pressed against his bearded face. While the distance between James and the soldier was too vast for him to hear the crackly, staticky message being relayed, the hungry look on the soldier's face told him all he needed to know. The face turned toward James, and the soldier's eyes brightened at the sight of the man on the motorbike. No doubt he'd just been dispatched a description of James and advised to intercept anyone matching that description.

James met his gaze unwaveringly. He couldn't blame the man for radioing ahead to tell people to scout for him. He would have done the same had he been the pursuer. It was best to act as though he belonged there. He had the right attire of the locals and the correct mode of transportation. His black hair was tucked beneath the sheep's wool hat, and his dense beard concealed most of the bottom half of his face. As far as anyone could tell, James was just another resident going about his business. If he continued to act like he belonged there, then perhaps he could keep up the farce for a little while longer.

Lowering his head, James revved the accelerator on the motorbike with a twist of his wrist. The bike lurched forward, and he picked up speed, moving steadily through the intersection. He kept his focus on the traffic moving sluggishly ahead of him, and as he moved past the scouting party that was searching the houses on both sides of the street, he kept his expression stony and his gazed fixed forward. Staring at the soldiers with a slack-faced gape would make him stand out, and the less attention on James, the better.

Other people could stop and watch the soldiers as they went from door to door in the neighborhood. It wasn't outright forbidden, after all. Hell, seeing someone get dragged out onto the street would provide a good five or ten minutes of free entertainment as far as most of them were concerned. Most people, however, didn't bother. While search parties out here weren't necessarily commonplace, the majority of the townspeople had grown to accept that the IRGC was a permanent feature in their community and didn't warrant a watchful eye. Paying an excessive amount of attention to them was a guaranteed way to make an individual stand out, and it was in James's best interest to act as though he were genuinely bored and disinterested in their methodical actions.

The motorbike picked up speed, and James felt the wind tug at his hat as he continued to navigate southward. He found himself growing warm in his layers of gear and clothing. The breeze was almost refreshing, despite the multitudes of stinging pinpricks of sand flying up and peppering his face as he drove the motorbike down the narrow street. He scanned both sides of the thoroughfare as he drove, his eyes watchful as he closed in on another intersection.

Yes, it was definitely unusually busy today. While he wasn't a resident expert on how active Mehran was typically, he knew that most smaller towns in these desert regions didn't usually have this much IRGC traffic on any given day. They were definitely picking up their security patrols and no doubt behaving like a pack of bloodthirsty hounds on his trail. It would be only a matter of time before someone eventually spotted him and pulled him over for an impromptu interrogation.

On approach to the next intersection, James slowed the bike down. The sunlight glittered off the Nhar Mirzabad River directly ahead of him, a murky and turbid slough of water cutting through the heart of Mehran. This intersection was a T-junction, splitting both left and right instead of directly over the river itself. A bridge would have required the use of too many resources, and instead of providing the community with direct access over it, locals were forced to diverge at this juncture. James drew the motorbike to a stop, craning his face in both directions as he idled at the intersection. If he bore east, he could circumvent the river and empty out on the other side of it. The left side of the street was clear of any activity, so he turned the handlebars of the motorbike and gripped the throttle in preparation to accelerate out of the turn.

A flurry of movement to the right side of the street drew his attention to the west, and he hesitated at the juncture. Here, more soldiers moved along the street in a similar pattern as the two prior clusters and another blocky armored personnel carrier lumbered down the street on the west side of the intersection. Two soldiers loitered outside the truck, their mouths moving as they discussed something of vague importance between one another. The taller of the two guards reached up, his hand snaking for the handle on the side of the truck, and then he froze. His finger extended toward James and the other soldier craned his neck around, fixating on James as he watched them from his motorbike. The shorter soldier turned back to his companion, and without further comment, they both piled into the truck.

James watched the exchange with mounting dread. No doubt his description had been broadcast to everyone with a radio, and it was only a matter of time before someone intercepted him for questioning. His ruse would be blown the moment someone tried to talk to him. He could carry himself like a native, dress in the fashion of the locals, and even keep his head low and posture the same as the residents of the town, but if someone tried to interrogate him, he was, to put it simply, screwed. He knew a scant handful of words in Farsi, and while he could infer the general gist of what someone was trying to say by their body language, he would be unable to respond to them in their native tongue. Playing dumb could buy him only so much time.

Lingering at this intersection wasn't going to help his cause any, though, so he turned his face back toward the east. At this point, he wasn't even sure he was going to be able to make it out of town with all the guards stationed throughout the area. He pulled the throttle toward him, and the motorbike picked up speed. The speedometer ticked steadily upward, showing him encroaching on thirty-five kilometers per hour, then fifty. The bar wavered unsteadily for a moment, then crept up again. The little bike was going over seventy kilometers per hour, or around forty-five miles per hour according to James's hasty mathematic calculations. It was as fast as it would go, and the truck fell steadily behind him as the distance between himself and the intersection widened.

Another intersection unfolded ahead, and James read the green sign as the bike sped past it. He was closing in on Road 64, one of the major arteries in the town. If he followed this route, it would lead him north and eventually spit him out into the center of town. He slowed as he approached the intersection. Turning right would lead him south, which would take him to the desert and eventually get him to his destination. The urge to bear south was compelling, but he shook his head. Going north, into the heart of Mehran, seemed counter to his objectives. Nevertheless, he knew he had a better chance of throwing the soldiers off his trail if he successfully managed to lose himself in the city center. It would cost him some time, but it was better to encounter a few extra delays than a handful of bullets into his back. It was a no-brainer. North it was.

James veered left, and the town's beige skyline loomed ahead of him. The desert to the south faded away in the distance as he zeroed in on the bustling urban district.

CHAPTER THIRTEEN

THE CHASE

0909 HOURS – 15 NOVEMBER 2013

JAMES STEERED THE SMALL MOTORBIKE north, his face set in a determined line of concentration. The wind whipped past his face as he sped down Road 64, tugging at both his beard and his woolen hat. With one hand on the throttle, he reached up and grasped the lip of the hat, pulling it back down over his ears. While it wasn't the most fashionable item, it was still an essential part of his ensemble and a key component to helping him blend in with the locals. Very few men dared venture out without such an accessory, as it not only was an on-trend garment but also helped protect their head from the effects of the blazing sun.

The bike continued its northbound trajectory on Road 64. As the desert route to the Iraqi border fell away behind him, the traffic picked up in response. It wasn't as heavy as he might have found in Baghdad or even back home in the United States, but there were a decent number of motorists out and about this November morning. If he could slip between a few other drivers on the road, he might be able to lose his tail and successfully blend in with the commuters. He ventured a glance back over his shoulder.

Luck was not in his favor. A few car-lengths behind him, the ponderous IRGC truck was steadily closing in on him. The olive-green pickup wove aggressively through traffic, and the other drivers on the narrow two-way road had to make a quick decision: get out of the way or be forcibly shoved out of traffic and onto the curb.

James lowered his head, flattening his body over the handlebars of the motorbike. The muscles in his back tightened, and the injury in his shoulder called out to him in sudden protest at the maneuver. Ahead, two rust-scarred cars battled neck-to-neck to take the lead ahead of him, and he considered the narrow gap between them. It would be a tight fit, but he was sure the little bike could make it. He glanced back over his shoulder again. The pickup had overtaken another car and was making steady progress in closing the distance between itself and James.

Pulling the throttle toward himself, James drew his body as low as possible against the bike and steered it toward the pair of cars ahead. The space wasn't very accommodating, but it would have to suffice. James brought his shoulders up, making himself as small as possible on the bike, then slipped between the two cars. If he extended either hand out to the side of his body, he would be able to rap on the glass windows of the two parallel cars with ease. One driver glanced up as he passed before dismissing him, but the other sounded their horn in surprise. James kept his head low, then revved the accelerator and pulled ahead of them. They disappeared behind him in a sandy plume of dust.

The motorbike jostled and thrummed beneath James's muscular legs as he wondered how reliable the bike actually was. A part of him was certain the vibration would soon cause parts of the older-model bike to start flying off in all directions. It was obvious that its former owner hadn't used it for much more than routine chores, and they certainly hadn't driven it as hard as James was driving it now. It occurred to him that if one of the threadbare tires ran over a particularly sharp piece of road debris, he could wipe out and be thrown from the bike. Without protective gear on his body or his head, it could easily spell out an ugly end for James. It was a prospect he didn't like entertaining, so he shoved the thought out of his mind and focused on the road ahead.

James scanned the horizon again. There had to be another gap opening up in the traffic. Ahead, a sun-faded blue Peugeot was moving along at a steady pace. To its right, a small gap by the shoulder of the road buffered it from passing traffic. This channel would be adequate enough for him to slip through.

A shot rang out, and James reflexively drew back from the sound. Ahead of him, a hole appeared in the rear window of the Peugeot and the car jerked sharply to the right, filling the space he'd been eyeing a moment before. He released the throttle, falling back. *Damn it.* Had he tried to zero in on the gap, he might've been pushed off the road by the other driver's panicked reaction. He would have to wait for another break in traffic for his chance to slip ahead.

Traffic was slowing down, and after a moment's hesitation and a wary glance back, James pushed himself upright to get a better view of the road ahead. A hundred yards ahead, traffic was starting to merge into a traffic circle, and the every-man-for-himself attitude about the roundabout was evidently to blame for the delays. The sounds of drivers pressing impatiently against their horns as they cut one another off in the circle created a symphony of repeated beeps in the morning haze, and James lowered himself back over the handlebars, considering this new development.

While traffic had slowed to a crawl at this roundabout, it was still moving steadily along on the straightaways. James glanced in the direction of the straight-moving traffic. Already it was thinning out as the handful of motorists cleared this pocket of congestion. He nodded thoughtfully to himself, then turning the handlebars to the right, nosed the bike in the direction of the traffic circle. It was easier to weave in and out of traffic in this corridor, so he coaxed the bike between the meandering cars and trucks that were branching off from the circle.

Behind him, the IRGC truck steadily gained on him. James ducked between two dusty cars, then peered over his shoulder once more. A couple minutes ago, it had been four car lengths behind. Now, even though it was moving more slowly, the distance between himself and the pickup was steadily shrinking. In front of him, a rear window spontaneously shattered as two shots rang out in rapid succession. A third one collided with the tire of the car he was following, and the vehicle fishtailed. Its rear swung erratically first to the left, then to the right, and James could see the driver yank the wheel sharply as they careened out of the roundabout.

Traffic was thinning out again as the roundabout finished its circular route, and James sped the bike up to stay with the flow of the neighboring vehicles. He twisted the throttle toward himself, and the bike moved quickly through the almost vacant road.

Here. This is as good a spot as any. He released the throttle and squeezed the brake, causing the bike to skid toward a reluctant stop and pivot on its nose. It skidded several feet, then with a squeal of rubber tires on sandy asphalt, slowed to a complete stop.

James moved rapidly, throwing his leg down as the motorbike toppled over with a clatter. The sound of the bike colliding with the blacktop was almost drowned out by the sound of the horns and traffic, but it wasn't the sound James was going for. As far as the Revolutionary Guardsmen could tell, he'd overcorrected, fallen, and was now pinned helplessly beneath the bike. From their perspective, they had easy prey they could pick off while James lay prone beneath the wrecked motorbike.

The pick-up rounded the smooth bend of the traffic circle, and from this distance, James could almost make out the scowling visages of the Revolutionary Guardsmen. He knelt beneath the bike, one knee pressed against the warm blacktop, the other one extended out next to his body, ready to propel him upward. He slipped his hand beneath the front of his tunic and let his fingers brush over his 1911 as he watched the truck steadily bear down upon him. His thumb found the safety on the back of the weapon, and it clicked quietly in his hand.

The truck finished its journey around the corner, and James watched it closely as it turned straight. Cars made a wide berth around him, but the truck picked up speed as it targeted him. The passenger, a dark-skinned man with a beard that was not unlike James's own, threw his shoulder out the window. James watched the soldier raise his body into a standing position with a weapon clasped in his hands. The truck closed in on him, and James regarded it warily as it coursed down the road. It was going to be a close maneuver, and he had no margin of error that would afford him any leeway. If he misaimed or timed things incorrectly, it could very well end with him painting the asphalt with a crimson spray of his blood.

The truck was a hundred feet away, then seventy, then fifty. As it closed in forty feet away, James made out more features of the drivers, their eyes wide and their lips pulled back in a rictus of grim pleasure as they bore down upon him. The passenger was raising his weapon, training it in James's direction.

Now! James leapt to his feet, yanked his pistol out from beneath his shirt, and raised the weapon in one smooth motion. His stance widened and he raised his left arm, supporting his pistol as he squeezed the trigger.

The weapon bucked in James's hands as two shots flew smoothly and silently from his 1911, the report muffled from the suppressor attachment. The bullets pierced perfect holes through the windshield, and the man leaning out of the window jerked, then slumped over. His body hung laxly from the open window, his pistol falling from his fingers. The man was no longer a threat, so James turned, pivoting on his booted heel, and aimed his weapon at the driver. The truck continued to bear down upon him, and if he didn't decommission the driver with this shot, he would be in serious trouble. He shifted his body, moving the firearm until the weapon was aimed at the driver's side of the truck. The expression on the driver's face hadn't changed. If anything, the sneer on his face widened. James drew his lips down in a frown, his eyes narrowing as he fixed the driver in his focus. A dazzling beam of sunlight bounced off the windshield, momentarily blinding him, then the moment passed. James squeezed the trigger—one round, two, then three—and the truck lurched as the rounds planted kisses of lead through the neck and face of the driver.

The nose of the truck veered to the left as the driver's body fell forward onto the steering wheel, then the slumped form fell from view and the truck righted itself again. Its pace slowed with the soldier's foot no longer on the accelerator, but it still steadily progressed toward James.

James sized it up with a sweeping glance. It was going to continue to roll until momentum no longer propelled it forward or it encountered an obstacle large enough to stop it. He wasn't interested in being that obstacle. Beyond the truck was a large fountain, its basin pumping a deluge of reclaimed water through the three-tiered concrete pillar. He leapt nimbly aside, jogging toward the center of the roundabout as the truck trailed harmlessly past him.

Traffic slowed even more. Some drivers affected no pretense of ignoring the actions of the man standing on the lip of the fountain, and a few of them shook their heads at him before turning back to the road ahead of them. A couple of others honked, but the majority of them seemed merely vexed by the new obstacle. From their limited perspective, they had no idea that the soldiers driving the truck were now dead. Their own cacophony of horns had been integral in preventing the sound of the reports from carrying across the street.

The truck's tires rolled over the motorbike, the chassis of the vehicle rocking slightly as it drove over it. The motorbike was dragged several yards, the plastic body splintering on the road as the tires crushed it, then it was left behind as the truck progressed onward. This was enough to slow the truck, and James watched as it crept to a lumbering pace of perhaps ten miles per hour. He tucked his 1911 back into its holster and then leapt down from the stone barrier surrounding the basin.

Moving quickly, James sprinted toward the truck, his arms pumping alongside his body as he ran. Even at its reduced pace, it was still moving fast enough that he needed to jog parallel to it in order to keep up. His hand groped for the handle, missed, then reached again. His fingers closed over it, and he grasped it, pulling. The door swung open, and James hoisted himself into the body of the truck, his legs dragging below him as he fumbled for footing on the floor of the cab.

The lifeless eyes of the driver stared at him. James met the gaze unflinchingly. Using his left arm, he gripped the forest-green lapels of the soldier's uniform and pulled him from the driver's seat and out of the truck. The body pitched past him, and he glanced down as it bounced against the road and tumbled away. Another driver rolled over it, then the body was swept away in the current of traffic. A grip handle hung from the ceiling of the truck, and James reached out for it with his right hand. His left moved from the handle of the door, and he reached into the truck. His hand found the lip of the bucket seat and, with his legs dangling out of the driver's side of the truck, he pulled himself inside.

The prone and lifeless body of the other soldier lay sprawled across the passenger seat. James gripped the steering wheel with one hand, then cast a wary glance behind him. No other soldiers lurked in the cab of the truck, but he didn't have time to thoroughly examine the vehicle. He needed to get the hell out of town, and his ride had suddenly been upgraded into a surprisingly efficient mode of transport. If nobody became any wiser of his usurping of it, he might be able to sneak out of Mehran without further interruption.

It was a nice thought, but James shook his head wryly at it. As much as he would like to believe he would get out of Iran in one piece, until he crossed the border safely into Iraq, he wasn't going to waste any time clinging to empty hope. He was now living life literally by the second. Each breath was a notable milestone, and he counted every one of them with gratitude. Every time he released air from his lungs, it served as further proof that he'd thus far successfully avoided getting killed or captured.

James met his own gaze in the rearview mirror. The dark colored eyes that peered back at him sported deep creases in the corners. Bluish smudges had set up camp beneath them, lending a bruised appearance to his tired face. The wool hat on his head cast a shadow across the upper portion of his face, making the whites of his eyes stand out in stark relief on his visage. At a glance, James looked almost feral, uncaged. In a way, it was true. Until he got out of Iran, he was a trapped animal. The only difference between him and a lion pacing its cage was that his cage was much more spacious.

James reached up and adjusted the mirror with his right hand as he steered with his left. The driver had been much shorter than him, and while the angle of the mirror had afforded him a solid inspection of his own bearded countenance, it did nothing to reveal the road behind him. He shifted his weight in his seat, and with another minute adjustment of the mirror, the stretch of the highway behind him bounced into view. Road 64 had ground to a standstill. A couple passengers had gotten out of their cars, their hands above their heads in a display of stunned disbelief as they swarmed the body lying crumpled in a heap on the road. The mangled corpse of a Revolutionary Guard was something these townspeople didn't encounter very often. Usually the soldiers were regarded as an unflappable figurehead of power. Even in a region where casual murder was a common feature, seeing a body close up like this commanded their complete attention.

Now that James had the luxury of a few seconds to examine the truck, he wanted to know exactly what sort of assets he'd acquired when he took over this vehicle. He turned in his seat, craning his body to view his new traveling companion. The corpse had slid farther down in his seat, gravity tugging at him. An AK-47 rested between his knees. The butt of the weapon was wedged between his booted feet, and a glance at the floor between the seats revealed what appeared to be four full magazines. If James needed another weapon, he'd just been bestowed an operational one with enough ammunition to help him hold off the enemy for at least a couple minutes.

James shook his head. With the knowledge that he was being pursued nipping at the back of his mind, he knew it would be prudent for him to create as much distance between himself and this traffic jam. Although it might take some time for any local authorities to work their way into this mess, he didn't want to be there when they finally did arrive. To do so would be the equivalent of him cheerfully signing his own death warrant. While the flow of traffic behind him had been staunched, the road ahead of him was relatively clear. James pressed his foot against the accelerator, and the truck picked up speed.

A quiet crackling sound and a rising crest of voices drew James's eyes toward a gray box sitting in the dip between the two seats. A voice rose suddenly, loud and strident in the enclosed cab of the truck, and James realized the speaker was not happy. Either they were demanding a status update and were livid about not getting one, or they were relaying vital information about James. He listened to it with one ear, but none of the rapidly spoken words stood out. If they were saying anything relevant, he was none the wiser to it.

He reached for the radio to turn it off, but his hand paused, hovering over it. While he didn't speak Farsi, there was a curious fascination about having a front-row seat to the discourse about him. Even though he didn't speak enough of the local language to make the conversation worth more than a modicum of his attention, the rise and fall of their voices gave away almost as much as their words. He drew his hand back, returning it to the steering wheel.

While he wasn't entirely certain as to how he would get out of Mehran yet, he was fairly confident as to what might afford him the most direct route. With his lips flattened in a determined line, James pressed his foot more firmly against the accelerator and guided the truck back into the flow of traffic and the direction of his escape.

CHAPTER FOURTEEN

THE TRUCK

0914 HOURS – 15 NOVEMBER 2013

WITH A CLEAR DESTINATION IN mind, James found himself experiencing a subtle shift in mood. He hadn't realized it before that moment, but his entire body had been taut with tension ever since he awoke in Da'wud's basement cave. The stress and uncertainty of the situation had held him locked in an exhausting fog of stress and uncertainty, perhaps how an animal felt when it knew it was being hunted and had little chance of evading its hunter. Knowing he was being pursued and with no concrete plans in place to escape his enemy, he was operating on a steady stream of instinct and adrenaline.

James knew that he had to get out of town, out of Iran, and back within the Iraqi borders, but it seemed that every turn threw another obstacle in his path. A full battery of enemy troops had been dispatched with the sole intent of capturing or killing him. From the moment he awoke in Da'wud's subterranean cave, he'd allowed his training to take over in the hopes that it would eventually guide him to safety. Even that, though, wasn't guaranteed. And James knew that too.

The tides seemed to be turning with things finally looking to be in his favor. The truck was a vastly superior ride over the motorbike, and it would allow him to blend in with the enemy soldiers for at least a little while. Before long, someone would figure out that it was James driving it, but for now? He had a good setup. He might actually make it out of Iran after all.

A familiar green vehicle nosed its way out from a side street, and James tapped on the brake as the lumbering body of an APC merged into traffic. The armored vehicle slowed down, and James paused. The drivers had a familiar bearing to them, and he realized he was looking at the same APC that had been part of the party clearing the street back in the residential part of town he'd just come from. Without preamble, the hulking vehicle parked itself in the middle of Road 64. James tapped his index finger impatiently on the steering wheel. So much for an easier escape. The entire southbound flow of traffic was effectively staunched.

James pried his gaze off the APC, lowering his head slightly as he steered to the right. If they couldn't see his face, perhaps they wouldn't be able to identify him. It might buy him a little bit of time, though the chances of that were admittedly slim. He'd recognized them, so it wasn't outside the scope of reason that they may just as easily identify him. Instinct kicked in again, and he coaxed the truck across the road and onto a westbound side street.

This was just a minor hindrance. Now wasn't the time to get discouraged. He could still get out of Mehran. He would just have to take the scenic route. The truck completed its turn, and James's foot found the accelerator once more. The truck picked up speed, bouncing as it flew over the potholes that pockmarked this narrower road. From the radio in the seat next to him, the voices continued to chatter, and James trained his ear on them as he drove. Nothing that was said made sense to him, but based on the rhythm of their voices, they didn't seem to be aware that their own truck had been hijacked by the American just yet.

Traffic on the side street was both more sparse and slower. James found himself moving along steadily, and like Moses and the Red Sea, the cars parted as he approached them from behind. They seemed to recognize the type of vehicle he was driving and understand promptly that it wasn't one they wanted to hinder. He'd assumed a position of power and authority, and with it came liberties that lent him ease of access through the town. It would be an unpredictable privilege, and it was only a matter of time before his charade was discovered. Until then, though, he drove on steadily. The city center was now several blocks behind him, and he had a good general idea of where he was heading. While the turn onto the side street had interrupted his internal map, he could easily get back on track. He needed to find his way back to the sewage treatment plant and use the landmark of the churning waste processing center as his guide out of Mehran.

James had always had an uncanny ability to quickly assess landmarks and estimate his location around them. This skill had saved his skin many times before. When other soldiers were fumbling through their topographic lessons, he was able to glance over the sheath of paper and categorize the landmarks with a lingering sweep of his eyes. Because he could easily interpret his location on a site, he could broadcast a three-dimensional map behind his eyelids and navigate his way out of almost any terrain.

He'd been peering out the window when the Blackhawk helicopter made its descent into Iran in the early morning hours. While Mehran had been dark and quiet before they landed, he distinctly recalled the glow of the lights coming from the waste processing plant. Da'wud's compound had been in its shadow, and James was sure that when the wind wasn't in Mehran's favor, the smell could get fairly pungent on hot summer days in the Iranian desert. If he could find his way back to the sewage plant, then he would be able to find his way out of Mehran. The border to Iraq, and his freedom, lay some five hundred yards west of the plant.

The politics of the region were highly divisive and tremulous. While Iraq and Iran were locked in an uncertain stalemate for many ways, there was still a sort of careful dance the two countries were engaged in due to the uncertain climate between them. Iran had a long-held historic tendency to assert its dominance over its neighbor, and ever since the fall of Saddam Hussein, it had been sending out feelers to see if it could successfully influence Iraq in this shifting social tide. The upper hand over the smaller country would give Iran a vast political advantage, providing it an opportunity to assert itself in matters of policy, trade, and religion. Because of this, James was certain they would not attempt to follow him into Iraq. To do so would be a political indiscretion that could potentially deal a devastating blow to the burgeoning rapport forming between the duo. They would not be happy to lose him in Iraq, and it wasn't necessarily guaranteed that someone wouldn't take initiative and try to harm him once he actually was in Iraq. But what good was a country's word if they never actually kept it? No, nothing was set in stone, but he knew that getting into Iraq was his best chance for survival.

James had company. Some eighty yards ahead of him, three soldiers congregated on the sidewalk. They were grouped together, their bodies only a couple feet apart. And, James realized with mounting dismay, they were looking directly at him. The crackling in the radio hadn't indicated word had gotten out, but perhaps that was on James for not understanding Farsi. A sole driver with a corpse slumped in the passenger seat wasn't exactly the very definition of discretion, but he'd hoped he still had a few extra minutes of cruising incognito before he was intercepted.

He reached down, lifting the hem of his shirt with his right hand. The truck swerved, and James shifted his weight, bringing his legs up. He guided the vehicle back on its trajectory with his knees, and the truck continued onward. He cast another glance at the men. They were now facing him, and he could see their mouths moving as they spoke amongst themselves. In a few moments, he would be driving past them. If he didn't have his firearm ready first, he would be sporting a new hole shortly.

Closing his hand over his 1911, James moved quickly to depress the magazine release. The half-spent magazine clattered to the ground, and he kicked it away absently with his booted foot. His left hand slipped beneath the shirt and, patting his flat abdomen, closed over a full magazine. He loaded the magazine into the pistol well, then locked it into place with the flat of his palm. Now he was armed, and the playing field between himself and the soldiers on the sidewalk had evened out somewhat.

The soldiers raised their weapons, their bodies moving simultaneously as they turned toward their prey.

James assessed the men with a brief glance, taking note of their formation. They were standing close enough together that it wouldn't require much adjustment to his aim to pick them off one by one. Had he been standing stationary or hiding behind some sort of barrier, he might have been granted a steadier aim. Moving toward his target in a jostling truck, however, would lend an extra element of difficulty in taking out the three men.

He wasn't about to wait and see if they would have any success with their rifles. He raised his pistol and, as the truck closed in on thirty yards away from the enemy soldiers, he depressed the trigger on the weapon. The first bullets cut through the glass windshield, the initial report resonant in James's ears. He let out his breath, tracking the trajectory of the first bullet without blinking. It was a no-go. A bounce in the truck had caused a slight tremor in his outstretched arm, and the bullet flew high, soaring harmlessly over the head of the closest soldier.

The middle soldier was given no opportunity to appreciate the miss. James adjusted his aim, raising his knees higher to keep the truck moving in a straight path. The second bullet soared out of his .45, and this time, its aim was true. A stunned look crossed the face of the second soldier as the round entered his chest. A second round embedded into his stomach, and the look of surprise melted away from the middle soldier's face as his rifle tumbled from his fingers. He collapsed to the sidewalk, his body thudding heavily to the ground where he lay still.

One down, two to go.

James drew in a breath, his eyes surveying the two remaining men on the sidewalk. They exchanged a glance, looked down at their fallen companion, and promptly dropped to their knees. James lowered his pistol, aiming it toward the remaining pair of men who were now huddling by the ground. The farthest soldier crept away from the corpse of the middle soldier, and with a shout that cut through the air, turned his rifle toward James.

A stream of bullets cut through the air, and James drew his body away from their trajectory, bracing himself behind the dashboard of the pickup truck. The panicked impulsiveness of the enemy soldier overrode his military training, and the hasty response to James's skillful array of rounds perhaps played a role in saving James's life. A hollow thud sounded as the first bullet collided with the side of the truck, piercing the metal body right above the right wheel well. Two more rounds followed in rapid succession, landing in a similar pattern against the side of the truck. Had the bullets been another two inches lower, the wheel might have blown out. Instead, the truck merely sported a new array of holes in its exterior.

Another stream of bullets clanged against the passenger side of the truck, each round burrowing into the side of the door as it cut effortlessly through the solid steel body.

James braced himself as he counted four resonant thuds, and the corpse next to him jerked when three of those rounds landed against the lifeless form with a meaty thud. A final round met the bed of the truck, settling in just beyond the door. Had the enemy not been retreating and had his angle been better, those bullets may have just as easily had James's name on them.

He peered over the edge of the dash and examined his remaining enemies. The two soldiers were crouched together in a staggered formation on the sidewalk. James fixed the closer guard in the sights of his 1911, bracing his right arm against the steering wheel. If the man saw him aiming at him, he didn't indicate it. He dragged himself backward along the sidewalk, trying to regain his footing so he could retreat, and rose to his feet. He turned his back to James, but the man wasn't going to get far. James would see to that.

He slowly tightened his finger around the trigger and released a series of bullets in the direction of the third man. The round met with the enemy's left hip. A shrill scream pierced the air and the soldier dropped his AK-47, his hand flying automatically to his shattered hipbone. His leg buckled beneath him, and he fell heavily to the ground.

The enemy's chest heaved, and he fixed James in a glower of blank fury. Even with a devastating injury, his hatred for the American overrode his pain. One of his hands pressed firmly against his blood-soaked hip, but the other patted the ground behind him as he searched for his AK-47. His good leg flexed and bent at the knee as he tried to stand, but the agony of his wound kept him firmly planted on the sand-dusted sidewalk.

James didn't wait to see if the man would recover his weapon. He released two more bullets in the enemy's direction, firing them in rapid succession at the now-fallen guard. The fourth and the fifth round from his firearm delivered their wordless message to this downed soldier, both landing squarely in his chest. The fight left the man's eyes as the force of the bullets dropped him to his back. He lay still and prone in the morning sunlight.

There was still one enemy remaining, and the man didn't appear interested in waiting patiently to determine his odds of survival against James. He glanced first at his two fallen companions, then at James, and made an executive decision. He spun on his heel and darted away. There was nothing strategic about his retreat. The soldier was on the edge of panic, and his flailing arms clinging clumsily to his AK-47 told James everything he needed to know about the enemy's training. Despite his initial display of bravado, the man had lost his nerve.

Nevertheless, a fleeing enemy was still a threat. If James allowed him to escape, the soldier would regroup and possibly come back in larger numbers. There was also a good chance that he would report to someone within his ranks everything he knew about James. The limited amount of intel he'd managed to gather in their fleeting encounter included data such as exactly what kind of vehicle James was driving, the license plate of the truck he'd co-opted, and whatever other trivia he could remember about James's appearance. No, this remaining enemy needed to be eliminated, and quickly. The longer James engaged him in armed combat, the longer he was stuck in Iran.

His escape from this country was contingent on killing this final man and continuing his trajectory out of the country. In a moment, if James didn't move swiftly, the panicked enemy soldier would slip around a corner and disappear out of sight. If James allowed this to happen, he might lose his chance completely to remove this threat.

He extended his arm once more, aiming in the direction of the retreating soldier.

The man hurried past a little grocery store, no doubt planning to slip into the alley between two buildings to escape.

James drew in a breath, holding it, then tightened his finger around the trigger. The last two rounds flew from his firearm, and he watched as they flew high and missed their target completely. A large chunk of plaster broke free from the side of the beige building as the bullets from his 1911 buried themselves into the edifice.

The enemy glanced up at the new scars in the building and, making a spontaneous decision, veered left. He dove for the ground, flattening his body next to a parked matte gray automobile, his chest pressed against the sun-warmed ground. His rifle fell from his hands as he landed, clattering loudly just out of his reach. He fixed James in a wide-eyed expression of both terror and rage.

James considered the soldier on the street. His magazine was empty, and the final survivor had managed to wedge himself into a position where he couldn't easily aim at him. He sighed, then returned his foot to the gas pedal of the pickup truck, steering it past the sheltered soldier. He would have to let him go. Because the enemy was at a tricky angle beneath the parked car, James would have to emerge from the truck just to get a clear shot at him. It wasn't worth the extra effort, and exposing himself to the receiving end of an AK-47 didn't appeal to him. A frown furrowed his brow. The enemy would survive to fight another day.

The man tracked James coldly as he maneuvered the truck past him, and James met his furious gaze evenly. Even though the chamber of his 1911 was now empty, he kept it trained steadily upon the soldier on the ground even as the truck gained speed and moved past him. While he himself had counted every round that had been aimed at him, it was possible this guardsman hadn't had the same foresight. If he knew the American was bluffing with an empty weapon, he didn't reveal this insight to James.

Now that he was past this particular obstacle, James's mind shifted to other concerns. Almost absently, he released the empty magazine from his firearm. The motions were fluid and swift as he switched out the empty mag for a fresh one. The spent magazine fell to the floor of the pickup truck, and he nudged it away with his boot. He slipped his hand up his shirt, withdrawing another full magazine from his vest, and loaded the fresh magazine into the pistol well. He slapped it into place with his open palm. The slide moved forward, loading a round in the chamber. With the weapon now loaded, he tucked it beneath his right thigh. Access to his holster was limited, and he had other things on his mind now, like how he was going to get out of Mehran.

The sun was high in the sky, casting harsh November shadows on the landscape. James reached above his head, pulling the sun visor down. It did little to cut the glare of the brilliant sunlight, but it did lend a degree of assistance in allowing him to see the road ahead more clearly.

Getting back to the sewage treatment plant was key to his escape. He recalled the layout of the region in his mind. One single road led to the plant, but it wasn't the easiest one to access, especially from this side of town. The map inside his head changed, and he could see with almost distinct clarity the connecting road he needed. He'd already driven along it once today, and its layout was still distinct and fresh in his memory. It was the road that ran both east and west alongside the Nahr Mirzabad River.

James recalled that he'd driven past it on the motorbike on the southside of town not too long ago. He needed to backtrack and find that road again. From there, he would have a clear chance at getting out of both the town and the country.

The sound of glass shattering broke his reverie.

James jerked his body away from the sudden sound, and the steering wheel turned slightly beneath his hands in response. The pickup truck turned to the left, and he quickly righted it as he assessed the damage in the truck. Someone was firing at him, and their aim had been close. Too close. James cast a glance in the rearview mirror, but nothing stood out to him as unusual or suspicious.

He recalled the enemy soldier he'd left behind a minute before, and he let out a quiet sigh. The man had clearly recovered his wits and his weapon and continued his pursuit. James should have taken him out when he had the chance, while the man was cowering behind the gray car. He suspected that the soldier was not only fulfilling his orders to either kill or capture James, but a part of him was more likely fixed on exacting his revenge upon James for humiliating him. For all James knew, the enemy soldier had radioed for backup.

Another shot rang out, and the wooden veneer of the dashboard splintered from the impact.

James pressed his foot against the gas pedal, and the older pickup truck groaned in protest as it accelerated. He needed to widen the distance between himself and his current assailant. The last thing he needed was to be followed to the rural regions of this town. A showdown between himself and a battery of enemy soldiers would more likely than not end poorly for him.

He briefly entertained leading the pursuer back into town to see if he could lose him in traffic again when a third shot rang out. A sharp crest of pain captured his attention, drawing his focus away from his escape plans and to the fact that he'd just been shot.

CHAPTER FIFTEEN

NAHR RIVER

0925 HOURS – 15 NOVEMBER 2013

J AMES GLANCED DOWN AT HIS right arm. The bullet had managed to thread the sleeve of his tunic, and a small trickle of blood was already starting to weep out of the half-inch laceration on the upper part of his arm. He took his left hand off the steering wheel and tugged on the fabric of his shirt, prying his eyes off the road long enough to briefly examine the wound. The injury stung, but it was more of an annoyance than a serious threat to his person. He prodded the hole, and his fingertips brushed against the wound. He hissed through his teeth at the sharp crest of pain that followed his touch, and he yanked his hand away.

No, it didn't hurt much, but he didn't want to probe the wound too deeply and risk infection or further irritation at the injury site. Already the blood flow seeping from the bullet wound was starting to staunch, and in a few minutes, it would taper off completely. It had been a close call, though. A couple inches closer, and it might have shattered his humerus. The idea of being quite literally disarmed in enemy territory wasn't amusing to James in the least.

He returned his hand to the steering wheel and cast a brief glance upward. The Big Guy had been looking out for him again. His foot bore down on the accelerator of the truck, and the needle on the speedometer nosed its way up a little more. The truck skimmed over the pockmarked road, bouncing and jostling along the blacktop. He couldn't really justify going much faster, as one wrong move could lead to a blown tire. There was a fine balance he needed to tread to ensure he evaded this enemy and actually kept his current set of wheels operational.

Ahead, the road split off, veering left. James turned the wheel sharply, and the truck's tires spun on the sandy road, sending up plumes of dust as he merged onto the southbound road. The body next to him shifted in response to the change in trajectory, sliding lower into its seat. A glance in the rearview mirror showed there was nobody in immediate pursuit of him. Either they'd consciously fallen back, or he'd successfully managed to lose them. He wasn't about to complain. Losing his tail was integral in ensuring he survived this spontaneous and largely unwanted adventure in Mehran.

This road was smaller and less busy than Road 64, but based on the sporadic traffic moving along it, it was evidently one of the main roads that cut through the town. It was narrower, with less defined lanes, but it had seen its share of activity. It also had fewer potholes blemishing its surface, but the increase in traffic still required James to release his foot from the accelerator. He cast another wary glance behind him, but if anyone was still following him, he couldn't see them.

The radio on the seat crackled, and James realized the voices were still continuing their monotonous chatter in the background. A few words jumped out at him, but without context, they were largely nonsensical. He reached down with his left hand and turned the volume dial with a twist of his fingers, and the amplitude of the sound increased incrementally. The sounds coming from the radio were mostly the droning hisses of static, but the occasional urgent voice punctuated the white noise emanating from the device.

The sidewalks on this stretch of the road seemed less active than Road 64 too, and James nodded to himself as he drove. It made sense. The sun was creeping higher into the sky, and even though the day was still cool, pedestrian traffic would be dramatically reduced as the sun migrated higher. Most people, as a general rule, preferred to do the majority of their domestic chores earlier in the day. As the day progressed, people would slip indoors to tend to their household responsibilities. A few might head out to perform urgent tasks such as picking up last-minute goods at the corner market or stopping by a neighbor's house to settle a debt, but for the most part, the sidewalks had quietened down considerably.

James alternated his attention from the road ahead to the twin sidewalks lining the street. So far, no discernible threats commanded his immediate attention. Another traffic circle staunched the flow of traffic just ahead, causing the pace to trickle to a meandering pace. As he maneuvered the truck closer to it, he realized he was starting to notice parallels between this quieter street and Road 64. Many of the stores and other businesses dotting the street were more or less the same, as were the tired faces of other drivers on the road. Even this roundabout was a smaller-scale version of the one he'd seen on Road 64. There were also a few differences, though, James mused as he nosed the truck into the roundabout. While this particular traffic circle diverted traffic into a mandatory circular route like the other one had, it had no ornamental fountain decorating its center. Perhaps this side of town had a smaller budget for such niceties. Still, it gummed up traffic just as effectively as it had on the other road. There was something about traffic circles that brought out the worst in a person's driving skills.

James tapped his fingers on the steering wheel impatiently as he navigated the pickup truck through the circle. The sounds of a few horns pierced the air as drivers expressed their frustration at the slowly moving traffic, but it seemed more like a conditioned action than genuine outrage. Bad traffic was a given, no matter what city a person drove in. He would have been just as likely to find blue-haired old ladies puttering along at an excruciatingly slow pace in Florida as he encountered the blank-faced drivers occupying their vehicles in Mehran.

The road straightened ahead of James, and he continued to follow it. This particular road would take him to the intersection back at the Nahr Mirzabad River, and he knew that if he remained steadfast on his southbound journey, he would eventually find the correct route to the sewage treatment plant. The traffic thinned out slightly on this section of the road, and he picked up speed. The growing urgency to find the exit out of this town pressed against him in a knot of anxiety in his chest. It wasn't a matter of if, but rather, *when* the enemy would find him again.

Ahead, an intersection bisected the street. He cast a wary glance in both directions as he drove though the juncture, but there didn't appear to be any unusual activity on either side of the road. So far, so good. The truck continued south for another couple hundred yards, and again, another intersection split the flow of traffic. This time, there was a heavier volume of cars traversing the westbound route, and James reluctantly shifted his foot from the accelerator to the brake pedal. A steady trickle of cars poured through the intersection, then the road was clear again.

James moved his foot back onto the accelerator, and as the pickup truck gained speed, he saw it out of the corner of his eye: the olive-green APC. It had found him again. He flattened his lips into a determined line as his eyes brushed over the angular panels of the heavy personnel carrier. The driver's eyes were obscured as James drove past the vehicle, and if the driver and his passenger recognized him, their expressions didn't indicate it. From behind this bulky vehicle, two more trucks came into view. James flickered his gaze over them as he sped past. These two new trucks were identical to the one he was driving, and the dual sets of guards driving them were evidence enough that he was about to be discovered again.

It could be worse. The thought manifested into James's mind with almost obnoxious good cheer. *I could still be driving that damned motorbike.*

It was true, though. The little bike had served its purpose in getting him out of the courtyard and the residential neighborhood, but considering that its speed had maxed out at no more than forty-something miles per hour, it had been a vastly inferior mode of transportation. Even worse, though, was the fact that it had left him exposed from all angles. Had any of the shots taken at him while he'd been mounted upon the bike actually landed, the small nick on his arm would have been the least of his worries. While this pickup truck with the IRGC crest displayed boldly on its side made him stand out, at least it provided him with a modicum of protection against enemy bullets.

James had always considered himself a man of cautious faith, but throughout the years, his relationship with God had waxed and waned. There had been a particularly quiet period of about six months after the end of his first marriage when he hadn't uttered a single word to God in prayer, and in retrospect, he imagined that the Big Guy had viewed his silence as petty and sulking. He didn't especially mind if God viewed him as a petulant child, but he'd eventually set his bitterness aside and worked on striking up a rapport with Him again after the deeper wounds healed. These days, the silence between himself and God was more companionable than hostile, but James found himself turning to prayer more often than not. And for the third time that day, he uttered a silent prayer heavenward. No, he wasn't in the best of situations at the moment. He would have much rather preferred to be back with his men in the Green Zone, but he knew that he'd been issued the tools and resources to navigate his way out of Iran. He still had his intelligence and his wits and had upgraded his ride to this truck. Yes, things could be better for him, but they could also be much worse. James wasn't an ungrateful man, nor was he a stupid one. Someone was watching over him, and he had his own inklings of who it was.

If James had any misgivings as to whether or not the APC and the dual pair of IRGC trucks were following him, they were dispelled with a glance into his rearview mirror. Instead of continuing westbound at the intersection, they'd fallen in line behind him. They continued along at a steady pace, neither speeding up or slowing down. There was almost an attitude of smug indifference to them, as though they knew they would catch up to him regardless.

James squashed the wave of anger trying to well up in his stomach. While it would be both satisfying and reasonable to be pissed at their relentless pursuit, it wouldn't be conducive toward his objectives. Succumbing to his annoyance would only distract him from his goals. It was better to ignore the emotions that tugged at him, and instead of giving into them, he needed to channel his energy toward escaping.

James forced his eyes off his pursuers and returned them to the road ahead. The truck approached another intersection, this time a T-juncture that went both east and west. Beyond it, the glittering body of the twisting Nahr Mirzabad River snaked across his field of view. A reluctant grin spread across his face as his gaze lit upon the familiar landmark. Bingo. He was back on track. The murky depths of the river were a welcome sight, serving as a subtle reminder that he was on the correct path. While the majority of the city was an indistinguishable series of bland buildings and meandering roads, the Nahr Mirzabad River was a distinct beacon of familiarity. Finding it proved he was indeed heading in the correct direction.

James turned the steering wheel to the right at the intersection. The river had a subtle smell of sulfur and methane emanating from it, and he cast a glance out of his window at the waterway running alongside the road. While the river was the primary source of water in the city, the stench radiating from it didn't surprise him. Running an aqueduct beneath the town was a far less efficient way of providing potable water to the community, but clearly the locals didn't care for such logic. To them, it was easier to dump the byproducts of the sewage into the river than actually process them in a sanitary way, and evidently the locals had long since stopped worrying about the minor issues of hygiene and clean water. It was just another clue as to the corruption dominating the rural regions of Iran, and while it made for an unpleasant smell, it was probably nothing new to the locals.

The road curved to the right, and James guided the steering wheel slightly in response to the subtle bend in the road. The body next to him swayed and slid farther down into the seat, and as James shifted the wheel toward the left, it slipped the rest of the way to the floor. The unseeing eyes of the corpse stared accusingly up at him, and he found himself meeting the expressionless gaze with one of his own. The radio on the seat crackled again, and another burst of voices spilled out of it. Like before, a few of the words were familiar, but nothing stood out as something that commanded his attention.

Despite himself, James found his pulse quickening in anticipation. He was so close to freedom and escape. He lowered his booted foot onto the accelerator, and the pickup truck gained speed as it navigated the paved road. The Nahr Mirzabad River faded out of view, and James noticed the stench of the river had been replaced by a new scent. He wrinkled up his nose, taking in the acrid odor with a deep breath. It was a distinct smell, and he recognized the scent of burning immediately. The tarry scent was coming from within the vehicle, and he frowned as he realized that a white cloud of smoke was rising in patchy tufts from beneath the hood of the truck.

James wasn't sure how much longer the pickup truck was going to last, but with how close he was to the Iraqi border, he hoped it would survive long enough to help him cross into the neighboring country. One of the bullets from the three guards he'd encountered earlier must've pierced through to the engine, severely damaging it. Moving along the uneven road at a high rate of speed hadn't helped the situation any, and as the distance between James and the border narrowed, he knew the pickup truck was now operating on limited functionality. It would only be a matter of time before the engine overheated and petered out. He silently hoped it would last at least another couple of miles. That was all he needed to get out of Iran and to safety.

Up ahead, the paved road transitioned into a sandy dirt track. The truck bumped and heaved as the road beneath him changed, and as if almost in response, another cloud of smoke spat out from beneath the hood. The burning smell was growing stronger, and James debated rolling down the driver's side window. He resisted the urge. While the pane of glass wasn't much of a shield between himself and any rogue bullets that might be looking for him, it was better than nothing.

Like a mirage on the horizon, the sewage treatment plant materialized into view. It lay like a squat and sprawling cluster of mechanical and spartan buildings in the distance. Based on the landmarks separating James from it, he estimated it resided some two miles off in the distance. The border was literally close enough that he could almost see it. At his current rate of speed, he could be driving into it in just a matter of minutes. He glanced down at the speedometer. While his foot was pressed heavily against the gas pedal, the truck was chugging along at a meager forty miles per hour. The damage to the engine was making it harder for it to pick up any more speed than that, despite his weight on the accelerator.

An inky smudge of smoke in the sky to the right drew James's attention, and he turned his head to peer out the passenger side window. The sight that greeted him caused his mouth to fall open in dismay. Where Da'wud's compound had once resided, a charred skeleton of rebar and smoldering embers now stood. Disbelief clouded his vision, and he shook his head in astonishment as he assessed the scene before him. The entire compound was completely destroyed. Not only had the building itself been flattened by flames, but the scorched and smoldering frames of two helicopters lent to the eerie scene where the house once stood. The odor of burnt metal and wood greeted his nose like a jolt of electricity, and despite himself, James lifted his foot off the accelerator. The vehicle slowed down as his dark eyes swept over the ruins in the distance. Even though the compound lay in charred disarray, it was no ghost town. Several vehicles were parked around the destroyed building, and from the markings on their doors, he could tell they were Iranian military and IRGC. From the looks of it, a large number of medical support vehicles had been dispatched to the remains of the compound.

"What the hell…?" The words slipped out of his mouth, and he was barely aware that he'd said anything as his neck craned in the direction of Da'wud's compound.

The panorama of destruction was almost surreal, and James found a numbness creeping into his peripheral extremities. He shrugged the sensation off. With the border so close, he couldn't allow himself to be distracted by the chaos in the distance. He could wonder about what had happened later.

A cold knot twisted in his stomach, though, and despite trying to silence the barrage of questions that arose at the grim sight, he found himself wondering what exactly had transpired in the hours since he'd fallen through the stairs. How had he not noticed it when he emerged from the courtyard earlier? Well, he couldn't blame himself for not picking up on it then. The residential area had been packed with buildings and enemy troops, and he'd been more focused on escape at the time. Seeing the charred remains of the helicopters, however, made him distinctly uneasy. How many of his men had perished in the firefight? What would he eventually learn when he finally made it back to the safety of the Green Zone? If he made it back, that was.

The radio crackled, and James tore his gaze from the skeleton of Da'wud's compound and lowered them to the gray box between the seats. The voices pouring from it sounded both frantic and urgent, and he realized they were talking over one another on the radio in their newest report. Something had riled them up, and he had his own mounting suspicion that he played a significant role in this outburst. He returned his gaze to the road ahead, and as he drove, one single word rang out from the speaker: the Farsi word for border.

As if on cue, the two trucks and the armored personnel carrier popped into view in the rearview mirror.

James cast a glance at the reflection, and the corners of his mouth turned down as he recognized their familiar shapes. They hadn't given up on him yet, and knowing that their quarry was so close to the border had probably sent them into a frenzy. The voices emanating from the speaker were sharp and impatient, and he had no doubt they were discussing his proximity to the line of demarcation that separated Iran from Iraq. If they let him cross the border, they would lose their rights to him. The overlapping voices indicated they had no interest in allowing such a thing to happen, and the speeding pair of matching trucks steadily gaining upon him belied their panicked desperation.

Behind him, the APC seemed to fall behind, but James knew it was an optical illusion. The APC wasn't slowing down. The two guard trucks were speeding up. A faded yellow plume of sand fogged out his view of the pair of trucks in the mirror. The distance between himself and his pursuers was rapidly shrinking, and the failing engine of his own truck wasn't facilitating his escape any. James threw his weight onto the accelerator, and another cloud of smoke poured from beneath the hood. The vehicle was taxed enough as it is. He wasn't going to be able to go any faster no matter how desperately he pushed down on the gas pedal.

The gates to the waste processing plant loomed ahead, taunting him with their proximity. Once he made it past them, the border to Iraq would be within his reach. Despite the knowledge that the truck couldn't go any faster, he bore down on the accelerator with renewed urgency. The tires churned over the unpaved road, kicking up a dense fog of sand behind him. Even if the engine hadn't been damaged when the guards shot at him, he wouldn't have been able to drive much faster than he was currently going. The only consolation was that the trucks behind him had the exact same type of tires, and the only advantage they held over him was a fully functional engine.

James could hear the mechanical churning of the sewage processing plant directly ahead. If he could somehow lose his tail in this sprawling facility, he might be able to gain a little bit of leverage. The repetitive thumping of the waste processing plant droned on monotonously, surprisingly loud in his ears. Despite the noise of the facility, though, it couldn't drown out the sound of AK-47s as they began firing upon him.

CHAPTER SIXTEEN

THE IRAQ BORDER

0936 HOURS – 15 NOVEMBER 2013

J AMES CAST ANOTHER GLANCE IN the rearview mirror as the sounds of rifle fire drew his attention away from the waste processing plant. Despite his vigilant efforts, the soldiers had managed to narrow the distance between themselves and him. They were now close enough to justify expending their ammunition on him, and James could see the green-clad body of one of the enemy soldiers leaning out the passenger-side door as he aimed his AK-47.

As James maneuvered the truck alongside the perimeter fence of the waste processing plant, he waited for the telltale sound of the enemy's rounds bouncing off the body of the truck. To his surprise, no resonant clang alerted him that any of their shots had successfully found their target. He shifted his eyes from the road ahead to the rearview mirror once more, but the trucks behind him were obscured by a vast cloud of dust. With a small shrug, he returned his focus to the road. If he couldn't see them clearly through the plume of sand, it was reasonable to assume they couldn't see him either. While it offered a temporary mask, he knew their aim would improve as they closed in on him.

The road turned abruptly to the right ahead, and he considered this new route as the truck sped toward it. After a fleeting moment of deliberation, he jerked the steering wheel sharply, and the pickup's wheels skidded along the dirt track. Gravel flew up from his tires as the truck bounced along this new route. James's body swayed and bounced as the tires skimmed over the perimeter road. This route wasn't designed to handle a pickup truck moving at high speed, and James briefly entertained—and dismissed—the idea of buckling his seatbelt.

Now he could see the enemy to the right of him. This new route ran perpendicular to the two pickup trucks and the lumbering APC, and without the sand billowing out behind him to conceal his precise location, he could make out their shapes more clearly. In turn, that meant they could also see him as well. James had a moment to assess their new location in relation to his position before the first shot rang out. The guard was still leaning out of the passenger's seat, and James could see the AK-47 firmly clutched in his hands.

Each shot met against the side of the truck with a hollow clang, and James felt the vehicle rock with each blow. The bullets peppered the side of the pickup, landing in an erratic spray against the righthand side. James forced himself to remain focused on the road ahead. Either he was going to get shot or he wasn't. Taking his eyes off the road would only distract him and slow him down.

The road completed its route around the front of the waste processing plant, and a curve in the road gave James no other option but to veer left. He turned the steering wheel of the pickup hand over hand, and the truck had momentary air before the tires skidded against the dirt road. His body lurched to the right in response to the truck's steep change in direction. Then his body swayed violently when the truck met solid ground once more.

The sand beneath the tires was dense and hard-packed, a combination of years of use beneath the blazing desert sun. Here, James was able to pick up speed, though the acceleration was nominal. The truck fought his orders, simply unable to muster up the energy to go any faster. Like an old, beaten horse, the truck didn't have much life left.

Will this thing actually take me to the border? James wasn't sure it would.

The APC had fallen significantly behind, designed for strength and not speed, but the two guard trucks were not deterred by James's attempts to lose them. From the rearview window, he watched as they mimicked the route he'd taken a moment before. Side by side, they sped down the dirt road toward him, both trucks sporting an enemy soldier hanging out of its passenger side window. While he'd gained a little bit of distance by taking the side roads, it had only bought him a few seconds. The trucks were no more than a hundred yards behind him now, and even though he was pushing his damaged pickup truck as hard as it would go, the distance between himself and the enemy was still closing rapidly.

James frowned as a new scent assaulted his nose. A variety of unpleasant smells vied for his attention: the acrid stench of smoke that was pouring out with renewed vigor from beneath the hood of the truck, the fetid odor of decay and human waste radiating from the waste processing plant, and the new smell joining the unpleasant brew. He took in a deep breath and sighed. It wasn't just the engine that was giving out. The slightly sour and fruity smell was distinct and unmistakable, and he recognized it immediately. Antifreeze. One of the bastards had managed to puncture the truck's radiator with his bullets, and antifreeze was leaking out of the coolant recovery system.

Damn it. Damn it all to hell.

He tossed another glance over his shoulder through the rearview mirror, but the sight that greeted him wasn't reassuring. At the rate the enemy trucks were still gaining on him, they would be on top of him in just a few minutes. He adjusted his gaze down to the instrument panel embedded in the dashboard, and the readout confirmed his suspicions. The white arm of the temperature gauge was firmly positioned on the righthand side of the readout, and as he watched it, it moved another millimeter toward the red overheating tick mark.

Shit.

Had the truck been fully operational, James might have stood a chance at evading his enemies. Even with one of the truck's systems failing, he may have still been able to milk just enough life out of the dying engine to help him make it across the border. But having several punctured components instead sounded a death knoll for the truck. At this rate, his chances of succeeding at this mission had just been dramatically reduced. He was so damned close, and the tantalizing promise of freedom that lay on the other side of the border was frustratingly elusive.

James set his jaw firmly as he returned his gaze to the road. His dark eyes were cold as he scanned the horizon. From here, he could almost see the border just out of his grasp. He would be damned before he let the Iranian military capture him. He was too close to actually escaping from this forsaken country to simply succumb to the enemy soldiers pursuing him. After all of his successful parries against enemy forces, something as stupid as a leaking radiator made a mockery of his unrelenting efforts.

A thought flashed across his mind, and he acknowledged it with stark resolve. *I'll die fighting before I let those bastards capture me.*

Fear had tried to grab at James, but he overcame its slippery grip once more. With renewed determination, he continued his route on the westbound perimeter road. Speed was no longer an option in the severely damaged truck, so he needed to change his approach to evading the enemy's bullets. If he couldn't go fast, he could at least try to dodge them. He turned the steering wheel slightly to the left, drifting to the left side of the narrow road. The tires skimmed the shoulder, and he inched the wheel back toward the right. The zigzag pattern should, at least, make it harder for the rounds to find him.

Despite this, a small weasel of anxiety found its way into the pit of James's stomach and nibbled on his intestines, making his gut clench as he maneuvered the truck back and forth on the road. This maneuver might make it harder for the enemy to aim their weapons at him, but it wasn't stopping them from trying. As he drove, he was acutely aware of the distance between himself and the enemy trucks still shrinking. The sound of a round pummeling against the back of the truck rang out at interment pauses, and James was grimly certain one of those shots would be lucky enough to stake its claim on his back.

The Iranian desert lay ahead as he realized the perimeter road was about to complete its course. In a few minutes, the enemy trucks would be nudging his rear with their bumper. As much as he wanted to go faster, he knew his new path would force him to drive even more slowly. With a resigned sigh, James lifted his foot off the accelerator when the truck glided over the boundary of the perimeter road.

He tightened his grip on the steering wheel as the truck coursed over the desert sand. The uneven terrain caused the truck to sway and shake on its suspension, and he knew that one wrong move could spell the end for the limping vehicle. The sprawling expanse was marred by an assortment of small but wickedly jagged rocks and the occasional sandy patch blemishing the landscape. He released the pressure from the gas pedal another millimeter, and the truck slowed down even further. As much as he wanted to fly over the stretch of land, he knew the risk to the tires was too great. He was literally stuck between Iraq and a hard place. If he slowed down, the IRGC would catch up with him. If he sped up, he ran the risk of blowing out a tire and permanently incapacitating the truck. Or, if he wasn't careful, he could wind up ensnared in a silty patch of sand. He was damned if he did, and damned if he didn't. It was a losing hand that he'd been dealt, and as poor as his odds were, he knew he needed to ignore the seductive voice of defeat nipping at the base of his brain. A man with less mental fortitude and training than James might find that voice almost reasonable. It would be too easy to pull the truck over, hold his hands up, and try to plead for his life. No, James wasn't going to give up so easily, not with the border within reach.

It was a common misconception that the desert was a vast and flat stretch of land. The wind coursing through it carved rolling dunes in the rapidly shifting sands. James's pickup truck closed in on one of these valleys in the desert, and he slowed the vehicle down in order to descend it. He raised his foot off the accelerator again, and the needle dropped to a paltry forty kilometers per hour. A quick conversion of the numbers in James's mind told him the truck was moving along at a sluggish twenty-five miles per hour. The truck's nose pointed down, and he transferred his foot to the brake in an automatic gesture. The pickup bounced as it settled at the bottom of the dip, but another one loomed immediately ahead. The truck slowed down even further, and he lifted his foot off the accelerator pedal when the pickup crested the three-foot incline.

With a sigh of impatience, he returned his foot to the gas pedal. This bothersome little obstacle had cost him significant distance between himself and the soldiers. Then the truck gained speed on the flatter surface he finally reached, and he ventured another peek into the rearview mirror. The two trucks had eaten more of the distance between them. From this angle, it appeared that the APC had fallen significantly behind the leading vehicles. He squinted his eyes, but his initial assessment had been correct. While armored personnel carriers weren't known for their remarkable speed, they were veritable all-terrain workhorses. It might eventually catch up, but he would worry about that later. The four goons in the two trucks posed a more impending threat.

Silence prevailed as James drove, and he realized that the enemy soldiers had ceased firing upon him. A visual confirmation in the rearview mirror confirmed his suspicions. Nobody was hanging out the passenger side of either truck. The lull in the barrage of bullets aimed in his direction had only one plausible explanation: they'd run out of ammunition and were reloading. As primitive as their methods were, the IRGC made up for the shortcomings in their training with ample dependence upon firearms. No doubt they had many more magazines hiding beneath their seats, and once they reloaded, they would return their attention—and their AK-47s—back onto James.

The needle on the speedometer ticked upward as he continued his westbound journey. He kept his foot on the accelerator while navigating carefully across the desert terrain. So far, he'd successfully managed to avoid any of the hidden sand pits lying in wait to hold his truck's tires hostage. No rocks had carved out a gouge in them.

Things were looking up for James. He scanned the terrain ahead, alert for any new obstacles that may try to hinder his progress.

He didn't have to look hard for obstructions, however. The truck meandered along another two hundred yards, the smoke pouring out from beneath the hood at a faster rate. Perhaps it was the smoke obstructing his view that had caused this new obstacle to sneak up on him, or maybe the light bouncing off the monochromatic terrain had something to do with it. James let out a low cry of surprise and frustration when he saw it, his foot leaping from the gas pedal to the brake pedal in one fluid motion. The truck jolted to a stop, and the tires ground against the desert earth, sending sand flying out from around the truck. James squinted in stunned disbelief at the yawning channel that loomed directly ahead of him.

A wide channel had been carved either by the relentless desert winds or a particularly torrential downpour during the region's rainy season. He glanced back over his shoulder. The soldiers would be done reloading their weapons shortly, and then they would undoubtedly take advantage of his unexpected stop. He slapped his palm against the steering wheel and shook his head, a low curse flying from his lips as he considered the gully below him. He couldn't drive down into it—the grade was too steep—and even if he didn't lose control of the truck on the way down, there was no way the disabled vehicle would be able to make it back up the other side.

James craned his head to the left. The southward route was completely blocked by the sandy gorge. The gully here was steep and pronounced, leading to what appeared to be a stark, forty-five degree slope straight down. It was completely impassible at this location. He turned in the seat, peering to the right. His eyes trailed along the edge of the gully, and finally he spied it. Some three hundred yards ahead of him, the angle into the valley was less pronounced. It would take him out of his way, and it would expose him to the enemy soldiers, but it was the only way around. He had no other option but to turn the truck and attempt to descend into the channel from that location.

As he steered the battered pickup truck toward the passage, he heard the first in the newest series of rounds from the enemy soldiers clanging against his vehicle. They must have completed their task of reloading weapons, evident by the resuming of a relentless stream of bullets in his direction. With them so close and the gaping chasm directly to his left, he couldn't afford to zigzag the pickup truck. Instead, he applied as much pressure as he could justify against the accelerator, and the truck gained speed as it barreled toward the passage.

As the truck approached the narrow path carved across the gully, James assessed the situation. The path's sharp grade would make getting in and out of it a challenge, but the dual pair of IRGC trucks bearing down on him provided no alternative. He couldn't continue driving alongside the gully until he found another way down. It was here or nothing. He lifted his foot off the gas pedal and turned the steering wheel to the left, sending the nose of the truck dipping into the channel. The tires dug matching grooves into the sand, and James felt them slip beneath the truck as the sand shifted and filtered down into the channel. Then the truck was down into the bottom of the ravine, and he pressed his foot against the accelerator once more. The truck picked up speed, its bumper rising as it clawed its way back out of the pit.

James was halfway up the far side of the gully when the two trucks behind him aimed their own noses down into the channel. One by one, they slipped in and continued their pursuit. James could see the face of the closest driver, the bearded countenance contoured in a frown of concentration as he drove. Sand poured down beneath their tires, flooding the bottom of the pit with a stream of coarse powder. He had no time to monitor their actions, though. Even as the drivers of each truck struggled to gain purchase on the unreliable sandy wall, their passengers were training their rifles at James again.

Once he rounded the top of the anterior wall, he would be able to recover the distance he'd lost between himself and the enemy soldiers. He gritted his teeth as the tires struggled with the sandy surface and the edge of the precipice loitered just out of the truck's reach. The rear tires churned up sand, spitting it out behind the back bumper. Then the pickup lurched forward, and James felt a momentary rise of triumph in his chest.

I'm going to make it over! This enfeebled truck is actually going to summit this unstable wall!

James was so focused on getting the truck the final few inches over the side of the sandy wall that the sharp pain of a bullet colliding with his body came almost as a surprise. A searing jolt of pain blossomed from his upper thigh, and his right hand flew down instinctively, clapping over the warm blood that promptly gushed from the wound. The truck rocked from the impact of the bullet and backslid several inches down into the channel, almost as though it too were responding to the unexpected injury. Then the truck rounded the lip of the wall, and James was on the other side.

I've been shot. The thought came to James almost distantly, and he peered down at the crimson fluid leaking out between his fingers.

The pain was remarkably muted, and he realized the injury must have triggered an instantaneous adrenaline response from his body. His adrenal glands must have been working overtime to subdue the pain in his thigh, and as he sped across the desert sand, it occurred to him how fortunate he was. He cast a cautious glance down at his hand pressed against the wound. Had the bullet landed another inch higher, or had the door not blocked the majority of the impact, it might have nicked his femoral artery. He was no doctor, but he knew he was damned lucky the wound wasn't worse.

Without preamble, the Iraq border unfolded directly ahead. James found himself curiously detached from emotion as the truck moved toward it. He pressed his right foot down onto the gas pedal, and a renewed jolt of pain coursed through his injured thigh. He consciously ignored the darkness that fuzzed the corner of his vision, shaking his head. His safety lay just ahead, a hundred yards to the west, but there was something disappointingly anticlimactic about it.

The first of the two enemy trucks appeared in James's rearview mirror, and he watched as the second one clamored over the lip of the gully. In a few seconds, he would no longer be in Iranian territory or under their jurisdiction any longer. He drifted his hand back and forth across the steering wheel, moving the body of the truck just enough to sustain the zigzag pattern for as long as it took to cross the border into Iraq.

The abused pickup truck crossed from Iran into Iraq without fanfare, and James found himself sitting in the cab in a frenzy of adrenaline and disbelief. He'd made it. He'd actually succeeded in making it into Iraq alive. His heart thudded in his chest as he allowed the reality to sink in. His head pounded and his leg throbbed from the bullet wound. His mouth was parched from not having a drink of water in hours, and he was dizzy with fatigue and elation, but he'd done it.

James glanced in the rearview mirror, and to his alarm, realized the IRGC did not seem deterred by this new development. Of course they were still following him. They were rabid bloodhounds and had picked up on James's scent. Something as trivial as another country's border was not enough to deter them. And why would it?

He glanced around. The desert stretched out interminably in all directions. This particular stretch of border had no armed guards, no gates, no checkpoints. As far as the enemy soldiers were concerned, he was still fair game, and they weren't going to let something as trivial as his arrival in another country stop them if there was no one watching anyway.

James knew with sudden and acute certainty that his enemies were going to pursue him until they had him captured or killed. Making it across the border hadn't been enough to stop them. Until there were witnesses to the fact that he'd made it out of Iran and into Iraq—actual witnesses other than these four men who had been chasing him relentlessly across Mehran—he wasn't going to be safe. As much as he'd hoped they would accept Iraq's sovereignty, he'd been proven wrong. He still needed to delve deeper into the neighboring country to get these soldiers off his back.

The next checkpoint was in the nearby town of Zurbatiyah.

Crushing fatigue descended upon James. He wasn't safe. He wasn't free. According to the internal map tucked away inside his memory, he still had another ten miles across the Iraqi desert in a destroyed pickup truck and with a bullet wound in his leg. The chances of him actually making it there were slim, verging on impossible. But if he wanted to survive, he needed to press on. He was so close now...too close to give up.

With a resigned sigh, he pressed his foot back on the gas pedal and, ignoring the warning cry of pain that shot up his leg, he continued his journey toward salvation.

CHAPTER SEVENTEEN

SAFE HAVEN

0945 HOURS – 15 NOVEMBER 2013

THE SMOKE POURING OUT FROM beneath the hood billowed up at a higher rate now, and James knew the end was coming soon for the abused pickup truck. He could try to push it as much as possible to ease every tiny sliver of life from it, but this would probably only buy him a few more minutes from the dying vehicle. Slowing the truck down wouldn't aid him much, either. Yes, it might prolong the life of the scarred engine and radiator and allow him to coax a few extra miles out of the pickup, but with his entourage narrowing in on him, it was a wholly impractical idea.

He was ten miles away from the nearest semblance of civilization, and despite the subdued optimism that had propelled him across the Iraqi border, his hope had been largely misguided. The two guard trucks were still bearing down upon him and showing no signs of slowing down or stopping. If anything, they were now driving faster, as though they knew they were engaging in highly unethical tactics and wanted to get their unsavory task over as quickly as possible.

James consulted his internal map, trying to recall the most direct route to the nearest oasis of civilization in this barren desert expanse. He knew there was a former United States Coalition base located ten miles within the limits of Zurbatiyah, but how could he get there as quickly and safely as possible in this disabled pickup trick? Even as he frantically checked his mental database, he knew his odds of successfully getting there were slim. Still. He needed to try, at the very least.

Had James been stranded in Iraq two years before, he might have been relatively confident that he would be welcomed into Combat Outpost (COP) Shocker with open arms. Familiar faces, or at least familiar uniforms, would greet him when he knocked on the doors of the outpost. If he tried to stroll onto the base that sunny and cool November morning, however, his outcome could vary wildly. They might greet him with cautious cordiality or train their firearms upon him and shoot before launching a more intensive investigation as to his presence in their country.

It was a risk he would have to take, though. He had no other options. If he didn't make a beeline for the former American outpost, then he may as well turn himself over to the IRGC. The uncertainty of what he would find when he arrived there far outweighed what he knew he would encounter at the hands of his current pursuers.

James knew he wouldn't be able to negotiate with these enemy soldiers. There were several barriers in place that helped ensure that fact. Not only would the lack of communication prove to be an obstacle, but these soldiers hadn't been dispatched to capture James and bring him back alive. Their haphazard shots fired in his direction helped crystalize this fact. No, they didn't care if they were able to keep him alive. If they did, it would be a bonus for them, but it certainly wasn't their primary directive when they set out after him.

The public executions of captured entities—whether they were civilians, soldiers, or even journalists—were not only a sickening reminder of the enemy James and all of America was up against, but also a grim sort of mass entertainment for the curious eyes of the public. He'd seen the grainy videos of these executions himself. He'd heard the muffled screams dispatched over the audio feed as the rusty and dull knife labored methodically over the flesh and tendons of the victims' necks. No, James was not going to give anyone the satisfaction of detaching his head from his shoulders.

The IRGC pickup trucks bounced over the sandy landscape as they sped across the Iraqi desert toward the fleeing American soldier. As far as Reza Mohammadi could tell, the American infidel was a prize worth risking his life for, and he wasn't going to stop his pursuit until he'd successfully captured or killed him. However, Reza had his own suspicions that no ill was going to befall him on this glorious day. For starters, the American wasn't even expending bullets on them. He was so focused on keeping his truck moving along, he hadn't fired a single shot in their direction in several minutes. Time was running out for the infidel, and Reza wanted to be there when it finally did.

His companion, a man of diminutive build and a remarkable enthusiasm for killing, leaned out the passenger-side window. His weapon gripped firmly in his hands, he squeezed the trigger repeatedly from his perch in the open window while releasing an unbridled cry of joy, his voice rising over the rattle of the firearm. The sound of rounds firing from the man's AK-47 and his trilling bellows lent an extra air of exhilaration to Reza's already thrilling morning. How lucky he had been to spot the American driving the pickup truck through Mehran! The passenger shouted something at him from his position in the open window, and Reza nodded at the comment, not hearing him over his thoughts.

Yes, he was going to capture or kill the American soldier. He was certain of it. And oh, how he was going to be rewarded handsomely for his work when he delivered the infidel to his commander.

He pried his gaze from the desert ahead and peered down at the weapon in his lap. The Browning HP pistol wasn't as powerful or effective as his companion's AK-47, but he favored it over the larger firearm. Sure, it required a closer range, but that was what Reza liked about it. He liked being able to see his targets' faces before he pulled the trigger. It made the kill more satisfying and added an extra element of excitement to his otherwise routine role in the Islamic Revolutionary Guard Corps. Reza Mohammadi was a man who took his job very seriously and who took great pride in his work.

After all, it wasn't every day that he was at the forefront of a high-speed chase with an American. Usually their targets were smaller fry, locals who had been caught spouting off blasphemous rhetoric and needed to be taught a public lesson. This was a special occasion, and Reza was acutely aware of how fortunate he was to be at the forefront of it. The message that had filtered through the radio hadn't divulged too many details, but based on the urgency emanating from his commander's voice, the enemy soldier was a high-profile target. Maybe he was one of those American Special Forces soldiers? The idea excited Reza.

He checked the Browning HP once more. The safety was off, and it was ready to be used at a moment's notice. He reached down, cautiously removing his hand from the steering wheel, and patted the weapon with his open hand. The cold metal body seemed almost alive in his lap, as though it were as eager to be used as Reza was to use it. He stroked the butt of the weapon with his fingertips. This weapon had been issued to him and he'd had it throughout his service in the IRGC. It was his faithful companion through numerous encounters with enemy targets. While he didn't know if he could trust the man in the seat next to him, he had ample faith in the pistol in his lap.

The terrain ahead was bumpy and unsteady, and Reza swore under his breath as his truck lurched over one of the valleys, taking great pains to not use Allah's name in vain as he cursed. In the very slight off chance that he were to die out here today, he wanted to stay in good graces with Allah. Instead, he redirected his frustration as praise. Allah had been good to him today. Because of the gift he'd been given—an American handed to him on a silver platter!—he would be going home today as a hero. His livery lips turned up in a jeering smile.

But the smile was short-lived on Reza's face. Had he been able to cut the American off back by the waste processing plant, he wouldn't be having to steer his pickup truck over this impossible terrain. That was his failing, though, and not Allah's. He needed to make sure he didn't deflect blame when the responsibility was entirely his own. He'd been given several chances to disable the stolen truck, but he'd failed. So far. The pickup's tires caught a divot in the sand, and he released his foot from the gas pedal. The truck slowed slightly, bobbing as it worked its way through the silty patch, then it was moving over the Iraqi desert again. His truck gained speed once more, and his pursuit of the infidel resumed.

As he drove, his thoughts went to what he would do when he finally stopped the American's truck. Well, it wasn't the *American's* truck, for starters. The thieving infidel had stolen it from the IRGC. The thought offended him. Americans had no respect for their culture, and this one would pay dearly for his crimes. Even if he weren't a war criminal, and Reza had no doubt that he was, his theft was something he looked down upon with unconcealed disdain. It almost justified his entry into Iraq, really. Even if his commander found out about it, there would be no reprimand if he delivered the American to him.

Reza hoped he would be permitted to help with the execution. The thought sent a thrill coursing down his spine. That was a thought! He had no doubt he would be able to do it flawlessly. His hand wouldn't even shake as he sawed through the infidel's neck. Realistically, however, he knew such an honor was usually reserved for someone else, someone higher up in the ranks. If he captured the American, though, there was a good chance he would at least be able to stand in the background of the execution video. Watching the life drain out of the infidel would be a pleasure like none other.

But first, he had to actually capture him. Reza picked up his semi-automatic pistol again, wrapping his fingers around its grip. His hands tingled from anticipation. As soon as he got the truck close enough to justify firing, he would actually use the weapon. For now, though, he had to focus on driving. There was no point in fantasizing about shooting the American if his pickup truck was too far away. He knew it would be a matter of minutes, though, at most, before he would be able to complete his mission.

Ahead of him, the stolen truck that was concealing the American belched out another opaque cloud of smoke. The plume was no longer white. The engine was overheating, and the smoke pouring out from beneath the hood was the color of soot. Reza's passenger had already succeeded in dealing a serious blow to it, and the bullet had evidently landed somewhere near the engine block. One more good shot would do the trick. Or, like a rabbit that was chased to exhaustion until its heart gave out, Reza merely needed to continue his pursuit to overcome his target. And once he did, he would take great pleasure in using his Browning HP on him.

Reza reluctantly removed his hand from his firearm, returning his attention to the American soldier in the truck ahead. A calm resolve drifted over him as he closed the gap between himself and his target. Today was shaping up to be a very good day indeed. As he drove across the Iraqi desert, the cheerful smile never left his face. Perhaps if he'd known the lethal capacity of the soldier he was going up against, the smile might have been slightly more reserved. Instead, it radiated continuously from his face, a black beam of dark cheer on this sunny November morning.

James cast another glance back in the rearview mirror. The enemy soldiers' pursuit was fervent and almost frenzied. The IRGC soldiers knew they'd disabled his pickup truck with their lucky shots, and it was only a matter of time before the vehicle seized up completely. While they may not have known what part of the truck had been disabled by their rogue bullets, they could see the smoke with their own eyes. They also knew that he wasn't half-assing his retreat, and the fact that his truck wasn't going any faster than it currently was further gave away his vulnerability.

James was a sitting duck in a failing truck. He had no recourse and knew he was operating on borrowed time. The pickup shuddered again, and he returned his focus to the road ahead. The tires kicked up sand as they maneuvered over the desert terrain, but at his reduced pace, that did little to conceal his location from his enemies. Had he been able to drive any faster, he might have been able to hide behind the dust rising up from behind his wheels. It had worked earlier, at least. Now, though, he was moving along at a slow enough pace that he was easy pickings for his enemies.

Despite himself, James grew angry. A throbbing pain had formed between his eyes, playing out a monotonous beat in his head. He knew it was a combination of stress and dehydration, but there was little he could do about it in his current position. There was no sign of the current stressors relenting, so he couldn't dismiss them with any degree of ease. As far as drinking water went, he knew how to sustain himself for long stretches of time without it. The loss of his hydration pack had been more than a minor inconvenience, though. James knew his life could be in serious danger shortly from dehydration. While he wasn't quite yet in danger of passing out from thirst, he was operating on limited time. It wasn't just his head's pounding rendition of an amateur drum solo causing the mounting fury to well up in James, though. His left shoulder ached from landing on it hours before, and his right arm pulsed from the superficial laceration. The numbing analgesic of adrenaline was also starting to wear off, and the pain in his leg was amplifying steadily. For the time being, it was still a droning ache in his upper thigh. However, every unexpected movement and jostle of the truck caused sharp tendrils of pain to jolt through the wounded limb.

If James didn't come up with another plan soon, he would be—to put it mildly—screwed. He was already in a precarious situation, and with each foot that the enemy gained on him, it grew progressively worse. He stared out at the desert ahead, his thoughts churning wildly. He wasn't a quitter, that was for damned sure. And he wasn't going to merely roll over and play dead for these enemy bastards. No, if he wanted to survive, he needed to approach his escape from these Iranian soldiers from another angle.

James had always been a man who thought on his feet. Even when the situation seemed insurmountable, he'd always regarded various crises with an unflappable, dry optimism. He had a survival instinct the majority of the population lacked, and it played into his ability to devise innovative new plans on the fly. Had the men in The Unit not been so hasty to dub him Gator, he might have been called

QT, short for Quick Thinker, instead. The fact was, catastrophic emergencies had nothing on James. It didn't matter what sort of precarious situation he and his men found themselves in, he always had a plan to extract them from it.

James had no delusions about the complexity of his plans. It wasn't so much that they were flawless and brilliant in their execution, but rather, they were direct and effective. If things turned south while they were on a mission, faces would turn to James, and they would wait for the words to inevitably pop out of his mouth. "Well, it's time for Plan B, then."

James considered his recent plan. It had been going great until it wasn't. It had been a simple and straightforward plan. Get a reliable set of wheels, get to the sewage treatment plant, and get the hell out of Iran. To his credit, he'd flawlessly executed this plan. He'd upgraded his motorbike to a pickup truck, lost his initial tail in the downtown region of Mehran, and managed to successfully navigate his way back to the waste processing plant. In that regard, the plan had been a rousing success. It wasn't his fault that his enemy kept finding him, and he couldn't be blamed for being outnumbered and outgunned.

But James knew something that these enemy soldiers didn't know. He'd only made it through his first plan of escape and hadn't even begun to draft his backup plan yet. As much as his enemies had tried to thwart him, they didn't realize he was only just getting started. Getting out of Da'wud's compound, escaping the enemy's residence on a rickety motorbike, and seizing a pickup truck to escape Mehran had been just a handful of his many survival techniques. James had so much fight left in him, and they were about to find out for themselves what the acts of a highly trained and equally desperate Delta Force Operator would be. And, more importantly, they were going to severely regret ever messing with James Chase in the first place.

CHAPTER EIGHTEEN

PLAN B

0946 HOURS – 15 NOVEMBER 2013

ANOTHER SHOT RANG OUT, SHATTERING the outside rearview mirror next to James. He jerked the steering wheel to the right, and the truck skidded across the sand. The sons of bitches were getting better aim. He glanced down at the mirror, which was now hanging limply from the driver's side door, what was left of it. The only thing he would be viewing from it moving forward would be the sandy desert. James straightened the steering wheel, then peeked behind him through the interior rearview mirror. The enemy soldiers were almost on top of him now. He needed to come up with something, some sort of viable escape plan to help him elude them and he needed to do it fast.

James ruminated on his options. The needle on the speedometer was still dipping lower, the truck progressively slowing down. That made it easier to maneuver the obstacles in the rocky terrain, but it also made it easier for his enemies to approach him. Almost in response to the dwindling speed of the truck, the engine temperature gauge continued to climb. The needle was easing closer toward a position within the overheating parameters. If he didn't come up with a new plan shortly, he would find himself without a truck *and* without a plan. James needed to think quickly, but he also needed to stay calm and rational.

Like the melodious voice of a muse whispering in his ear, a thought came with stark clarity. The enemy soldiers in the trucks behind him thought they would be able to chase him down until the truck ground to a stop and was no longer operable. Once the pickup seized up completely, they likely believed James would have no other option except to step out of the truck and plead for his life. They weren't wrong about the state of the hole-riddled pickup truck. It wasn't going to go much farther, and it damned well wasn't going to be able to take him to the safe haven known as COP Shocker. But he sure as hell wasn't going to beg the IRGC soldiers for any sort of mercy. That was for damned sure.

The truck was nothing more than a formality, a set of wheels reluctantly supporting a steel chassis. The body of the truck had already been peppered with holes, and if one of the tires blew out? It was only a matter of time before one of the enemy soldier's rounds met rubber, completely crippling the pickup truck. No, the truck wasn't going to be his salvation. Clinging onto it with the same panicked desperation that a drowning man might have when clutching a life preserver would only serve to hinder his progress. The truck was no longer of any value to him. It was his albatross, a burden that he needed to discard. It was nothing more than a heap of scrap metal at this point, and its worth was rapidly diminishing by the second.

A smile tugged at the corner of James's lips. There it was: Plan B. Its brilliance lay within the heart of its simplicity.

The truck continued to slow down as James regarded the speedometer with renewed serenity. The needle dropped down another five kilometers per hour, and a glance into the rearview mirror confirmed that the enemy soldiers were still growing closer by the second. He shifted his attention back to the desert ahead and, with fluid grace, withdrew his 1911 pistol from beneath his thigh.

At the speed he was currently maintaining, the truck needed very little assistance from James to move forward without deviating much from its course. He lifted his left leg, and his knee pressed the lower rim of the steering wheel. With his hands now freed, he transferred his firearm into his lap. A cursory glance down verified that the safety mechanism wasn't depressed on the weapon. He didn't want to get this close to freedom, only to need his weapon and have it click uselessly in his hands. James gripped the suppressor with his right hand, and with a firm yank, loosened it. A handful of twists later, and he dumped the silencer unceremoniously onto the floorboard of the truck. Any subsequent reports from his firearm would be loud and booming.

James slipped the 1911 back into his holster, then returned his hands to the steering wheel. Even in the few seconds it took him to remove the suppressor from this weapon, the truck had lost another five kilometers per hour and was chugging along at a paltry twenty-seven miles per hour. If he didn't act quickly, he would soon be going no faster than a brisk trot in the handicapped vehicle.

A loud crash drew his attention. He recoiled from the sound, and a fragment of plastic flew through the air, gliding past his face. James's eyes went to the dashboard of the truck. The entirety of the dash was obliterated, and the radio was a smoking ruin. He blinked at the radio, confused. If the guards were close enough to group together enough rounds to blow out the dashboard, they were close enough to get a few of those bullets into his skull. Those shots had been a close call, too damned close for comfort.

James glanced down at the dead soldier slumped next to him. Coagulated blood oozed from multiple wounds. His firearm lay propped up between his knees, and James reached out with his right arm, readjusting the body in the bucket seat. The AK-47 fell forward, and James caught it in a fluid motion, pulling it toward himself. The weapon perched in his lap, and he let it linger there for a moment while he steered the truck around a silty patch of sand. Then he returned his attention to the firearm draped across his thighs. Did it have enough ammunition in the magazine? There was only one way to find out. He pressed his left knee to the steering wheel again, hoisted the weapon in the air and, reaching out with his left hand, ejected the magazine from the firearm. The mag dislodged from the magazine well, and he held it in his outstretched palm, checking its heft with a bounce of his arm. The wound in his shoulder flared, and he let out a low hiss at the sharp crest of pain. Then it subsided, and James nodded in quiet satisfaction at the momentary lull. The weight of the magazine indicated it was full, or at least, close enough to being full to be of good use. He slipped the magazine back into the AK-47, locking it into place with the flat of his hand. His thumb glided over the safety selector, and he verified with a glance that it was on the semi-automatic firing position.

All he needed to do now was make sure the weapon still fired. James pulled the firearm across his lap, running his hand over its smooth frame. A brief glance over its matte black body confirmed that the weapon had no new scars upon it, but until James fired a round, he couldn't be sure the AK-47 worked. He cast a cautious glance out the passenger-side window and then lifted the muzzle of the weapon higher, aiming it toward the glass panel on the opposite side of the truck. The pickup hit a bump, and the weapon bounced in his hands. James spat out a profanity. Had he tried to fire the AK-47 in that moment, he might have missed the window completely. Hell, the bullet might have sliced through the flesh of his new friend. James certainly didn't want that. Finding friends who understood the value of companionable silence were hard to come by these days, and blowing his new buddy's head off with a rogue round would surely damage their newly burgeoning relationship.

James tightened his finger around the trigger, then paused. His eyes scanned the sandy expanse through the windshield ahead of him. The desert stretched out before him, flat and featureless. If there were any silty patches or large stones obstructing his path, he couldn't see them from his current position. He lifted the weapon marginally higher, pointing it through the open passenger's side window. His finger tightened around the trigger once more, and the weapon bucked in his hands as a single round flew from the chamber. The bullet soared through the open window, cutting through the air with a low whine before vanishing on the horizon.

At least the weapon still worked. James's morning had thus far been punctuated by a seemingly incessant series of unfortunate luck, but having another operational firearm at least gave him some leverage. Satisfied, he returned the AK-47 back to its original owner. James pried his gaze away from the desert ahead long enough to confirm that the weapon was secured between the dead soldier's knees. Its muzzle was pointed down and its safety was off, and the weapon stood at a sort of inanimate attention, ready to be used at James's command. James moved his hand down to the dead soldier's knee and closed it with a brisk shove. There. The AK-47 wouldn't be moving anytime soon unless James moved it himself.

Uncertainty tugged at James, and he found himself glancing at the collection of ammo mags on the seat between himself and the dead soldier. He needed to double check them to make sure they had sufficient rounds, as having enough ammunition was key to ensuring his new plan would work. Two of the magazines had fallen to the passenger side floorboard, and he noted with a frown that they'd managed to wedge themselves between the dead soldier's boot and the crevice beneath the seat. James let out a low sigh of frustration. He would just have to hope they held thirty rounds each. The other two magazines sat within arm's reach, perched on the fabric seat next to him. He reached over and felt his fingertips brush over them. His hand closed over the nearest one, and he picked it up, then bounced the magazine in his hand, feeling its weight. Its ample heft indicated its contents. This one was completely full. James returned it to the seat, shoving it beneath his dead companion's left buttocks. His hand found the other magazine, and he held it up fleetingly before returning it to the seat. Also full. He wedged it next to the first one, securing it in place underneath the corpse's cheek.

James cast a glance at the dead Iranian soldier, a wry grin tugging at the corner of his lips. He reached out, patting the corpse's knee almost affectionately. "Thanks for helping me out, buddy."

The corpse slumped forward, and James shoved it back upright into a sitting position with his right forearm. He shook his head ruefully, his expression sardonic and vaguely bemused. He paid the dead soldier *one* compliment, and already it was starting to get complacent and slack off. James would have to keep an eye on this one. He didn't want to find out that the dead man wasn't pulling his own weight and only looking for a free ride. He cast one final glance at the body seated next to him and, assured that the corpse wasn't going to topple over again, returned his gaze to the sandy stretch of desert sprawled out in front of him.

Smoke continued to pour out from beneath the hood of the truck, thick and opaque now, and James marveled silently that the vehicle was still somehow operational without any antifreeze in the reservoir. The needle on the temperature gauge was now unambiguously positioned on the opposite side of the overheating range, and yet the pickup was still moving ahead. The speedometer had plunged another few kilometers per hour, and he could tell by the reduced amount of wind coming through the open window that the truck was moving at a fraction of the rate it had been earlier.

James reached into his front left pocket, feeling around for the distinct and familiar orb shape of an M67 grenade. His hand closed over the metal, and he slipped the fragmentation grenade out, taking care to avoid inadvertently tugging on the pull ring as he drew it out of his pocket. He lowered his hand to the space between the seat next to him and carefully wriggled the grenade between the seat bottom and the seat back, securing it between himself and his dead companion. James's hand returned to his pocket, cautiously patting the modified bullet-resistant vest beneath his shirt. The two remaining grenades were still where he'd left them. Their presence reassured him, and he found himself growing calmer.

Plan B was slowly starting to come together. James just needed to find the right window of opportunity to execute it. He let out a low, cautious sigh of guarded optimism. He'd been in numerous dangerous situations before, but this one was somewhat unique when compared to the others he'd encountered in the past. Nearly every time he'd found himself in a seemingly intractable scenario before, there had almost always been one common denominator: he was rarely ever alone. In nearly every mission he'd been on, there had been other men in The Unit by his side, silently goading him onward. Yes, James had been on a few select training missions on his own, but those were mostly to determine his mental fortitude and grit when separated from his team. He normally had someone else depending upon him for survival, and this was one of those very rare occasions when he was accountable for himself and only himself. With nobody else relying upon him, he found his methods turning slightly unorthodox. A little bit of chaos in his planning methods might be the kick he needed to actually survive this debacle. Hell, as long as it worked, he didn't care how he executed his Plan B. Yes, unconventional was the defining term of his misadventures in this wasteland, but James found himself easing into his plan with a kind of uneasy accord.

James turned his eyes up to the rearview mirror again, and the sight of the two trucks closing in reminded him that he still had a significant amount of work to do before he could even begin to consider himself safe. Evading these enemies was only one part of the equation, only a fraction of the work he still needed to do. Even if he did manage to escape them, he still needed to get to the Iraqi outpost, which meant he needed to secure one of their trucks too. Otherwise, he would be stranded in the desert. He knew he wouldn't be getting far on his wounded leg.

His pulse quickened, but he realized he was not afraid of his upcoming challenge. If anything, he was taut with anticipation, eager to see how they appreciated his handiwork. James knew that either he was going to survive this entire ordeal, or he was going to perish. If he were to die, though, he hoped he would be able to take out a few of the Iranian soldiers before they eventually got him.

James silently issued another prayer that luck would somehow fall in his favor. He couldn't afford to screw this up. Any hopes that his remaining lifespan would be measured in units of time that were marginally longer than a few extra minutes depended upon it.

CHAPTER NINETEEN

THE SHOOTOUT

0955 HOURS – 15 NOVEMBER 2013

ANOTHER GULLY LAY STRETCHED OUT across the desert landscape ahead. James considered it, sizing up its depth and width. It was almost as vast as the one he'd traversed earlier, but fortunately, the walls weren't as steep here. He glanced to the left, then to the right, but the slope of the channel was sharper in both directions. If he wanted to steer the truck down into it, this was the only place he could successfully do so. The lagging truck pointed nose-down into the gully as James gripped the steering wheel tightly and guided it down. The tires rolled clumsily over the sand, struggling and failing to stay aloft on the uneven sand. The truck skimmed across the soft terrain, and he found that the vehicle wasn't so much driving as it was gliding down into the channel. Streams of sand spilled out from beneath the weight of the truck bearing down on the loosely packed wall, and the truck skidded several feet before James regained control of it. The truck bounced and heaved, then finally settled into the bottom of the gully with a mild jolt before steadying itself. The momentum of the truck settling into the valley caused the truck to skid a few yards, and James jerked the steering wheel sharply to the right as it drifted across the sand. The tires spun wildly on the uneven terrain, and he pressed his foot firmly on the brake, coaxing it to an abrupt stop. The truck bounced once more, then was still.

James didn't hesitate. He reached to the right, wrenching the AK-47 out from between the dead soldier's knees. In the same motion, he gripped the door handle with his left hand, shoving the driver's side door open with his elbow. It flung wide, then bounced on its hinge, swaying back toward him. He shoved it open once more, a wave of impatience washing over him, and the door settled in place. While it wouldn't provide him with an excessive amount of coverage, it was better than nothing.

James threw a glance behind him, but the guards still hadn't approached the lip of the gully. He lunged his body out of the pickup truck and, moving swiftly, darted around the door. His knees popped audibly, vaguely muffled in the sandy gully, as he dropped into a crouch by the front wheel well. He shifted his weight, transferring it to his left hip. His right leg throbbed, and any motion caused the wound to cry out with renewed vigor. James hoisted the AK-47 in his arms, aiming over the hood in the direction of the gully where the guards would be emerging in a moment. His heart pounded loudly in his ears as he scanned the horizon.

A second passed, then another.

James's knuckles were blanched from the tight grip he had on the firearm, and he forced himself to relax his shoulders. Anticipation drummed at him in a persistent beat, and he took in a shallow breath, then released it. As the air flowed steadily from his lungs, his dark eyes lit upon the body of the first truck descending over the lip of the gully. The driver of the pickup guided its nose down the embankment, giving James a clear angle into the interior of the vehicle. The passenger had tucked himself back into the truck, but from the distance of a mere sixty feet, James could see he was still holding his weapon tightly in his grasp. As soon as the truck reached the bottom of the gully, the soldier would emerge from the vehicle once more to fire upon him.

James didn't want to wait to see if the man would point the AK-47 at him. He turned his own weapon toward the IRGC soldier, and with another shallow inhale, tightened his grip around the trigger. The AK-47 jerked in his hand, immediately responding to his touch. Bullets poured out of the muzzle in rapid succession, decorating the enemy's pickup truck with a string of holes. The windshield splintered under the sudden onslaught, then exploded inward from the stream of bullets. A rain of glass poured onto the passenger, giving the enemy soldier no time to react to the jagged shards. James could see the man dance a macabre jig in his seat as his chest was aerated by the four bullets. A fifth and final bullet silenced the man forever, slicing cleanly through his throat. A geyser of blood spurted out from the wound in the soldier's neck, and he went limp, falling forward in his seat.

One threat down, three more to go.

James released the breath he'd been holding, then helped himself to another, deeper inhalation. His nerves were steady now, his pulse an unwavering metronome in his veins. He shifted his weight, quelling the pain in his leg with a clench of his teeth, and aimed his weapon toward the driver of the pickup truck. The enemy soldier wasn't looking at him, though. The man's eyes were wide and fixed in an expression of disbelief on the stalled pickup truck stationed in the gully. James could see the enemy's stunned gaze fixed upon him as the stalled truck rose up to greet him. If he didn't respond quickly, he would be crashing into James's pickup truck.

The soldier's reaction was instinctive, and James could tell even from his vantage that the man's mind had reverted to a primitive state. Impulse was guiding the man now, as conscious thought had too much of a refractory pause to be of any benefit to him. He was responding to both the assault from James and the stopped truck directly ahead of him with an automatic and frantic sense of survival, and James could see the feral and detached expression on his face as the Iranian soldier jerked the steering wheel to the right. The truck careened wildly to James's left in response to the urgent maneuver, and the truck skidded to a reluctant stop some thirty feet ahead of James. The vehicle idled at the bottom of the gully, its body fixed horizontally to James's position.

With the truck stalled in a mound of sand, the driver of the truck was now directly within James's line of sight. James concealed a ghost of a smile behind his beard. The enemy soldier had played directly into his trap, affording him a clear view of his target. The soldier shook his head, dazed, and turned his face toward James. His eyes widened in recognition, as though he suddenly remembered his mission to capture or kill the American. His body turned away from James, no doubt trying to find his own firearm to aim. Despite having the wind knocked out of his lungs and being slightly disoriented from his crash landing, the soldier moved quickly.

James, however, was faster. He took in another breath, then squeezed the trigger of the AK-47. Six rounds flew from the chamber, zeroing in on the soldier behind the wheel of the pickup truck. The enemy soldier seemed to anticipate James's actions and jerked back from the bullets. He pressed his head against the headrest of the pickup, his face pointing forward and his spine rigid, as though he thought he could dodge the rounds plowing toward him if he sat still enough in the driver's seat. The first two bullets zipped harmlessly past him, skimming past his nose by a mere inch or two. One of the rounds collided with the dead passenger's head, and it exploded inside the cab of the truck, spraying pulpy red shrapnel in every direction.

That was no matter to James, though. There were still four more bullets flying toward the enemy, and their ability to find their intended target was vastly better than the first two rounds. They landed in a close cluster on the driver, blemishing him with an assortment of lead-centered circles. One of the rounds found its way into the enemy's left shoulder, and the arm shattered, sending a spray of fabric and flesh flying through the air. The enemy soldier had no time to react to the piercing wound as the next three bullets sought him out, spelling his demise. These final three rounds succeeded in decapitating the soldier, landing in an erratic pattern on his neck, jaw, and forehead. A deluge of red and gray matter decorated the steering wheel, seat, and whatever remained of the windshield.

James had no time to relax and admire his efficient handiwork.

As the final round pierced the driver of the first truck, the second pickup erupted over the lip of the embankment. The driver plowed toward him, a look of manic concentration on his face. The truck tore down the side of the slope, gaining speed as it bore down upon James. James had only a split second to react to the newcomer's arrival. He re-aimed the muzzle of the AK-47, sighting the driver of the second truck in the crosshairs of the weapon. Four rounds flew from the chamber, colliding with the center of the windshield. Hairline fractures erupted across the windshield of the pickup, but the driver and passenger remained unscathed.

"Shit," James said.

He leapt away from the oncoming truck, his legs pumping beneath him as he tore across the sandy terrain. He stumbled clumsily away, his feet slipping over the uneven sandy surface of the valley as he veered out of the trajectory of the oncoming truck. A moment later, the booming sound of the vehicle slamming against his own filled the valley with a deafening noise. James whipped his head around just in time to see the enemy's pickup ram against his truck at a rate of what had to be at least thirty-five miles per hour. The enemy's truck met the right rear quarter panel, shoving it forward several feet. An excruciating screeching sound followed the initial cacophony of the collision, and James flinched away from the grating noise. The rear portion of the truck spun in a lazy semicircle, twirling around in the bright sunlight that streamed down into the valley. The truck shifted another twenty degrees, then seemed to reconsider its actions as the left rear tire snagged on a patch of stones. The truck froze mid-revolution, ending its pirouette.

However, the truck wasn't done performing its acrobatics just yet. The crumpled nose of the enemy's pickup truck forced James's vehicle to rise, then tilt. The impact hoisted it dramatically off the ground, where it hovered uncertainly on its wheels as if considering its options. Would it right itself, or would it succumb to the inertia of the second truck? After a lingering second, the truck decided to obey the laws of gravity and toppled over onto its left side. Its wheels spun halfheartedly, the dying eruptions of a wounded animal.

"Holy shit," James amended, the words falling from his mouth in disbelief.

While he already knew he wasn't going to be able to make it out of the desert in the disabled truck, seeing it laying on its side in the bottom of the gully crystallized his conviction. The contents of the vehicle spilled out of window and open door, sending all of his weapons and the lifeless body of his passenger tumbling out. The corpse flopped gracelessly onto the sand, and James's scant belongings scattered around him like a mediocre offering to the dead that now called the gully their grave.

The upturned truck blocked James's view of the IRGC's truck. He could vaguely make out the shape of the enemy's truck on the other side, but the entirety of the cab was completely concealed. He raised his firearm, training it in the direction of the enemy's pickup, and took a cautious step toward it. A jolt of pain shot up his leg as he placed his weight on it, momentarily hobbling him. He hissed through his teeth as his right leg buckled beneath him. Bright spots danced before his eyes, blotting out his vision.

Evidently the adrenaline had worn off, and every movement caused a fresh stab of pain to course through his leg. James glanced down to assess the wound, which had started to seep fresh blood again. A dark stain spread across the fabric of his pants, the black cloth clinging to the tacky fluid weeping from the injury. It was a deep one, and he needed to stem the flow before too long. While a major artery hadn't been damaged, he was still losing a significant amount of blood.

He paused, gritting his teeth as he regained his composure. The shimmering lights faded from his vision, and he blinked, confirming he could see again. He returned his focus to the collision. The enemy's truck lay some forty-five feet ahead, sheltered by his own truck. He righted himself, holding his leg out stiffly in front of him. He still needed to examine the truck to see if the enemy soldiers had survived the crash, and while a wounded leg would undoubtedly serve as an inconvenience, he couldn't allow it to disable him. After a pause, he tightened his lips in renewed conviction and took another step toward the wreckage.

James made a wide berth around the pileup, keeping the barrel of the AK-47 pointed forward as he crept toward the two trucks and his gaze wary as he moved in an arc around them. While there was no movement coming from the driver's side of the truck, the passenger had evidently survived. The green-clad Iranian soldier had managed to extract himself from the wreckage and hovered next to the door of the damaged truck, his focus locked on something inside the cab. His head jerked up as James approached, and James watched as the enemy produced an AK-47 from the cab of the vehicle.

The enemy soldier may have been quick in his movements, but James was significantly faster. He barely had time to register the enemy raising his own weapon when James's fingers tightened around the trigger of his firearm. Three rounds burst from the chamber, following each other sequentially as they tracked the enemy soldier. Two of the rounds buried themselves into the man's abdomen, and the third one sliced through his lower chest. The soldier let out a gurgling sigh, and his legs folded beneath him. He collapsed to the ground and lay still, his eyes focused and unseeing at the sky above him.

James's eyes narrowed at the man outstretched on the sand before him. Even though he'd fallen, the enemy soldier's arms were still wrapped possessively around his AK-47. Until he knew for sure that the man was dead, he couldn't relax. An armed enemy was a lethal one, and James wasn't going to gamble with carelessness when he was so close to escaping their pursuit. He took another step toward the prone soldier, his weapon trained steadily on the fallen man. Sunlight bounced off the unmoving body, but James realized the enemy's chest was still rising and falling. He tightened his finger around the trigger, and as he closed in on the man lying in the channel, the soldier sat upright. A spray of blood flew from his mouth as he aimed his AK-47 at James.

"Not today," James informed him flatly. His voice was both reproachful and chiding, and even though he knew the dying man wouldn't be able to translate his words, he hoped the man could discern the disapproving tone in it.

James tightened his finger around the trigger, and two more rounds flew from his weapon.

The enemy soldier's face ruptured at the impact, bone fragments and gore flying from the shattered head with an air of aloof objectivity. The soldier fell back onto the sand once more, dead.

Threat successfully neutralized.

The sound of a body stirring inside the truck reached James's ears. He spun on his heel, ignoring the protest of pain coming from his injured thigh. The driver of the pickup truck had evidently survived the crash too and not been rendered unconscious from the impact. A large laceration marred his forehead, a flow of blood streaking from the wound. The man appeared to be stuck behind the steering wheel, and James could see him struggling to wrench himself free from his prison. The sunlight bounced off the passenger side window, causing a haze over James's vision. He blinked to clear it, and as the enemy sprung into focus once more, he realized the man was holding a pistol. And he was aiming it directly at him.

Time seemed to freeze as James transitioned his weapon from the corpse on the sand to the driver of the IRGC truck. His hands felt heavy as he aimed his AK-47 on the man seated behind the wheel. He had no time to catch his breath. He tightened his finger around the trigger, but he'd been a fraction of a second too slow in his reaction time. Even as the report from his own firearm rang out in the gully, he could hear the sound of the enemy's pistol discharge as he fired it at James.

CHAPTER TWENTY

THE FIGHT

1008 HOURS – 15 NOVEMBER 2013

J AMES HAD NO TIME TO appreciate his precise aim as his round
collided with the face of the soldier. Even as the bullet sliced
through the enemy's cheek, shattering the orbital bone directly
below his eye, the guard's own gift was threading through James's left
shoulder. The enemy soldier's head jerked back from the round, then
he slumped forward, his body collapsing over the steering wheel.
The pickup's horn let out a solitary, desolate honk as its driver's
face painted a trail of vibrant, scarlet red across the steering wheel's
vinyl surface. Then it was silent, and the gully was bathed in a
preternatural quiet.

James's body twisted away from the sudden anguish in his
shoulder, his body jerking to the left in response to the bullet
connecting with his flesh. His weapon tumbled from his fingers, and
even as his fingers instantly grew numb, a new sensation of agony
rose from the fresh wound. An ecstasy of pain flooded through him,
and bold spots of color flashed before his eyes. The sound of his own
heartbeat was deafeningly loud in the otherwise silent desert. James
clenched his teeth, biting back the involuntary cry that threatened to
squeeze through them. Pools of water welled up in his eyes, blurring
the technicolor haze wavering in his peripheral vision. He clasped
his shoulder, his hand closing over the new opening he found there.

He could feel the warmth of his blood spreading out across his tunic, and the hot liquid seeped through his fingers as he held them against the latest hole in his body.

He shook his head firmly. He wasn't going to die like this, not after getting this far. He was too close to freedom to quit now. Instead, he closed his eyes and drew in a deep breath. The cool desert air poured into his lungs, and he focused all of his attention on this seemingly trivial act. He let the air ease slowly out of his mouth, then immediately followed it with another breath. With every breath he took, he could feel the pain steadily fading away.

The scarred flesh beneath James's garments told a story of his life, a network of ropy knots that marred the tan-colored surface of his skin. Christina had once trailed her fingers across those scars and asked him about them, but his eyes had grown dark at the unwelcome intrusion into his past. The abrupt answer he'd given her had silenced any further probing. Even though he didn't like to discuss the blemishes on his body, they were as much a part of him as were his heart, his lungs, and his brain. No, this wasn't the first time James had been shot, and he didn't doubt it would be the last. If, of course, he survived these wounds.

He banished the fatalistic thoughts from his mind. He'd survived other bullet wounds before, and he was going to survive these too. Not everyone could boast having a method to help them stay conscious after being shot, but he had quite successfully mastered this particular skill. He'd learned early on that if he focused on his breathing after a major wound, he could maintain a grasp on reality. Today would be no different, and so he blocked out all sensation and allowed another deep breath to flood his lungs.

After the better part of a minute with his thoughts focused entirely on his breaths, clarity replaced the haze in James's brain. A numbing balm of adrenaline blotted out a nominal fraction of the pain in his arm, and the blackness that threatened to overtake him was gradually shoved aside. He could think again. He could see. With the back of his right hand, he wiped at the sweat trails on his cheeks. His vision cleared further at the motion, and he blinked at the Iraqi desert. Red streaks transferred from his fingertips to his face, but he paid them no mind. As long as he could actually focus again, it was progress worth celebrating.

James's hand cautiously returned to the wound in his shoulder. The pain wasn't as bad this time, but he found himself reluctant to apply overly firm pressure to it. He ignored that urge. If he didn't apply enough pressure, then blood would continue to flow from the injury. He rewarded himself with another deep breath, and the disorientation that threatened to claim him faded even further. He was almost back to normal lucidity. He needed to think. He wasn't in the clear yet, and he still needed to come up with a workable plan to get out of this desert wasteland. He wasn't about to give up.

The buzzing in James's ears was growing louder, and with dawning horror, he realized it wasn't the pain in his shoulder causing the rising droning sound he was hearing. In the distance, still faint but steadily growing louder, he could hear a distinct grinding rumble. His eyes widened, and he shook his head in disbelief as he realized that he knew exactly what this churning noise represented.

The words flew from his mouth, a stunned outburst yanked from his lips as he identified the heralding sound. "Oh, *shit*. The armored personnel carrier!"

Thoughts swirled around inside his head. How long since he'd last seen the APC? It had been, what? *Ages ago.* At least, it felt like it. Dismay wrapped around James in a suffocating shroud, and he shook his head, not wanting to believe what he was hearing. He lowered his right hand from his wounded shoulder, pressing his bare knuckles against the sandy ground. He pushed down and, with a low grunt, hoisted himself to a standing position. His vision faded out once more as he stood, and he shook his head sharply, clearing it.

This cannot be happening.

The growing rattle of the APC closing in on him grew louder by the second. The vehicle would soon begin its descent into the gully. Once it did, James would be cornered and helpless. The sun glinted off the metal body of the AK-47 laying on the sand, and his eyes flickered to the firearm resting on the ground in front of him.

There was no way he would be able to shoot the weapon with his current injury. Even if he could wield the AK-47, his accuracy would be abysmally poor.

James drew his wounded arm closer to his body, propping it against his torso to minimize any movement. The wound throbbed in response to the motion, and he pointedly ignored it. Instead, he turned his gaze toward the sandy wall of the gully. Even in peak condition, climbing it on foot would prove to be a challenge. In his present state, there was no way in hell it was going to happen.

I have to get out of here. The thought rose doggedly in his brain, and he turned it over, examining it. Even though the frank simplicity of the idea was almost insulting, mocking him at his most vulnerable, he recognized the voice of logic and knew it was right. He did need to get out of the gully, and quickly. He needed to create as much distance between himself and the APC. But how the hell was he supposed to do that?

James shifted his gaze to the three trucks positioned in various locations in the gully. Two of them were lying in a smashed heap directly in front of him, completely useless. However, one of the remaining trucks seemed to be in a decent state. He turned toward this remaining truck, considering it. This was the first one that had skidded down into the gully and swerved to avoid hitting James.

An insistent jag of pain wove its way through James's body, coursing through his wounded leg and completing its journey in his stiff arm as he limped across the sand toward the truck. He moved as quickly as his injuries would allow, and the pain that bloomed from the wounds threatened to steal his consciousness again. He kept his gaze focused on the truck. It became almost talismanic to him. If he could reach it, he would be saved. The truck meant all the difference between life and death for him.

Upon reaching the pickup, he gripped the door handle with his right hand. Its former driver still sat in the driver seat, slumped over the steering wheel. He reached into the truck and grasped the lapels of the dead soldier's jacket. With an impatient grunt, he yanked the body out of the truck. It tumbled gracelessly to the ground, and he stepped over it, then dipped his head into the truck. A low purr from within the truck captured his attention, and he paused, listening. The truck was still running. A quick glance down at the keys still securely in the ignition verified his observation. The truck still worked. That was good news, at least. James smiled wanly to himself. He would take all of the good news he could get at this point.

As he withdrew his head from the truck, his eyes lit upon the left front wheel. While he'd initially believed the truck not rolling away had been a modicum of good fortune for himself, evidence clearly indicated otherwise. The tire was securely embedded in the silty layer of riverbed sand that dusted the floor of the gully, stuck.

Perhaps he could dislodge it. James lowered himself back into the truck, lifting his right leg to support his weight as he shifted himself into a sitting position inside the cab. It was a decision he immediately regretted. As a new jolt of pain shot from his leg, he found himself stumbling and practically falling into the driver's seat of the truck. He kept his left arm secured to his body, and using his right arm, grabbed the steering wheel and used the leverage it provided to help him ease into the driver's seat. Crushing fatigue, dehydration, and blood loss was taking its toll on him, and he knew he was operating on sheer adrenaline. More lights danced before his eyes, and he found himself struggling to maintain focus.

The sound of the APC growing louder was enough to jar him back to reality. His eyes flew wide, and he turned his head in the direction of the sound. His gaze swept back and forth over the lip of the gully, looking for any indication that the enemy had found him. So far, he was still alone in the channel. He knew this wouldn't remain true for long.

James drew another deep breath, then slowly released it from his mouth. *Focus, dammit.*

Extending his right arm across his body, he pulled the driver's side door shut with a slam. He didn't even have the energy to yank on it to ensure that it was secured. He would just have to hope it stayed shut once he got the truck moving. If, of course, he was actually able to get the vehicle dislodged from the sandy patch it had managed to work itself into. Even from within the truck, James could still hear the APC bearing down on him. Its distinct sound was growing steadily louder, and in a moment, the armored personnel carrier would be visible.

James gingerly pried his right hand away from his left shoulder and raised it to the steering wheel. The wound on his shoulder released a warm trickle of blood in response to the gesture, and he grew distant and detached from the wound. His hand left bloody fingerprints on the wheel as he gripped it. A part of him realized he didn't care about the extent of his injury. He could worry about stitching it up later, when he finally got out of this gully. For now, he needed to release the truck's tires from their sandy prison.

A hint of movement at the top of the channel caught his eye, and James glanced up at the sudden motion. Dread rose in his chest at the sight that greeted him. The APC had successfully found him. The angular, olive-green body of the lumbering vehicle seemed to suspend indefinitely on the horizon as its driver maneuvered it alongside the ledge, then the personnel carrier's geometric nose dipped down into the channel. The APC began its slow and methodical descent. Clumps of sand preceded the vehicle, spilling down the walls of the channel. Its tracks gripped the sand with ease, as though it were designed for this very purpose, as it was. It was a ruthless hunting machine, patiently overtaking its prey in its natural habitat.

James forced his attention back toward the task in front of him. He pressed his foot against the gas pedal, and the tires spun obediently in response to his commands. However, the truck didn't move. The engine roared at the renewed pressure from his foot, and the nose of the pickup truck lurched forward an inch or two before falling back into its original position. He gritted his teeth, a wave of frustration coursing through his tired and aching body. His foot bore down on the gas pedal with even more weight, and a fresh wave of pain coursed up his leg. But the truck remained stationary, firmly planted.

"Shit," James hissed.

He glanced back over his right shoulder at the APC. It was

making steady progress and was almost completely down the wall of the gully. In another ten to twenty seconds, the driver would mosey right up next to him. And seconds after that, he would surely shoot James on the spot.

James moved his right hand from the steering wheel, lowering it to the lever selector between the driver and the passenger seat. He yanked the bar back, shifting the truck into reverse. Perhaps if he could rock the pickup back and forth, he could successfully dislodge it from the sand. He was grasping at straws, and he knew it.

The situation had steadily gone from bad to worse, and while he'd been so close to actually escaping his pursuers just a moment before, his plan was falling apart before his eyes. Even this close to death, he couldn't spare a single iota of pity for himself. Instead, a sliver of fury imbedded itself beneath the surface of his skin, prodding it with a blazing white heat. He'd been so damned close to escaping, and to be captured because the tire was stuck in the sand?

An indignant outrage tugged at him, flooding him with both anger and a fresh dose of adrenaline. Like *hell* he was going to let them get him. Not when he was this close to freedom.

James pressed on the gas pedal with renewed vigor, ignoring the surge of pain coming from the bullet wound in his thigh. The tires spun furiously in the silt, sending up visible plumes of sand behind the pickup. The truck rocked back in response to his efforts, and he felt a momentary wave of hope rise in his chest. Then the truck dipped forward once more, falling back into the sandy patch that held it captive. James pressed the gas pedal again, and the truck repeated the rocking motion before settling back into the hole. He was trapped.

A quiet cry of exasperation wrenched itself from between James's teeth, and he slammed his palm down on the steering wheel in disgust. So much for getting away. His shoulders slumped in dejection, and he reluctantly raised his gaze toward the APC. The enemy's final vehicle had caught up with him, and he watched as the driver coasted it toward the pickup truck. It rolled directly in front of the truck James was in and stopped. A dazzling beam of sunlight danced off the windshield, obscuring the driver from his view.

The back door of the APC swung open, and four uniformed IRGC soldiers streamed out of the vehicle, each bearing an AK-47 and a matching dour expression. Almost in unison, they swarmed the truck James sat in, their weapons trained steadily upon him.

James watched them with flat, expressionless eyes as they arranged themselves in a staggered formation around the front of the pickup truck. His breathing slowed, and he felt disappointment descend upon him like a bleak, gray cloud.

So, this is how it ends for me. He'd been so close. So damned close to getting out of Iran alive. Hell, he'd technically succeeded at that objective. Had the enemy soldiers not followed him into Iraq, he might have already been at the outpost in Zurbatiyah. Instead, they'd thrown honor and integrity to the wayside and stalked him even into the perimeters of this presumed impartial territory. Despite their pursuit, James had still been able to neutralize that initial wave of enemies. But now the APC had caught up with him. He swept his dark eyes over the four men, his lips tugging down in anger.

A movement from within the APC drew James's eye back to the enemy vehicle. A shadowy form moved from inside the cab, then a figure stepped out the passenger doorway of the APC. The body was tall and lean, a towering shape against the body of the enemy vehicle. Time seemed to slow down as the man stepped down from the vehicle and onto the sand with exaggerated ease. The sunlight played over the man's face, casting its defined features into sharp relief. Then he broke into a cheerfully malignant smile, and James realized he was peering into the grinning countenance of a high-ranking officer.

CHAPTER TWENTY-ONE

THE END

1019 HOURS – 15 NOVEMBER 2013

THE SHATTERED WINDSHIELD MADE IT difficult for him to see the men, but even without a clear view of their forms, he knew he was outnumbered and outmatched. James regarded the semicircle of men surrounding him with quiet contemplation. This was it. There was no chance in hell that he would be able to draw his pistol quickly enough to fire upon them one by one. Even if he didn't have an actively weeping bullet wound in his shoulder, his reflexes would still have been too slow to shoot them all before they shot him. Sure, he might have been able to pick off one or two of them, but all five? It was wishful thinking at best, suicidal at worst.

It had been a thought worth entertaining, at least. James shook off the growing cloud that threatened to envelop him. If he was going to die anyway, why not go out fighting? Either he was going to die right then, in a blazing gunfight underneath the November sun, or he would die in a day or two—or a week, if they decided to take their time with him—if he let them capture him. James shuddered at the thought, revulsion twisting in his stomach. No, he would never let them do that. His right hand snaked around his torso, grazing lightly over the butt of his 1911.

You haven't even tried Plan C yet. The voice popped into his mind, distant and darkly optimistic.

James tilted his head, considering this new option. His dark eyes once more swept over the crescent of men standing around him, peering at them through the cloud of dust and smoke congesting the inside of the pickup truck. *What about Plan C? Do I even have the strength to muster something up?*

His hand drifted away from the 1911, and he found himself reaching for one of the M67 hand grenades still secured in his vest. It wasn't much of a plan, but it was better than sacrificing himself in a bloody shootout with the enemy. Slipping his hand beneath the tunic, his fingertips grazed over the familiar orb of the fragmentation grenade behind the vest's fabric. Through the blurry haze in the truck, he could see the officer moving outside the window, navigating his way around the front of the pickup. *Good.* After the amount of effort James was expending to prepare this little gift for the enemy officer, he wanted to make sure he could see the reaction on his face when he finally presented it to him.

James's fingers felt clumsy as he fumbled to retrieve the grenade under his tunic. His hand prodded at the Velcro for what felt like a small eternity before his fingers closed around the freed M67. He withdrew it from his vest, then lowered his hand back down to his lap. Even this scant amount of effort sent fresh waves of pain coursing through his body, and he realized with surprise that the grenade felt surprisingly heavy in his weak grip. He wondered fleetingly about his blood loss. His tunic was coated in a thick layer of his own blood, and the tacky fabric clung to his body in limp folds.

He would worry about it later. James realized this thought was quickly becoming his new mantra. It occurred to him that this entire morning had been singularly defined by shoving his thoughts aside and compartmentalizing them to deal with at a later date.

Will there even be a later?

James hefted the grenade in his right hand and rotated it over clumsily in his grip, turning the pull pin toward his left hand. He aimed the pull pin toward the middle finger of his left hand, but his aim was poor and the loop missed the digit entirely. The ring skidded down his knuckle, and his right hand bounced against his left thigh.

James gritted his teeth and, taking in a slow breath, repositioned the pull pin, slipping it easily around his middle finger.

His timing couldn't have been better. As the warm metal encircled his finger, the driver's door to the pickup truck opened. A cool rush of air flooded into the cab as a shadow fell across James's body. He turned his face up to peer at the figure standing in front of him, his eyes meeting the dark, expressionless visage of the enemy officer. Despite himself, James felt a slow smile creep across his pallid face. He held the officer's gaze as he pulled his right hand back, revealing what he held in his palm.

The officer's eyes flickered down to James's lap, then back to his eyes.

A quiet ghost of satisfaction settled over James as he saw the look of surprise in the man's eyes, and he felt grimly pleased with himself. *At least I'll be going out with a bang.*

The pain in his arm was unbearable, excruciating. He took a deep breath, held it, and locked his gaze with the enemy officer's. With grim determination, he slowly drew his left hand away from the grenade in his lap. The pin pulled taut, and he felt the metal wire slowly drawing out from within the steel casing. Even as he tugged on the pin, however, the pain in his left shoulder crested and bloomed. Blackness wavered in the perimeter of his vision, and a cold sweat erupted on his temples. Then his left hand seized, and his hand fell open. He peered down at his splayed hand in disbelief. The pain was insurmountable, secondary only to the sensation of betrayal he felt toward his own body.

James raised his face back toward the figure looming over him, defeat evident in his eyes as he took in the appearance of the man. The enemy's emerald green uniform was freshly pressed, and not a single wrinkle blemished the crisp and clean fabric. The single button at the chest level of the uniform was tight and secure, and the seam running down the front of the fabric was flat and smooth. Shoulder boards decorated the broad stretch of fabric on each side of the officer's neck, a series of four golden eight-sided stars dotting the black material on each board in a line. James's initial assessment of this man had been correct. There was no doubt that he was a high-ranking officer in the IRGC.

"Allow me to introduce myself." The voice coming from the careworn face was silky and almost amiable, though thick with an Iranian accent. "My name is Captain Ahmed of the Iranian Islamic Revolutionary Guard." The man's silver-streaked beard was neatly trimmed and well-groomed, barely concealing the easy smile on his face. He leaned into the truck and plucked the grenade out of James's hand with fingertips sporting manicured fingernails, then stood up confidently again. From the soldier's bearing to his uniform, everything about this man exuded pristine self-control. "You will not be needing this."

Cold numbness pumped through James's veins. Despite all of his efforts to evade the enemy, the one thing he'd wanted to avoid the most had actually happened. The methodical escape from Da'wud's compound. His jaunt across Mehran on the rickety motorbike. Dodging bullets in the pickup truck. Evading the four men who had pursued him into Iraq. All of it...for what? James had vowed he would be killed before being taken prisoner, and the shame of his failure burned at him, creeping up his neck in a hot flush. He set his lips in a firm line, his eyes staring past the man who had introduced himself as Captain Ahmed. He could feel the captain's eyes crawling over him, the dark gaze taking in the wound on his shoulder and the blood streaked across his face.

The smile lingered on the enemy's lips, taunting James with its empty good cheer.

The captain leaned forward, close enough James could smell the stench of his sweat beneath his clean uniform. Despite his pretenses, the man was still nothing more than an animal. James didn't glance down, but he could see the enemy officer's shoulder shift, then the sound of the engine idling cut off abruptly. Captain Ahmed pulled himself back out of the cab of the truck, straightening his back as he quietly regarded James. His eyes moved toward the pistol secured beneath James's blood-soaked tunic, and a knowing recognition flashed behind them as he reached out. His hand lifted the tunic, and James could feel the damp shirt peeling away from his body as the captain found his pistol beneath it. He drew it out of the holster in a smooth motion, then returned his body to an upright position.

"Tell me," Captain Ahmed said, his eyes locking onto James's own fatigued eyes. "What is your name, American soldier?"

Silence followed.

The captain's eyes remained fixed on James's as he slipped the 1911 into the front of his own waistband and his right hand idly turned the M67 grenade.

James returned the emotionless gaze unflinchingly. Already he felt a detached serenity replacing the fear thudding in his chest. In a few minutes, he would be dead. He stared fixed and unblinking on the captain's face, and even as he held the enemy's gaze, he issued a silent prayer. *Dear God, please don't let him prolong my death.*

After what felt like ages but was surely no more than a beat or two, Captain Ahmed spoke again. The façade of joviality was still in his voice, but it sounded more strained and impatient this time. "Well, American? What is your name?"

James's face was an inscrutable mask. His eyes didn't budge from the sunken eyes beneath the thick and bushy gray eyebrows punctuating the enemy officer's face. His mouth was dry, and he swallowed, but there was no saliva left to coat his parched throat. It didn't matter anymore, though. The Geneva Conventions clearly dictated that during times of war, a captured prisoner needed only to reveal name, rank, and serial number to their enemy captors. James wasn't a POW, and he had no pressing obligations to speak. He took a bleak sort of glee in knowing that his silence infuriated the enemy officer. If it provoked him to use James's own firearm against him, it would be even better.

The smile melted off the captain's face. He raised his right hand up and bounced the fragmentation grenade in his palm as though it were nothing more benign than a baseball.

James glanced at it, then back at Captain Ahmed's face. *Is that how it's going to end? Instead of using my 1911 against me, he's going to slip the grenade into my lap and then duck for cover?*

The M67 spun in the captain's hands, a compact orb of destruction enshrouded in a steel case. The captain's motions were graceful, as though he was still going to give James an opportunity to speak. His left hand reached up, and his fingers seemed to caress the smooth body of the grenade with a reverent form of respect at the power contained within it. Then his middle finger hooked the pin ring, and Captain Ahmed arched a brow at the American soldier. The gesture was challenging. Who was going to call the other's bluff?

James's expression didn't change. He was no longer afraid. God had gotten him this far. If He was going to call him home now, then James was at peace with that. Besides, he reasoned, death by grenade was far more pleasant than death by a dull rusty blade.

Captain Ahmed shrugged slightly. If he were bewildered by James's lack of reaction, however, he didn't show it. In one swift, fluid motion, the captain yanked the pin from the grenade.

The enemy soldiers stationed by the front of the truck exchanged troubled glances. Even though the captain didn't seem concerned by this new turn of events, his men evidently were. They each took several hasty steps back, their eyes suddenly wary. Their weapons remained trained on James, though, steady and unwavering despite their newfound unease. Perhaps wisely, perhaps foolishly, none of them dared vocalize their concerns to their captain.

The scowl on the captain's face deepened. He bit off the words one by one, spitting them into James's face as he said, "You are going to tell me your name, American. Or I will kill you where you sit." The falsetto of cheer was gone from his voice, which was now a gravelly sound coming from deep within the officer's chest. The words were almost inviting despite the threat evident within them. The officer believed that he could reason with James.

James turned his face toward Captain Ahmed. He blinked slowly, and a slow smile crept across his face. The gesture didn't reach his eyes. There was a quiet peacefulness to it, and he knew in that moment that he genuinely wasn't afraid to die. It was almost curious, really. After all the training he'd undergone to help ensure he stayed alive at all costs, when he was finally faced with death, he accepted his fate with a tranquil dignity.

Captain Ahmed returned his smile with one of his own. Like James's smile, the expression didn't extend beyond his lips. His teeth flashed at James, surprisingly bright and white in the dazzling midday sunlight. "Have it your way, American." He took a step back from the truck, then with a swift motion from his left hand, slammed the door shut.

The captain turned his face slightly left and issued a barking order at the men standing in front of the truck. While James's Farsi wasn't adept enough to translate the command, it was no doubt an instruction to move back.

The men didn't hesitate. They took several shuffling steps back. The distance between themselves and James widened until a space of some thirty feet separated him from the enemy soldiers. Their AK-47s never wavered from their stance, and the barrels remained stubbornly aimed on him as though they thought he might bolt in a sudden display of cowardice.

James squeezed his eyes shut. His shoulders relaxed, and he rested his head against the fabric headrest of the pickup truck's seat. A renewed calm settled on him, and he felt hot tears spring up behind his eyes. His sons had loved to head to the Tampa Renaissance Festival with him every year, and while nobody would argue their fair costumes were historically accurate, it was admittedly more of a ruse to bond with his children. The knowledge that he would never be able to enjoy another overpriced smoked turkey leg while being entertained by anachronistic reenactors filled him with an aching grief he knew he would never be able to articulate. Hell, James was the one dying, not his children or Christina. Still, he found himself mourning the future that he would never have with them.

I love you, Jesus. The words rose in his head, sincere and unabashed. Despite all of his conflict with God throughout the years, James had always remained grateful for his faith. It made his fate more bearable, knowing what awaited him after death. His only fear was what would happen to his family. *Please take care of my boys for me.*

James had experienced many types of deaths due to his choice in career, but perhaps one of the more significant ones had been the death of his marriage. It was no secret that military life was a ruthless killer of matrimony, but everyone in The Unit would readily attest that being part of the Combat Applications Group (CAG) was much more taxing on a marriage. Before he met Christina, he'd been married to the mother of his children. While the marriage had lasted only ten years, Deana had given him four children, a daughter and three boys.

His daughter Tayler was in a league of her own. Both stunning and brilliant, she had a kind heart and a wry sense of humor. While she wasn't dating just yet, he knew it would be only a matter of time before she swept some unsuspecting young fellow off his feet. Tayler was the inquisitive type, but instead of taking apart clock radios to see how they worked, she was more interested in the inner workings of the human body. She'd professed a love for internal medicine and interest in eventually earning her X-ray technician certification. James was very proud of her.

Conner was a great student in school, and James knew the young man had a bright and promising future ahead of him. A natural athlete, he was already playing goalie for a local semi-professional soccer team. While his sights were firmly set farther than the local leagues, he'd already determined he was going to start out at Tampa University to play for the Spartans. James knew he was going to be an incredibly successful professional athlete.

Then there were his twin boys, both sixteen. Gage and Parker were polar opposites, and James loved them for all of their personality quirks. Parker was the academic type and loved to be on the computer, while Gage had already indicated he would be following in his father's footsteps. Parker was exacting in his studies and had told his father he was going to pursue a degree in cyber security in college. Gage was interested in enlisting, despite his mother's protests. James had told him to go to college and go the officer route, but the boy had laughed and told him he is going into the Air Force and going pararescue.

Every time James returned to Florida, he immediately found his way to his children. There was a rhythm they'd managed to work out, and despite the differences between himself and Deana, she had to admit that he was a caring and loving father. In March, he would pick them up from her house in Largo and drive the boys back into Tampa for the Renaissance Festival. In October, he would take them to Halloween Horror Nights in Orlando. They hadn't protested that part of the routine yet, but James knew they would have outgrown it before too long and that made it all the more precious to him.

Of all the things they did together, however, there was one thing that stood out as the most cherished to James. Every single weekend they were together, he would take the boys out to Denny's for breakfast. It was a humble routine, but it was theirs, exclusive to only the men in the Chase family. They almost always ordered the same thing, and while nobody would be writing Denny's any heartfelt letters thanking them for their gourmet fare, the atmosphere was only one part of the overall experience. One particular trip to Denny's stood out in James's memory, and in his last seconds of life, he recalled it with warm fondness.

Through a mouthful of pancake, Gage had casually informed his father, "Last week, Mom and Aunt Patty took us to this very Denny's. But you know what?"

"What?" James had asked him, handing him a folded paper napkin. The boy had a dollop of pancake syrup on his chin and was cheerfully oblivious to the sugary streak blemishing the lower portion on his face. He tapped his own chin, mirroring the smudge on his face, and the boy seemed to get the hint.

Gage rubbed absently at the spot as he talked. "It didn't feel right. This is our place to come with you, Dad. And I don't like it when Mom brings us here."

A tear carved out a path on James's cheek at the memory, and he didn't wipe it away. His chest ached at the recollection. It had been nice to hear that the boy valued their time together, and even the normally exuberant Parker had nodded in agreement at the statement. *I just hope they're able to continue this routine without me, after I'm gone.*

The reflection passed through James's thoughts in a flash, presented to him in stark clarity. It was like a highlight reel of the best parts of his life, vivid and sharp in his mind. James found himself grateful for this last moment of reminiscence. He had his regrets, sure, but who didn't? Fortunately, he'd been spared the rumination upon those. It was a small mercy, at least. He could die with a clear mind, free from the burden of guilt and anxiety about how he stacked up as a partner, a father, and a soldier.

A clanging thud of something landing at his feet told James it was over for him. The grenade skipped over his booted foot and settled on the floorboard somewhere to his right. He had no time to consider its location, only realizing fleetingly that it didn't matter. An instant later, a deafening explosion resonated loudly in his ears, blotting out the world. But James was ready, and he was at peace, and so he embraced his death with a faint yet serene smile on his face and tranquility in his heart.

CHAPTER TWENTY-TWO

THE INTERROGATION

1022 HOURS – 15 NOVEMBER 2013

THE WORLD DRIFTED AWAY. EVEN as the grenade detonated in a deafening explosion, James felt himself accepting his fate with a detached sort of acceptance. He was buoyant, weightless, his heart and mind unrestrained by the dubious laws of gravity. A comforting warmth enshrouded him, and he felt blissfully light and free from the burdens of mortality.

Is this what it feels like to die?

No archangel greeted him with a warm embrace as he made the transition from living to dead. There were no harps serenading him, heralding his arrival into the afterlife. Nobody coaxed him to head toward the light. In a way, it was almost anticlimactic.

Then laughter, loud and raucous, cut through his thoughts.

James felt himself slam back into his body with the weight of this sudden new awareness. His eyes flew open as the humorless laughter rose again. The sound was harsh and strangely vulgar in his ears, and he turned his face toward the sound. Disbelief obscured his vision, and he blinked, trying to make sense of the offensive noise. His eyes lit on the enemy soldiers still standing in a loose semicircle around his truck. Captain Ahmed punctuated the crescent, his hands on his hips and his mouth open in a derisive laugh.

"What the hell?" The words were raspy in James's mouth, and he dragged his dry tongue across his chapped and split lips. Nothing made sense. *If I'm alive, why did I feel myself drifting away from my body?*

That, at least, was easily explained. It was the blood loss. James had never fainted before, but he was certainly teetering on the brink of unconsciousness now. Disbelief tore through him, but there was no denying it. The pain he was feeling was testament enough that he was still alive. The bullet wound in his right thigh burned and throbbed, and the injury in his left shoulder still screamed at him in a persistent thrum of agony.

"Ah! I knew you were American." Captain Ahmed's voice wafted across the desert, smug and self-satisfied.

James instantly recognized his mistake. Despite keeping his lips sealed and refusing to offer a single word to the enemy officer, the surprise of being alive had somehow caused him to slip up. The careless phrase had also been a distinctly American colloquialism, betraying his nationality.

That was only one of James's many problems in that moment, though. If a grenade hadn't blown him to shreds, what had caused the explosion? More importantly, what had thudded into the pickup truck? He pried his gaze away from the enemy captain and let it drift to the floorboard, scanning for any sign of what might have landed at his feet. His gaze trailed over the frayed carpeting, and a moment later, he spotted it. He frowned at the offending object resting inconspicuously on the floorboard of the truck. A fist-sized stone lay there on the floorboard, and James considered it curiously. It all made sense now.

Evidently Captain Ahmed had a black sense of humor. When he saw James rest his head against the seat and close his eyes, he'd taken his chance to reach down and scoop up the stone to pitch it into the truck. But if the grenade hadn't landed inside the pickup truck, then where had the captain thrown it? James jerked his head up, scanning the vista outside the window. His eyes settled on the overturned pickup truck, a burning heap of ruin in the distance. The enemy officer must have first tossed the stone into the truck with James, then swiftly thrown the grenade over to that truck afterward.

Realization rewarded James with both uncertainty and, quickly trailing it, renewed fear. Yes, he was still alive. Captain Ahmed clearly had other plans for him. A surge of anger promptly followed these emotions, and he found his vision darkening with renewed anger. The knowledge of the cruel prank played by the captain offended him on a primitive level. Hate washed over him, and he wished he still had enough remaining strength to meet the laughing face of his enemy with his fist. He opened and closed his right hand, wadding it into a ball and releasing it in a repetitive motion. Punching this Iranian bastard would give him satisfaction like no other. He hoped he would be able to get at least one blow in before the enemy disabled him.

Captain Ahmed's voice wafted over the desert once more. His so-called joke had evidently lightened his sour mood, as the thinly veiled anger was again gone from his voice. His tone was almost singsong as he called out, "What is your name, American?"

James regarded the captain with a somber, unblinking expression. The temptation to respond to his question with a pointed and deliberate insult was tempting, but he shelved it. It was better to not give him anything at all. Furthermore, he was worried the epithet would come out as a froggy croak, small and petulant, instead of the defiant and cold response he wanted it to be. Silence prevailed, and James let the weight of his lack of response settle between himself and the enemy officer. He had all the time in the world, as limited as it now was. He felt no rush to fill the quiet with the sound of his own voice.

The smile slowly melted off the captain's face, a scowl quickly replacing it. Captain Ahmed was done playing with the American, and the furious expression on his face indicated that he wasn't going to show him any more mercy. He considered James coldly, his lips a flat line cut across his face, then said, "That is okay, American. You will talk to me very soon."

The captain regarded James for a moment longer, then turned

toward the collection of men standing several yards in front of the truck. His voice was sharp as he issued commands to the four enemy soldiers in his native tongue.

Even though the commands were clear and distinct, James still couldn't identify any of the Farsi words. It didn't matter, though. He didn't need to speak the language of the Iranian men to know they'd been instructed to get him out of the truck.

The men immediately sprang into action, striding toward James.

He watched them silently. *Is there another plan left in me? A Plan D, perhaps?*

He was unarmed, weakened by his injuries and blood loss, and he felt lightheaded. Coherent thought taunted him, evading him despite his fervent efforts to regain mental composure. Even though James was a practical man not prone to wishful thinking, he found himself issuing another prayer that it would be all over for him soon.

The captive American might have had his own suspicions about what his future would hold, but Captain Jafar Ahmed knew precisely what would happen to the quiet soldier. He hadn't risen in the ranks to become a top leader in the Islamic Revolutionary Guard Corps due to dumb luck or the flip of a coin. Ineptitude was punished strongly with strident measures, but military finesse was just as equally rewarded. Captain Ahmed had his own history of successes, and his prowess had helped him escalate through the ranks of the corps to become the respected captain he was today.

Indeed, Ahmed didn't like being disrespected. He'd encountered discourteous prisoners before, but this American was particularly brazen in his defiance. Ahmed would be sure to correct this behavior before he was done with his captive. That he would see to personally. The thought of teaching the American manners caused a hint of a smile to tug at the corners of Ahmed's mouth, and he forced it back down. Now wasn't the time to get complacent. Yes, he'd successfully captured his target, but he still had so much work ahead.

If Ahmed questioned the American about what he thought

would happen to him, perhaps the soldier would reveal that he believed Ahmed would slowly remove his head from his shoulders. This, of course, would be filmed and shared across broadcasts in several nations. Fear made a powerful and evocative propaganda tool, which is what made these public decapitations so effective. Ahmed himself had overseen many of these executions and he had to admit, the American would be right in his assumptions. There would come a day in the very near future when someone—ideally Ahmed himself—would hold the blade that would end the American's life.

The captain frowned as he watched one of his men yank the door handle of the pickup truck. A second soldier stood directly behind him, ready to catch his comrade if his legs buckled. The other two soldiers stood sentry, their firearms trained on their enemy. Except for muttering a single sentence under his breath, the American remained almost completely silent throughout this whole display. Ahmed wasn't surprised by this. It was still early in the day. He'd hoped the grenade would cause the man to lose his resolve, but the stunt hadn't worked quite as he'd expected. Ahmed knew he was working with someone special here. The challenge of breaking him would be all the more enjoyable.

The report over the radio had revealed to Ahmed all that he needed to know about his quarry. He'd suspected the soldier was an American, and hearing his distinctly western accent had confirmed the man's nationality. According to the message on his radio feed, the soldier was quite possibly one of those Special Forces soldiers. Ahmed knew about those too. He'd never actually succeeded in capturing one of them himself, but he'd heard about them from other officers. There had been Americans in his grasp before, though, and as far as Ahmed was concerned, they were all the same. This one would be no different. He would eventually fold, and Ahmed would derive great pleasure from the entire encounter.

That the American would be decapitated was only one part of Ahmed's plans for him. First, he would carefully and methodically milk all of the intel he could get from the soldier. He had his own ways of acquiring information and knew what worked on one subject may not necessarily work on another. That was no concern to Ahmed, though. He would start small. Physical pain was a powerful motivator. But as Ahmed watched his men yank the American from the scarred pickup truck and throw him onto the ground, he knew pain would not be enough to get him to talk. The man's body already bore two bullet wounds that Ahmed could see. Even though it was evident he was suffering from severe agony, it was equally clear that his spirit wasn't weakened by his injuries.

Even the fear of death was falling short with this man. That was no matter, either. Ahmed could still break him. Even if the American soldier wasn't worried about his own mortality, he could find other ways to terrify him into revealing information. He would carefully comb through the man's pockets for any clue to his weaknesses. Some men carried pictures of their loved ones in their pockets. Ahmed wasn't sure he would find such a treasure on this soldier, but he knew he would find something. If he didn't, though, a lack of food, water, light, and silence all went quite far in subverting a detained subject.

Ahmed had employed all of these tactics before with varying degrees of success, and he had no doubt that he would be able to get what he wanted from the American before too long. All of the closely guarded secrets the American held inside his brain would be revealed before he was done with him. This would go far in helping to guide him to another promotion and, with it, more respect. Ahmed had had his eye on becoming a major for some time now, and the increased pay grade and quality of life that went with such a promotion were just some of the perks of the job. He wasn't afraid to admit that he loved the fear and sway he held over other humans.

And after learning everything the American knew, then, and only then, would he kill him. If the American thought he was on the fast track to a swift and merciful death, then he was quite mistaken.

Captain Ahmed rubbed his hands together as he took a step toward his captive. He would show the American the errors in his thinking. The day was still young, and he was only just getting started. He had no desire to linger in Iraq any longer than necessary. The sooner Ahmed brought his prisoner back to Iran, the sooner he could start his interrogation. And, if he had to be truly honest with himself, he was quite looking forward to it.

———⸻———

Dread twisted into a bolus of bile within the depths of James's stomach. He watched as the Iranian soldiers approached and circled around to the driver's side of the pickup.

Two of the enemy soldiers paused and handed their AK-47s to the other two soldiers. They each accepted the weapons wordlessly, propping the firearms against their legs as they kept their own weapons trained upon James.

James's shoulders slumped, sending a fresh surge of pain through his body as he felt the rush of air soar through the open door. He had no fight left in him to resist these men.

One of the soldiers stood in the open doorway, watching James silently. The other one, however, moved quickly. He leaned forward, his hand reaching out toward James. He grasped the blood-sodden material of James's tunic, grabbing it directly above the puncture in the fabric.

James hissed in a breath of air through his teeth, choking down the gasp of pain that threatened to bubble out of his throat. He wasn't going to give them the satisfaction of knowing they were exacerbating his injury and causing him unspeakable pain.

He felt himself being wrenched from the pickup truck, and a moment later, his body was flying forward. As he fell face-first into the sand, instinct took over. His hands shot out, his palms striking the ground first. This time he couldn't bite back the profanity that flew from his lips. Pain ricocheted up his arms, white hot and excruciating. It would have been better to land on his face, but it was too late to regret his defensive reaction. His arms buckled beneath his weight, unable to support him, and he collapsed onto the sand. His shoulder bounced off the ground, and again, a low grunt of pain flew from his lips. Then his face was in the sand, plumes of dust flying away from his panting breaths.

Perhaps it was the immediacy of the agony that made it blot out all other instances of similar pain, but he truly could not recall ever feeling so much pain coursing through his body. Even the other times he'd been shot paled in comparison. He raised his right hand, pressing it against the fresh deluge of blood bubbling out from the wound in his shoulder. This new pressure against it caused black dots to blot out James's vision, and he reeled against the pain all over again. If he allowed himself to succumb to it, he would wind up unconscious. If he blacked out, he might never wake up again. As weakened as he was by fatigue and blood loss, he couldn't yet admit it might be over for him. He wasn't going to give up without a fight.

A voice muttered something in Farsi, then a pair of hands grabbed him from beneath each arm. The fingers dug into his armpits, and James felt the earth slip away below him as he was hoisted back to his feet. One of the enemy soldiers was saying something to him, but the words were a useless jumble in his ears. He couldn't translate it, but based on the annoyed expression on the enemy's face, it was probably a reprimand for James having the nerve to collapse to the ground in pain. Their viselike grips encouraged the pain in his wounded shoulder to announce its presence once more.

When will this agony subside? It seemed as though all James had ever known was pain, and he doubted he would ever know anything other than suffering for the short remainder of his life.

Captain Ahmed materialized before James's eyes, and he barely had time to register the enemy officer standing directly in front of him before a fresh wave of pain blinded him. The captain's fist connected with James's flat abdomen, and James let out a low *woof* as the air was forced out of his lungs. His vision swam, and he felt the beckoning call of blackness summon him from the edges of his consciousness. He drew in a short gasp of air, but his lungs seemed to have forgotten how to breathe. He was suffocating, the mere act of breathing seeming to be a foreign act.

If James thought he would be granted the opportunity to catch his breath, he was profoundly mistaken. The captain's hand found its way around his neck, his thumb and forefingers securely tucked beneath his bearded jawline.

James straightened his back, but his legs were limp and useless beneath him. His booted toes dragged against the sand, and he forced himself to stay upright. If he slumped down, then the airflow into his lungs would be completely cut off by the captain's grip. James wheezed and peered at the enemy officer through slitted eyes.

Captain Ahmed lowered his face toward James's, sending hot and fetid breath pouring from his mouth. "You are going to talk to me," the man said in English, each word carefully enunciated.

James realized the officer's accent had thickened since the last time he spoke. His anger was making it harder for him to speak clearly, and despite saying the words one by one, he was losing his composure.

"And you are going to tell me everything I want to know."

James fixed the man in his unblinking gaze while thoughts swirled through his brain. *After everything else I've had to endure this day, is it really fair that one of my last breaths on this planet should be tainted by the foul odor of Captain Ahmed's breath?* There truly was no justice in the world, and the stench emanating from his enemy only confirmed it. A ghost of a smile played at the corner of his lips, and he met the captain's eyes with his own steady gaze. "There's something I would like to know too."

Captain Ahmed seemed surprised by James's words. His eyebrow went up, and curiosity played on his weathered face. "I will indulge you, American."

"Would you?" James replied. He raised his uninjured arm, wedging his hand between himself and Ahmed. He waved the hand back and forth in front of his nose, wrinkling his face into an exaggerated expression of disgust. The smile remained on his face, mocking and derisive throughout the entire pantomime. "Would you like a breath mint? Because your breath smells like cat *shit*."

The look of black rage on the captain's face almost made the taunt worth his loss of life.

Almost. James wasn't afraid of the captain, but that wasn't enough. He wanted this Captain Ahmed to know he wasn't afraid of him. And it was the truth. This knowledge soothed James, and he straightened his back even more. He was in charge here. Even if he died today, he knew he wouldn't die a coward. He certainly wasn't going to let them take him without a fight.

James drew his body back away from the enemy officer, but Captain Ahmed tightened his grip around his throat. James didn't mind. It was a ruse, regardless. He was merely trying to divert the officer from his next and final act. He'd been told before that he was stubborn and hardheaded, and this wasn't a mistruth. His hard head would be meeting Captain Ahmed's face in a moment, and then the captain would also be privy to this insight.

As James squared his shoulders, tensing them in preparation for his final assault on the enemy officer, a new sound cut through the gully. His eyes widened at the familiar sound, and he jerked his head back to face the source of the new noise. Captain Ahmed tightened his grip around James's neck in response to the motion, but he was oblivious to the compression around his throat.

Am I hearing what I think I'm hearing?

It was a distinct and unmistakable sound, but the captain wasn't responding to it.

Momentarily unsure if he was experiencing another hallucination, James scanned the sky but found no evidence of his suspicions.

Then the APC exploded in a brilliant fireball, and James knew the humming noise was exactly what he'd thought—and hoped—it was. He could identify the familiar sound of an MQ-9 Reaper without hesitation, and today the unmanned aerial vehicle sounded precisely like James's salvation.

CHAPTER TWENTY-THREE

1035 HOURS – 15 NOVEMBER 2013

T HE PERCUSSIVE FORCE OF THE blast knocked James and the two men holding him up off their feet. He felt the world rushing up to greet him as his body fell heavily to the sand. His head thudded against the ground, and his shoulder met the sandy surface with renewed agony. Twinkling stars moved in his field of vision, blotting out his sight. Consciousness threatened to escape him as he lay unmoving on the ground. He closed his teeth over his tongue, biting down hard. The sudden pain rising in his mouth followed by the coppery tang of his own blood jolted him back to awareness.

In the distance, James saw Captain Ahmed on the ground as well, already struggling to his feet. Trails of blood coursed out of his nose, and the man seemed disoriented by the explosion. He shook his head, then took a staggering step toward James. Behind him, the other two soldiers remained sprawled on the ground. On his left and to his right, the enemy soldiers who had been holding him upright were lying on their backs. James could see one of them trying to sit up, and the man shook his head and blinked with wide, stunned eyes.

The APC was a burning mass of metal. The sole operator who had been loitering inside it, waiting for his command to start driving again, was an amorphous lump of gore and charred bone shards. The missile attack had seemingly come out of nowhere, and the driver never knew what hit him. Even James had to admit that he'd been caught off guard by the sudden assault. He'd been certain that he would have to manually summon a rescue party once he arrived at the outpost in Zurbatiyah. Seeing the APC ignite in a blaze both puzzled James and simultaneously roused the faintest glimmer of hope deep inside his chest.

Motion on either side drew his attention to his periphery, and he glanced around, taking in the scene unfolding around him. Captain Ahmed was revolving in a slow circle, his head craned toward the sky, scanning it. The two soldiers next to him staggered to their feet, and James could see them reaching out, extending their hands to the other two soldiers who had been keeping watch on the other side of the pickup truck. Traces of blood moved in slow rivulets down their faces, a parting gift from the explosion delivered by the Reaper. James could feel a trickle moving down his own face, and he wiped at it with the back of his hand. A cursory inspection of his knuckles revealed that he too was bleeding from his nose.

Everyone stared up at the sky. Even James's eyes were fixated on the deceptively clear expanse above. While the other men rose to their feet to get a closer look at the heavens to determine what had caused the explosion, James remained secure on his position on the ground. He lay on his back, the sun beating down on his face, beaming bright light directly into his eyes. He snaked his right hand up to his left shoulder and let his eyes flutter shut. If there was one attack from the Reaper, then there surely would be another following shortly. Standing up would only lead to him falling down again in order to take cover, and he had to admit that was something he wasn't looking forward to. His battered and wounded body couldn't handle much more abuse.

A second later, James's suspicions were confirmed. A low thumping echoed over the gully, its rising sound not even muffled by the poor acoustics of the sandy channel. A slow and uncertain smile crept across James's face. The reinforcements had come for him.

Thank you, God!

The distinct sound of helicopters rose in the valley, and an instant later, two ovoid shapes dipped gracefully down over the horizon. The smile on his face widened into an earnest grin as his gaze landed on a pair of MH-6M Little Bird helicopters. The agile aircrafts dipped into the gully, revealing their passengers to James. Two Delta operators perched on the ledge on either side of each chopper, a Stoner SR-25 Marksman sniper rifle clutched in each man's hands.

James drew in a shaky breath. Even drawing air into his lungs was painful, and as he watched the helicopters turn into the gully, he wondered if they'd come too late for him. Blood continued to seep out of the bullet wounds in his shoulder and leg, and despite him making a conscious effort to stay awake, he knew he was fighting a losing battle. Once the adrenaline of the whole ordeal wore off, it was highly likely that he would pass out from both shock and blood loss. Even as he felt a dreamy haziness wash over him where he lay on the warm sand, James found himself wondering how his men had been able to find him.

The enemy soldiers didn't stand a chance against the highly trained men descending into the gully in the pair of Little Bird helicopters. James watched as a pair of well-aimed bullets took care of the duo of men standing closest to him. From his vantage point on the ground, James could clearly see a perfectly clean hole form in each of their foreheads. The men fell to the ground with weighty thuds, bounced once, and then lay on their stomachs on the sand. James turned his head to the left, and his gaze met with the unseeing stare of the enemy soldier closest to him. A glance to the right confirmed the other man was dead too.

Captain Ahmed seemed to lose all control of his English vocabulary. A stream of incoherent Farsi flew from his broad lips, and based on the black expression in his eyes, he was teetering on the brink of a panic. His perfectly executed plan to capture James and bring him back to the enemy base was falling apart, and the jumble of Farsi words flying from his lips were easy for James to understand.

He didn't need to be a native speaker to know the man was spewing expletives, and the brunt of his wrath was divided between the aerial assault from the Delta soldiers in the Little Bird helicopters and the elite soldier lying on the ground before him.

The enemy officer reached into the waistband of his pants and, in a fluid motion, withdrew the 1911 pistol.

James remained unflinching, his gaze fixed on the ranting captain. *Is this really how I'm going to die?* Frankly, he was growing weary of wondering if he were on the precipice of death. He was so close to rescue—hell, he could almost make out the identities of the men sitting on the ledge of the helicopters—and this Captain Ahmed might instead dispatch him with a strategic bullet from his own firearm. Disappointment washed over James, bathing his body in cold chills. He was too weak to roll away from the trajectory of the bullets.

At least it will be over quickly instead of a lingering torture.

James let his eyes lock onto the face of his enemy as Captain Ahmed trained the pistol at him. The barrel of the weapon lowered toward him, and James justified a glance at the yawning opening. The captain was aiming at his head. This was good. A quick bullet to James's brain would mean he wouldn't even feel the lead colliding with his flesh. While it wasn't preferable to actually surviving this whole ordeal, it was better than the fate he'd thought he would be facing just a minute or two earlier.

Time seemed to slow down as he watched Captain Ahmed tighten his finger around the trigger.

A loud report boomed through the gully, but the pain never came.

A dark blossom formed on the front of the enemy captain's green coat. Two more stains quickly followed the initial shot, and the officer's body lurched forward suddenly, moving as though he were a jerky marionette on a short string. His hips wrenched to the left, then the captain took another jittery step forward on heavy legs. A tuft of sand less than a foot away from James's head exploded as the rounds finished their trajectory through their target, and he felt the fine grains settle on his face from the rain of sand that ejected upward from the impact.

Captain Ahmed's eyes were wide and blank, then the man's legs buckled beneath him and he fell face-first onto the sand, his body motionless.

Two more shots rang out, and James turned his head to identify the recipients of these rounds. A fresh surge of pain radiated down from his shoulder, and he gritted his teeth. The slightest movement was excruciating. James returned his head to its original position on the sand, his eyes squinting up at the clear blue sky overhead. Despite not seeing whose name was on those bullets, he suspected they'd found the two enemy soldiers who had taken shelter behind the pickup truck.

This is it, James thought.

Relief washed over him, and he sagged against the sand that supported his body. He was surprised to discover his body felt heavy and leaden and he couldn't move his limbs. Even as he tried to raise his hand to wave at the helicopters flying overhead, he was surprised to learn his body wouldn't respond to even basic commands. In a way, this disappointed him. He wanted to be able to greet the men who had risked their lives to save him, thank them personally for flying down and rescuing him.

That will just have to come later, he reasoned. Once they got him out of this damned gully and back into the chopper. Maybe after they hooked him up to some fluids though, first.

James ran his tongue over the back of his teeth. His tongue felt thick and swollen, a clunky foreign entity in his mouth. And his mouth was so damned dry. He made a mental note to ask one of the men in the Little Bird if they had a coffee with them, maybe one of those fancy drinks from the Green Beans coffee shop. James's mouth widened in a smile at the thought, the corners cracking and bleeding at the frail gesture.

The steady thumping of the helicopter's rotors grew louder as one of the Little Birds descended into the channel. James turned his head minutely, watching as the pilot eased the little helicopter onto a bare patch of sand some twenty yards away. The other helicopter maintained its position overhead, keeping a perimeter watch on the channel. The first craft landed softly on the sand, and James kept his gaze fixed on the two Delta operators unhooking themselves from their respective harnesses and leaping nimbly from the side of the Little Bird. They kept their heads low as they charged through the sandy plume kicked up by the rotors, and James found himself squinting through the deluge of debris to see if he could identify their faces.

"Who goes there?" The words came out of James's mouth in a froggy croak, and the dry rasp of his voice stunned him. He'd expected his words to be booming and resonate, fitting for his natural baritone. Instead, he sounded weak and tired. *To be fair*, he mused, *I am weak and tired.* He coughed, then tried again. His eyes lit upon the first Delta soldier as the man approached him, and genuine happiness sparked behind his fatigued gaze. "Well, I'll be a son of a bitch. If it ain't Twister."

"How you doing, Gator?" The man's lined face was concerned but friendly, and he offered the chief a thin smile as he knelt on the sand next to him. "Well, how about that. You look like shit, buddy."

"I *feel* like shit," James admitted, a smile tugging at the corner of his lips. "I'll be honest with you, man, I've felt better. Been a little bit of a rough day, but you probably know that already. Who'd you bring with you, Twister?"

Another face materialized into view. "Hey, Gator. It's me, Daisy."

"I'll be damned," James said, the grin on his face widening. The gesture hurt his bleeding lips, but he found he couldn't remove the smile from his face. Both Daisy and Twister were top men, and the genuine delight of seeing them was almost overwhelming.

Twister had come from Kansas and, despite being constantly reminded that he was no longer in the midwestern state, he still had a laugh for the tired joke. Daisy had a reputation for emerging from even the stickiest situations smelling, as the saying went, as fresh as daisies.

Seeing their familiar faces lifted a weight James hadn't realized he was carrying. He swallowed, then remarked, "They sent nothing but the best to chauffeur me back to the base, huh?"

"That's right, man," Twister agreed. His voice was distant, detached, and James recognized the note of concern in the first sergeant's voice. "We're gonna bring you back and get you cleaned up a little bit. You look like you've been through hell and back today."

James shook his head, then coughed again. "Nah, I'm fine. You're not going to ask me about my cat's name or anything?"

"C'mon, Gator." The man known as Twister nodded at Daisy, who returned the gesture.

James sensed the tension between the men, dense and tangible. They were trying to keep their voices light and even, but even as they patted him down, their concern was evident.

Twister said, "We both know you're not a cat person. Doesn't Christina have a dog, anyway? Fluffy, or some shit? Next thing you know, you're going to be asking us if the Rays won the World Series."

"That," James intoned with dry cheer, "would clearly mean that I'd died. We both know that's never happening."

"Hey, maybe someday, huh?" Twister wiped his hands off on the front of his FRACU fatigues, then cast an apologetic glance down at James. "We gotta get you on the bird, you know that, right? This is gonna hurt a little bit, okay?"

James nodded. There was no need to answer the man. He knew there was no graceful way to hoist him up, and even as gentle as Twister would try to be, shifting him onto his back to carry him out of the gully would lead to a fresh wave of pain coursing through his body. He relaxed his body, and Twister bent down, hooking his hands beneath James's armpits. He lifted the injured soldier, and James sounded off with a grunt as he was hoisted into the trademark fireman's position over his battle buddy's shoulders.

Even as he tried to maintain his composure, the pain was far too great, and darkness slipped over James.

—✳—✳—✳—✳—✳—

"You got him?" The helicopter pilot's voice was muffled over the sound of the rotors thudding overhead, but a glance over his shoulder confirmed the answer to his question. A remark rose in his throat at the sight of the limp and lifeless body of the chief, and he bit it off. Gator was in bad shape, and even as Twister eased him into the passenger seat of the helicopter and buckled him in, the pilot could see that the man was unconscious. "He even alive?"

Twister gave him a curt nod, followed by an annoyed glare.

This wasn't the time to be asking pointless questions. A highly skilled chief warrant officer, the pilot knew better than to interrogate him with questions he couldn't answer at the present time. At the very least, communication was limited over the sound of the rotor blades.

Twister had no status report he could offer beyond a terse, "Yeah."

Daisy climbed up onto the lip of the Little Bird and reached around his body to secure the harness. He glanced over his shoulder, and Twister nodded at him. When his own harness was secured into place, he raised a thumb at the pilot. Daisy mimicked the gesture, and then the pilot was easing the helicopter back into the air.

The ground fell away as the pilot peered down at the gully below. The APC was a smoldering mass of sooty smoke, flames licking at its geometric metal body. The nine bodies of the fallen IRGC soldiers lay in a haphazard formation on the sand, the only witnesses to what had happened to James that day. They would never reveal their secrets now.

Behind them, the second Little Bird rose in the air once more and fell into place behind the other helicopter. The Iraqi landscape faded from view as the pilot and the two Delta soldiers turned to face the horizon. They'd rescued Gator, but they still had many more miles to go before they made it back to the Green Zone in Baghdad.

Gator was in bad shape, very bad shape. He was alive for now, but it was obvious by the glances exchanged between Twister and Daisy as they worked to staunch the bleeding that they weren't sure if he was actually going to make it.

CHAPTER TWENTY-FOUR

THE RESCUE MISSION

1045 HOURS – 15 NOVEMBER 2013

EVERY SINGLE STEP JAMES HAD taken that fateful day, from the moment he made that phone call to the Tactical Operations Center onward, had been observed by several sets of eyes monitoring him with precise interest. Even as he'd sped across the town of Mehran on the borrowed motorcycle, those eyes had been following him. When he'd hijacked the IRGC pickup truck, these individuals had known. Each bullet that had met with his flesh had been met with grimaces and genuine concern by parties carefully observing him.

The entirety of the 15th of November had been a day of tense missions. The initial mission had begun just after midnight early that morning, when James and the rest of The Unit descended upon Da'wud's compound in Mehran. That mission, by all accounts, had been an exorbitantly costly endeavor in human lives. The second mission had begun when James awoke in the subterranean basement below the compound. His fervent attempt to survive had become his own personal mission, and that too had soon begun shaping up to be a disaster. Then the third mission had begun when James picked up the phone in the neighboring house and made his outbound call to the TOC.

Even as he lay dying in the Iraqi gully, James had still believed this call had been largely ignored. James Chase was not the type of man to hold a grudge, and even as he'd believed he'd been abandoned by his men, he held no anger or disappointment at them for their supposed inaction. Hell, he didn't blame them for evacuating the compound and leaving him behind. Why wouldn't they? They'd erroneously mistaken him for dead and fled only after they'd verified that their companion was beyond rescue. The state of Da'wud's compound only confirmed for James that they'd done everything they could to retrieve his body before they'd evacuated, and he didn't doubt they'd employed a tactical retreat only under the immediate threat of death.

Even as James had attempted to flee Iran, he knew rescue was outside of the scope of possibility. It was too dangerous for the remainder of The Unit to attempt to cobble together any semblance of a rescue operation on such short notice. He'd known if he wanted to see the sun set on that cool November day, he needed to take the initiative himself to get out of the country. His first plan had taken him only as far as the Iraqi border, and his second plan had implored him to live long enough to knock on the door of the COP Shocker outpost in Zurbatiyah. If his allies could pick him up from this new location, then James would have been perfectly content with their efforts. He'd expected no more and no less from them.

The United States Government, as well as the remaining Delta Team, regarded James from an entirely different perspective. James wasn't just one of their top soldiers. He was a highly valuable asset they'd invested a significant amount of time and resources into honing. Furthermore, letting him be captured or killed in Iran would have triggered a massive political upset that could paint the United States in an incredibly poor light. It was also worth noting that the men had a selfish interest in rescuing James. To put it briefly, they liked him, and so rescuing him was also something they wanted very much, for personal reasons. So even as James was trying to mount a one-man operation to save himself, he'd had no idea that his government and his friends were desperately trying to rescue him too.

Gator was living on borrowed time. He knew it, and Twister knew it. But while James had ample reason to believe there would be no rescue party coming for him—the risk of danger, as well as political repercussions, were far too great—Twister knew that the only thing separating him from moving forward was the word from the CIA deputy executive director at Langley. And once that word came, he would be part of the party swooping down into Iraq to recover his friend.

Langley just needed to get off their asses and give them the damned word already.

Twister was ready. Hell, they were all ready. Daisy exchanged a glance with him, and they both cast a pointed glance at the clock on the wall. James had successfully completed his transition from Iran to Iraq nearly a half hour before, and from where Twister was standing, things weren't looking too hot for the chief warrant officer. What the hell was taking them so long?

Like everyone else back in the Green Zone, Twister had been among those who had erroneously believed Gator was among the dead at Da'wud's compound. It wasn't just Gator he was grieving that morning. It was all of the men lost in this damned mission—his friends, his brothers-in-arms, and almost all of them, dead. He'd caught a glimpse of the shellshocked expressions on Tex's and Ginger's faces and knew there was a strong likelihood that he would never fully know what had transpired earlier that day.

Then James's call to the Tactical Operations Center had been patched through, and the atmosphere in the Green Zone instantly changed. Gator's voice, firm but staticky over the poor connection, managed to introduce a fresh wave of hope surging through the Green Zone.

After the call to the TOC, Osborne had sat in his seat for a few seconds in stunned disbelief, even as he heard James's voice fade out in a hiss of static. Three of those seconds had been used to confirm the call had been dropped, and two of them were employed to corral his racing thoughts. Then Specialist Osborne had flown from his seat, knocking the battered metal chair to the floor in his frenzy to reach out to The Unit commander.

His words had met dumbfounded ears as he sputtered in disbelief to his commanding officer, "Chief James Chase is alive! He is *still alive!*"

Up until that point, everyone at the base within the Green Zone had unilaterally believed Chief James Chase, also known as Gator to his closest friends and brothers in arms, had been killed in the assault upon Da'wud's compound. Then, to all of their surprise, the presumed-dead man had somehow managed to place a call to the TOC. This new intel meant that instead of trying to mount an operation to retrieve his corpse from the rubble, which would have been a strategic stalemate in itself, they needed to revise their approach to rescue their fellow soldier.

Thus, Operation Gator had been born.

Before any actions commenced, however, Specialist Osborne's report needed to be cross-referenced with the CIA for verification. Twister waited with as much patience as he could muster for this task to be completed. Because Operation QuickSand had been a CIA-run operation, it meant the organization had their fingers deeply embedded in the entire mission and bore an especially large responsibility to help extract James from the region. That also meant they needed to help verify the man Osborne had spoken to on the phone truly was Chase. While the phone call itself had been very convincing, and the specialist even insisted that he'd personally recognized the man's voice, blind faith could be a lethal error. After all, anyone could research the TOC's phone number and make such a call.

Even if it were the man they knew as Gator on the line, how could they verify he wasn't making the call under coercion or duress? Before Operation Gator could be implemented, all of the men in Delta at the Green Zone, as well as the CIA, had to first confirm that it was actually Chief Chase on the line. Fortunately for James, the CIA had several ways they could verify the accuracy of this new intel. Their first step had been to eavesdrop on the two-way radio communications from within Mehran. This was relatively simple for the CIA, as they already had an extensive communications surveillance operation in the region.

Within just a few minutes of James's call to the TOC, the CIA had been able to pick up radio chatter on a presumed private radio comm line of the IRGC. Their base translator had been roused and ordered to report to the TOC, and with his guidance in interpreting the Farsi messages, the CIA was soon able to verify that the IRGC was actively pursuing an unknown entity within the same area as Operation QuickSand. The enemy soldiers themselves hadn't known the specific identity of their target as they chased him throughout Mehran, which could have ended in a dead-end for the CIA. That was where their second surveillance tool had stepped in: the M-Q9 Reaper.

The Reaper, also known as Predator B, was a Remotely Piloted Aircraft (RPA) that had already been used extensively in the area. Because the CIA had already been using the Reaper for surveillance in the region, having it transfer its focus onto James had been as easy as instructing its operator to train its video feed upon Mehran. The Reaper had been diverted to the small town, and within minutes of flying over the area, they were able to verify it was indeed Chief James Chase being pursued by the IRGC. This discovery had been met with restrained cheers from within the TOC. On one hand, James Chase was still alive. On the other, they needed to get him out of the region in the same condition.

Tired of waiting, Twister's body was tense and a dull ache was forming between his eyebrows, the first hint of a stress headache. Instead of a couple ibuprofen, though, the only thing that could relieve this tension would be the opportunity to actually *do* something. He was taut with anticipation. Again, the thought rose in his mind: *What the hell is taking Langley so long?*

In reality, it hadn't been that long since Specialist Osborne had taken Gator's call. In the scope of mission planning, it was actually a very narrow window of time, and the speed with which the CIA sprang into action was nothing short of impressive. The issue was that James was, unfortunately, still in Iran. And while the chief was still within the boundaries of this hostile country, the men were not authorized to undertake any actions to rescue him.

With this exciting revelation fresh in their minds, the men at the TOC suppressed their enthusiasm and shelved their desire to simply reach into the country and scoop Chase out. Following the strict protocols of a bureaucracy, they'd instead gone through the proper chain of command to authorize his rescue. The CIA station chief residing within the Green Zone had promptly picked up his STE phone and dialed the CIA deputy executive director at Langley. He reported their findings to the man on the line and requested authorization to conduct a rescue operation. He'd also forwarded all his intelligence to the director. Then he held his breath and waited.

Sitting idly on their asses wasn't something the men in The Unit were particularly known for, so while they'd waited for authorization from Langley, they decided to begin their preparations for this new mission regardless. They'd already strongly suspected that Operation Gator would be a go. It was just a matter of *how* they would execute it.

The Delta commander had gathered a team of Delta operators, as well as Task Force Brown—another group of elite men known as the Night Stalkers—to fly the Delta Team in for the rescue operation. The commander had quickly assigned two pilots for this duty, and even as they'd waited to hear back from Langley, the men prepared two MH-6M Little Bird helicopters for action.

While this entire act had taken no more than a quarter of an hour to implement, it felt like a small eternity to the men within the Green Zone. Nervous energy could be felt through the base, an almost electric charge running through them as they'd executed preparations. Twister was wearing a path of erosion on the floor from his pacing back and forth. Finally, just after the pair of pilots started their work on readying their MH-6Ms, the word had come back from Langley.

They had two key points that they firmly emphasized as they

relayed their instructions to them. One, Operation Gator was officially "green lighted" as a high priority mission. And two, under no circumstances would the men involved in the rescue operation ever cross into Iran. And now, these entities were springing into motion, activating their carefully devised plan to extract James from enemy territory.

A grin spread across Twister's face. His waiting was over. And, if all went well, he would be reunited with his friend again very shortly. He just hoped they weren't too late.

⸻ ⚬⚬ ⸻

The rescue team had suspected these strict policies would be the case, and because of this, they were largely unfazed by their instructions. Hell, they would have been surprised if the CIA *hadn't* been so exacting in their demands of the rescue team.

The pilots quickly loaded up in both Little Birds, and four Delta operators strapped themselves to ledges jutting out of both sides of the helicopter. Then they began their journey to the Iraqi border. Back in the TOC, every pair of eyes was glued to the video feed streaming back to their multiple computer screens. The Reaper served as an additional set of eyes as well. Even though James had sincerely believed he was completely on his own, he had no idea how close he was to rescue as he drove his truck into the neighboring country. His quick thinking had arguably saved his life, as he himself knew he had no chance of survival if he stayed within the perimeters of Iran. His own intellect, combined with his relentless resolve, had been integral in the success of Operation Gator.

As his battered pickup truck puttered across the border into Iraq, a shout of heartfelt elation had arisen within the TOC command center. The voices in the room rose as one, and a few of the men even clapped in delight as James crossed into the neighboring country. The Delta commander, Captain Edwards, couldn't conceal his own joy as he declared over the overlapping voices, "Operation Gator is a *go!*"

Even as they saw the chief defeat the quartet of enemy personnel from within the two pickup trucks that had followed him into Iraq, they knew that Chase wasn't in the clear just yet. The APC had steadily churned its way across the desert landscape, unrelenting in its pursuit of its target. Both the Reaper operator and the APC were closely monitoring James's progress, and while it appeared that James himself had forgotten about the armored personnel carrier following him, the Reaper hadn't. The tension within the TOC was thick and palpable as they watched James spar with the unknown officer who had emerged from the APC, and a chant of, "C'mon, *c'mon*," rose inside the room as they watched helplessly from their position. At one point, they were certain that they'd been too late, and they were going to fail to rescue James.

Eliminating the enemy had only been one part of their mission. What good would it be to them if they neutralized the APC and the enemy officer if Gator died in the process? The Reaper operator waited patiently for the MH-6M helicopters to zero in on James before he launched his missile. Even that was a carefully weighed tactical decision. The operation was a surprisingly delicate one, and one wrong move could result in them inadvertently killing the man they were trying to save. The chief was approximately fifty feet from the APC, which meant that he could be within the blast radius of the missile when it collided with the APC. Conversely, with a truck between himself and the APC, perhaps it could act as a sort of buffer, shielding him from the explosion.

But they needed to act fast. If they didn't fire the missile soon, there was a good chance that they would completely fail at the mission. The way the enemy officer was maneuvering around Chase, it was evident that he was preparing to subdue him before shoving him into the APC in order to bring him back to their own headquarters. If this were to happen, then the chances of them rescuing James would diminish dramatically. The men in the TOC watched as James was shoved to the ground, then hoisted back up by two IRGC guards.

It was now or never. The operator of the Reaper drew in a deep breath and, with only a momentary pause to confirm with himself that this was indeed the ideal time to act, he squeezed the trigger. The missile released from beneath the wing of the M-Q9 Reaper, raining literal hellfire upon the enemies down below. While James might or might not survive the explosion, the operator hoped he'd gauged his strike accurately. The Reaper had come to do its job: to harvest its quarry, and with the aid of the men piloting the Little Birds, they would be collecting some souls that morning. He just hoped that one of them would be a living one.

CHAPTER TWENTY-FIVE

THE HOSPITAL

18 NOVEMBER 2013

WHEN THE LITTLE BIRD LANDED in the Green Zone, a medical team was already waiting. James's eyes remained shut and his breathing shallow as he was lifted out of the helicopter onto a waiting litter. He didn't stir as his Unit members sprinted across the landing pad with him in tow into the medical building. There he waited, unconscious, as life-saving procedures were performed to stabilize him. However, the medical building was no match for a fully equipped treatment facility, which is why another flight was summoned for him not long after.

Two hours after James Chase arrived back at the Green Zone in Bagdad, he was airlifted in a C-130 Hercules to the Landstuhl Regional Medical Center in Germany. As the largest and best equipped hospital for wounded American soldiers in the region, it had been unanimously decided that he would have a much better prognosis if he received treatment there. The nearly eight-hour flight, which spanned over 2,600 miles and numerous countries, saw the soldier weaving in and out of consciousness. James never reached full alertness during the entire flight, though many times he shouted out from within his fitful slumber. The medical team assigned to him exchanged concerned glances at these spontaneous outbursts as they worked to keep him alive.

The medical team waiting for James in Landstuhl immediately leaped into action. The surgery took nearly four hours, the majority of it focused on addressing the bullet wound in his shoulder. It had pierced the front of his shoulder and shattered his scapula, and stitching it up turned out to be a major task. He would not be using that arm again for quite some time. However, the surgeons all agreed that James had been very fortunate. The wound in his thigh was a clean through and through and had luckily avoided any major arteries. As the surgeon probed the wound, he shook his head many times. It was a wonder James hadn't bled out, and had the bullet landed another inch higher, the soldier would have surely perished from the injury.

James remained oblivious to the lifesaving efforts going on around him. The fight for his life had taken its toll on him, and his fitful slumber continued for the greater part of several days.

The military nurse assigned to him had taken note of him when he arrived. At first, she'd dismissed the unconscious soldier as just another casualty. His dark curls were matted with sweat and blood around his face, and his face was disfigured by angry, purple bruises.

It hadn't taken long, though, for word to get back to the petite nurse about who exactly was in her care. It had started with reverent glances in his room as various personnel walked down the hall, then evolved to offhand comments about what had happened to the mysterious soldier. The nurse, a first lieutenant by the name of Reynolds, was not in a position to coax gossip out of the medical staff at Landstuhl. It turned out that it was unnecessary. Over the next couple of days, she slowly became privy to who exactly lay prone in the hospital bed.

It didn't help that James Chase was evidently an attractive man beneath his injuries. Reynolds could readily admit that. As the bruising and swelling subsided, his high cheekbones and full lips became more evident. Based on the hue of his skin, she was sure he had a pair of piercing and intelligent brown eyes beneath the thick eyebrows set above them. Despite herself, the lieutenant had slowly taken to the gravely injured soldier over the three days he was in her care. His physical appearance was only part of his appeal. His understated yet ruggedly handsome appearance had certainly caught her eye, but the rumors of his escapades in Iran had crystalized her respect for him.

She'd made a point to check his left hand while changing his dressings, and while she knew better than to indulge in fraternization, she couldn't help but feel her pulse quicken every time she stepped into his room. Her gaze lingered on his flat and muscular abdomen as she carefully bathed him with a sponge, and despite her guilt for these cresting feelings, she couldn't ignore them. Nevertheless, she did her best to suppress them. Developing a silly crush on a fellow soldier was the very definition of forbidden.

Three days after he'd been rescued from Iraq, James finally opened his eyes. His throat was dry and sandpapery, and his entire body ached. He fumbled for the call button, and a military nurse hurried into his room.

Her hair was pulled back into a sleek bun at the nape of her neck, lending a harsh severity to her demeanor. However, when her eyes lit upon James, her face widened into a sincere grin. "So you're finally awake, huh?"

James nodded. A bolt of pain shot down his spine from the motion, and he winced. He ran his dry tongue over his chapped lips before speaking the single word that defined his immediate needs. "Water?"

"Of course." The nurse turned away from James and pulled a cup from a row inside a tightly packed dispenser hanging from the wall. She filled it from the tap at the sink, then offered it to him.

His hands trembled as he accepted the drink. He was so damned weak and wondered fleetingly how long he'd been in the hospital. That thought was dismissed as the tepid beverage hit his lips, coating his parched tongue. He quickly drained the first cup down, followed by another one that he was admonished to sip by a mildly chiding voice, and then the nurse took the cup away. She crumpled it in her hands and let it fall into the nearest wastebasket.

Quiet fell over her, then she said, "I think you have some visitors. You feel like you're ready for some company?"

James didn't, but he nodded anyway.

The nurse filed out of the room, and a few minutes later was replaced by Captain Edwards and the CIA station chief. He recognized Daniel Gibson—*how many days has it been?*—who had led him to Mehran in the first place.

The slim man greeted James with a slight nod as he pushed his wire-framed glasses up his nose.

Captain Edwards leaned over the side of the bed with a bleak expression on his face.

James frowned at the look of concern being cast on him, frustrated that he couldn't find his voice to ask any questions, but that proved to be a non-issue. After a perfunctory clearing of his throat, Edwards started telling him everything he needed to hear. And more.

"I'm damned proud of you, James," the captain began. He didn't blink. He didn't shift his eyes. He didn't remove his gaze from James's face. "We all thought you'd died out there, but fortunately you went and proved us all wrong. I wish to hell that I could say the same for the rest of the men on your team."

James found himself without words. Despite sucking down two cups of water, all moisture was gone from his mouth. He knew what was coming. Even as he felt the sinking dread in his stomach, the memory of the charred compound in Mehran swam before his vision. As he'd driven past it on his way to the waste processing plant, he'd fleetingly wondered why Da'wud's compound was a smoking heap of rubble. Specialist Osborne's words on the phone filtered back into his memory, suddenly clearer today than they'd been when he'd first heard them. He'd mentioned that he thought James had died, but there had been more to his comments.

The stunned specialist's voice rose in his memory as a sharp reminder of the conversation with him echoed clearly in his head. *"Holy shit! You're still alive! ... thought you had ...!"*

"We lost some team members." Edwards reached out to take James's hand, and James found himself unable to resist the calloused grip of the base commander. Edwards patted it, an uncharacteristically compassionate gesture from the normally reserved captain, then he released James's hand and continued his speech. The words fell from his mouth, clipped and steady, almost as though he'd rehearsed them. Maybe he had. "The intel itself for Operation QuickSand was good. We got it from someone we thought was a trusted informant. We didn't know at the time, but the informant was also working for the Iranians."

Behind Edwards, Gibson shifted from one foot to another. His face was blank, but guilt danced behind his hooded eyes. He knew he was partially to blame for this, and James felt a rising surge of anger in his chest. He suppressed it, then returned his gaze to Captain Edwards.

"The informant had told the Iranians we were coming. He told the Iranians the Americans were actively searching for Da'wud Al Muhammad and knew where he was." Edwards cleared his throat, then resumed. "So, they knew we were coming, but they just didn't know when. They were on high alert, waiting for us. When we landed, the Rangers were performing perimeter support. You already know that part, but I don't think you know the rest. That's when they were attacked."

"What happened?" James asked quietly. He knew the answer but needed to hear it. The smoking ruins of the compound flashed in his memory once more.

"The Rangers and the Night Stalkers tried to repel the attack, but they were outnumbered and outgunned. The Iranian force was too large, so they tried to fall back. You know Tex. He wouldn't let his men get slaughtered. He tried to get the men to the helicopters to evacuate." Captain Edwards swallowed hard, his gaze never leaving James's face. "The IRGC fired multiple rockets into the compound. They thought all of the Delta Team was still inside."

"But they weren't?" James asked.

"No, they'd already headed out to lend ground support to the Rangers and the Night Stalkers. Tex said he tried to get your body, but the sound of artillery fire and explosions outside drew his attention to the firefight. He thought he could come back and get you later. He met Benjamin downstairs."

"Wait," James said, and he held up a hand, interrupting his commander. "Where did you get all of this information? Who reported it back to you?"

"Everyone but Tex and Ginger were killed in the firefight. I took their statements, which match the intel we have. Hell, we thought you'd died in there too, James. Then your call came through to the TOC."

"How did you find me?" James asked, his head swimming. The words seemed to come from a far distance, hollow in his own ears.

Edwards reached out, patting James's hand once more. "That's enough talk for now. You need to get some rest. A couple friends have come to see you, and once you're feeling better and more alert, they'd like to say hi. But I don't want you pestering Ginger and Tex for more information until you've recovered more. You hear me?" The base commander knew better than to expect James to comply with his request but issued the instruction regardless. His face was unreadable as he peered down at the wounded soldier.

Already James was feeling tired, so tired. It couldn't be true. Almost all of his friends were dead. Their faces moved in shadowy shapes behind his closed eyes, and he felt the hot sting of tears moving behind his eyelids. Disbelief and grief lapped at him, and he drew in a shuddering breath, then let it back out. Finally, he returned his gaze to the captain and managed a slight nod.

This seemed to satisfy Edwards, but both men knew James would be interrogating Ginger and Tex the moment they were reunited.

James would have to grieve silently. He'd thought he would be pouring out a drink on the sand for Hank, for Marmaduke, for whomever had been killed downstairs when Kermit stepped on the pressure mine. He'd never fathomed that he would be losing almost every one of his closest friends on that mission. Even as sleep once more stole over James, he knew he would forever carry the memories of his fellow men who had sacrificed themselves that chilly November morning. For Chief Warrant Officer 2 James Chase, also known as Gator to his friends, that was exactly how it should be.

And so James drifted back into a deep sleep, and it was the last time the elite American soldier ever had a dreamless respite again.

⸺ ✳ ✳ ✳ ✳ ✳ ⸺

James gazed out the window from his hospital bed, his eyes flat and expressionless beneath his black eyebrows. Outside, tree branches swayed and nodded in the November wind like bony skeletons against the bleak gray sky. The clouds were low and heavy on the horizon, spitting out snowfall that clung wetly to the window.

Dead. Almost all of his friends, the men who had become his brothers in arms, had perished back at Da'wud's compound. His brow knit into a frown, the only sign that the otherwise stoic man was struggling with his emotions beneath his seemingly-indifferent exterior. But James was feeling anything but indifferent. He couldn't recall the last time he'd felt such inner turmoil.

Tex and Ginger had been by that morning. Tex was quiet and reserved, and only a ghost of a smile remained on his face when he talked to James. James could tell the smile was more of a grimace, for James's reassurance instead of based on any genuine happiness. The only time the smile had any warmth behind it was when his eyes had first lit upon the solider lying in the hospital bed. Tex hadn't said it outright, but he was a changed man. The mission had molded him, shaped him into someone different. While he would eventually recover to bear a passing semblance of the man he was before they'd descended upon Da'wud's compound, he would never be the same again, James had thought as he listened and nodded to the reserved Texan speaking.

Ginger, on the other hand, had a little bit of the manic energy he was known for thrumming through him as he filled James in on his version of what had happened back on the compound. James could tell, however, that there was no heart in it. And instead of having an easy grin ready for James, the man's green eyes had darted around the room as he spoke, as though he expected an enemy to materialize through one of the beige hospital room walls.

They'd left hours ago. The nurse, a first lieutenant—James hadn't bothered asking her name, and she didn't volunteer it—had brought his lunch by, then reluctantly wheeled it away untouched two hours later. She'd tried to coax him to eat, but a steely look from James had silenced her. She'd set her lips in a firm line and hurried back out of the room, making a mental note to slip him some extra food at dinnertime.

Tex and Ginger hadn't been his only visitors during his tenure at the hospital. Sometime after they trailed off—time was starting to lose meaning in the hospital—a man knocked on the heavy wooden door. James glanced up sharply, and surprise flashed across his face as an unknown figure slipped through the door, eased up to his bed, and peered down at him. He wasn't sure who he'd expected, as Tex and Ginger had already paid their regards, but this unfamiliar face immediately piqued his interest.

Despite his interest in this new party, James was too weak to muster up any enthusiasm for his visitor. Through the fog of pain and disorientation, he managed only a cursory grunt in greeting. "Who are you?"

"Name's Marc." Then the man fell silent as he considered James.

There was an air of expectation to him, as though he expected James to start speaking after the initial introduction. Maybe he thought James would introduce himself to him in return. James regarded him silently, taking in his appearance. The man seemed to be slight of build, a little bit shorter than James, probably falling about four inches shy of being six foot in stature. He was dressed in a crisp, albeit slightly crumpled, white button-down shirt. The collar lay tucked beneath a navy-blue sport coat. His hair was a sandy blond, and his eyes were an alert and intelligent shade of gray.

After a lengthy pause, Marc spoke again. "I, uh, I was out in the hall yesterday and I couldn't help but overhear you talking to Captain Edwards."

"Yeah?" James's reply was noncommittal, but if the stranger was put off by his blunt answers, he didn't indicate it.

"From the sounds of it, you've been through hell." Marc's face was sympathetic, and as James searched it with his dark eyes, he realized the man was being sincere. James felt himself soften slightly, and he nodded marginally at him. Marc added, "It's a wonder you're alive."

"No," James replied, and his voice was instantly dull and flat once more. "It's not."

Marc seemed to weigh the injured soldier's words, then finally nodded. "From what I've heard, recovering from a bullet wound is going to hurt like hell. But I have a feeling you're going to come out on the other side of this with nothing more than just a few physical scars. And maybe a few mental ones too. But you're going to make it through this."

James sighed, and it was a weighty sound from deep within the recesses of his lungs. Finally, he said, "You might be right. What did you hear out there?"

"Just enough." Marc reached up to his face and rubbed his thumb against the side of his nose, then folded both of his hands in front of his body. The gesture caused his jacket to fall open, and James noted what appeared to be a badge on his hip, looped around his belt. He glanced at it, then raised his eyes back to the man's face.

"What, am I in some kind of trouble with the law or something?" James turned his face away from the man.

Outside, the snow had not yet started to fall. He knew his escape from Da'wud's compound had probably broken a few local laws and perhaps toed the line on a few international ones too, but this was a little bit early for anyone to be showing up with a set of metal bracelets for him to wear.

"No. I *am* from CID, but you're not in trouble." Marc let the words hang heavily in the air. If he expected James to be impressed that a man from the Army's Criminal Investigation Division was talking to him, then he was going to be sorely disappointed. He pulled his jacket back farther, revealing not only his CID badge but also a 9mm Sig pistol. "I don't think anyone's going to be chasing you down for what happened to you in Mehran. Your actions out there were very impressive. Heroic, even."

James slowly turned his face toward Marc, ignoring the surge of pain that flared in his bandaged shoulder as he shifted his weight. "I guess you didn't hear enough, then. I'm not a hero. Those men who died out there on the mission? They're the real heroes."

"You always sell yourself short like that, Chief?" Marc raised a brow at the man lying on the hospital bed in front of him.

James had no answer for the CID agent. He lowered his gaze to his own hands, which lay palm-down on the blanket draped over his body. They were bloody and bruised, swollen with the fluids that the doctors had been pumping into him. "What are you doing here, anyway?"

"I wanted to talk to you." Marc cleared his throat, then rested his fingers lightly on the bedrail. He leaned forward slightly, looming over James. "I've been working an investigation. There was an attempted murder, and the victim is recovering here at the hospital. I just happened to wander by yesterday when you were talking to Captain Edwards. I heard the tail end of it, but it didn't seem right to waltz in after you got such somber news. It just so happens that I had to re-interview the victim today, so I figured if you were awake when I was passing by, I'd pop in and introduce myself."

"Okay." James's voice was dubious. The man had an angle, and James had his own suspicions as to the man's true motives for visiting him. He wasn't about to ask him outright what he was doing here, though. He suspected that if he waited long enough, the CID agent would eventually reveal it. "How's the investigation coming along, then?"

"Better than expected. The victim's statement's is going to lead to the identification of the suspect." Marc nodded as though he were answering the question more for himself than for James. "How are you doing...James Chase, is it?"

"It is." James gave him a perfunctory nod. "I'm holding it

together. Been better. Can't say I've been much worse, though, if I had to be completely honest with you."

"That's understandable. What about your buddies? What were their names?" Marc furrowed his brow as he tried to recall what he'd overheard the day before. Then he shrugged at the lapse in memory. "How are they doing?"

"Tex and Ginger?" James considered the question seriously. There was something about Marc that somehow lowered his guard. He knew he could trust the man, despite having only just met him. "They're hanging in there. They're strong men. Some of the best, really." His voice grew quieter as he spoke, the last words almost a whisper coming out of his parched and raspy throat. "I'm not sure I can continue working in the Combat Applications Group, though. Just realized, maybe a little too late, that constantly saying goodbye is starting to take its toll on me."

"I wouldn't expect you to feel any differently." Marc's voice was quiet.

James recognized the note of respect in the man's voice. Everyone, in fact, had been treating him very well since his arrival at the hospital. He was starting to suspect that being one of the few survivors of a highly costly mission afforded him a certain degree of reverence. He would have given it up in a heartbeat if it would bring his friends back.

"It sounds like you lost some good friends out there."

"Some of my *best* friends," James said, his voice surprisingly steady. Even he was surprised at how strong it was.

"I'm sorry as hell for your loss, Chief. I mean that. Being part of CAG is a big deal, and knowing what *could* happen doesn't make it any easier when it really *does* happen." Marc's hand was back at his face, his index finger and thumb worrying the folds of his nose. "But if you're thinking about leaving The Unit, I can help get you into CID if you're interested? You may not realize it just yet, but CID has its perks, and we could use someone with your training and skillset."

"You think so?" He sized the CID agent up. Despite himself, the idea appealed to James. He'd been telling the truth when he mentioned that he was thinking about leaving The Unit. There was nothing left for him there. And the thought of losing another one of his friends? The thought was more than he could bear. Maybe later, when the wounds weren't so fresh, maybe then he could reconsider his doubts. But for now, he wanted to distance himself as far as he could from The Unit and everything it represented. "It sounds like it could be interesting."

"Don't make any decisions just yet." Marc patted his front shirt pocket and, after a moment, pulled a small, white rectangular card from it. He extended it to James between his index and middle finger.

After a moment's hesitation, James reached up and tugged the card out of the man's grip.

Marc said, "This is my number. Think about it. And if you decide that joining CID is something that makes sense to you, then go ahead and give me a call."

"Yeah," James said, his voice growing distant. He was already looking out the window again. Whatever sedatives they'd given him to conk him out were working, and he was struggling to keep his eyes open. He fell silent, listening to Marc's feet shuffling next to his bed.

A minute later, the man turned and walked out of the room, his heels clocking quietly on the tile floor. The door shut with a muffled click behind him.

James continued to doze for the greater part of the afternoon. When Lieutenant Reynolds brought him his dinner, he roused out of his groggy stupor. He had no words for her and barely acknowledged her presence when she placed his tray, stacked high with dinner rolls and a towering scoop of mashed potatoes, over his bed. As he gazed out the window, watching the snow cling to the ledge in a sticky and dingy film, he found himself replaying Marc's words in his head. When Marc had initially told him about CID, there had been a certain appeal to it. But James had been groggy and his emotions had been high after talking to Tex and Ginger earlier that morning.

After sleeping on it, though, it made perfect sense to him. He'd been right in his initial assessment. James had heard of CID before, but it had never really resonated with him until now. Maybe there was an opportunity for him there. He sighed and let his thoughts go back to the faces of the men he'd lost. Quitting The Unit wouldn't bring them back, but James didn't care. He'd lost his ability to conjure up any emotion other than aching grief since learning about their deaths.

A career in CID, on the other hand? That might give him ample diversion, something to draw his thoughts away from his mourning. And as the wind picked up, howling its own sorrowful dirge outside the foggy window overlooking Landstuhl, James realized that maybe he'd found his new calling. He was no longer going to be part of Delta. Instead, he would call Marc once he was released from the hospital and see about how he could start the process of joining CID.

After all, Marc had said he was looking for good soldiers to join his ranks. James had no delusions of false modesty. While he wasn't sure just yet how CID would put his talents to use, he was admittedly curious to learn more. In that moment, he couldn't think of any better use of his abilities.

A sort of cautious peace descended upon James, shrouding him in something that vaguely resembled closure. It was still too early, and the wounds were still far too fresh, but he knew this day marked the ending of one chapter of his life and the beginning of another. And James Chase was ready for that change.

TO BE CONTINUED

Thank you for reading. I hope you enjoyed this reading adventure and will leave a review on your favorite retailer to let me know. Please join our mailing list for more information on upcoming books at tonyperezbooks.com

SNEAK PEEK

There were several cameras perched along the body of the house, sending a constant video stream feed to the agents monitoring it from within the building. While there were no cameras inside the house, a safeguard for the SecDef's privacy, James knew there was at least one pair of eyes watching him over the feed as he stepped through the two-and-a-half foot gate encircling the house. Crickets sang their morning tune as he approached, not bothering to pause their interlude to announce his arrival. He angled his way down the three steps leading to the back door and paused, listening for any sounds of activity inside the house. From James's vantage, the house was quiet, belying the already-bustling activity of the men stationed inside.

Excerpt from *James Chase, The Dragon and The Eagle, War with China (A James Chase Military Thriller Book Two)*
Coming December 2020
Sign up at www.tonyperezbooks.com to learn more

ABOUT THE AUTHOR

Chief Warrant Officer 2 Tony Perez is an American soldier, defense contractor, and now the author of the James Chase book series. His debut novel, The Delta Mission, is inspired by his experience as a soldier during his extensive military career. His notable accomplishments during his military career earned him several awards, to include the National Defense Security Award, Army Commendation, NATO Award, Afghanistan Campaign Award, Global War on Terrorism Award, Global War on Terrorism Expeditionary Award, among many others. Perez has a master's degree in Information Technology, specializing in Cyber Security. He currently works full time for a defense contractor in Florida and part time as a CID Special Agent in the US Army Reserves, both of which require him to maintain a security clearance.

You can follow his upcoming projects at tonyperezbooks.com
You can also follow the author on
www.facebook.com/author.tony.perez
and
www.instagram.com/tonyperezbooks/

ACKNOWLEDGMENTS

I want to thank all of our military members in each of our armed forces. I also want to thank all the members in my current unit, 307th MP DET (CID), for the great times we had, and looking forward to several more years together.

Made in the USA
Columbia, SC
03 November 2020

23874186R00137